GLOSS

GLOSS

JENNIFER OKO

MIRA®

ISBN-13: 978-0-7783-2442-3
ISBN-10:   0-7783-2442-7

GLOSS

www.MIRABooks.com

Printed in U.S.A.

For Michael, who makes everything possible.

ACKNOWLEDGMENTS

Gloss would not exist if it weren't for the support and encouragement of some very special people. So to my agent, first reader and my personal Queen of Swords, Stephanie Kip Rostan, thank you again and again. Selina McLemore's enthusiasm for the printed page is contagious and I am lucky that not only did she fall in love with *Gloss,* she was able to help me whip it into a more readable shape than I could have alone. I am grateful that Selina was able to usher the book into Linda McFall's able hands and that Linda has been able to guide me wisely through the rest of this adventure. Thank you to everyone at MIRA for making this project so pleasurable.

Every writer should have a support group like the one I had with Roomful of Writers: Elaine Heinzman, Kevin Ricche, Martha Heil, Peter Reppert, James Riordon, Contessa Riggs and (briefly) Eric Roston. A special shout out to Jennifer Ouellette and Erica Perl. On the face of it, it would seem that the authors of books such as *The Physics of the Buffyverse* and *Ninety-Three in My Family* might not necessarily be the best readers for a book like *Gloss,* but in fact a little Einstein mixed with some excellent children's literature was precisely the medicine *Gloss* needed. John Elderkin, wherever you are, thank you for the title. Thank you to Elizabeth Shreve for your endless publishing wisdom.

Thank you to Janet Leissner, Michael Bass, Linda Mason, Hardy Spire and the rest of my friends and colleagues at CBS News and *The Early Show* for your support and good-humored encouragement.

Writers usually work in solitude, but this writer wouldn't be able to get anything done if it weren't for friends like Tula Karras, Jenny Trewartha, Jan Trasen, Julie Ziegler, Jennifer Howze, Sasha Gottlieb and Liza Vasilkova.

This book was sold shortly after the birth of my son, Jasper, and it took an amazing amount of help from my family to assure that I had the time, space and energy to be a producer, a writer and a good mother all at the same time. Annette Oko, Ben Oko and Helen Dimos—thank you for the love you have showered on Jasper and his mom. And to my parents, Sue and Arnold Cohen, it sounds trite but I really have no words to thank you enough. My husband, Michael Oko, continues to amaze me with his patience, his kindness, his enthusiasm and his belief in me. And it is Jasper who has helped me see all the blessings and joy. Thank you.

PART ONE

gloss (glôs)

n.

1. A surface sheen, often referring to cosmetics used to enhance the lips.

2. A superficially or deceptively attractive appearance.

3. A smooth-coated, slick media format.

The obscure we see eventually. The completely obvious, it seems, takes longer.

—Edward R. Murrow

PROLOGUE

I digress.

When I was little, the adults laughed and said I had a vivid imagination. It was a good thing. But by the end of my elementary years it was a source of heated conversations in parent-teacher meetings, and then, by high school, it became a source of parent-psychologist conversations, leading to parent-neurologist conversations, leading to a career as a television news producer, and ultimately, to where I am now. Which is to say, my tendency to take off on flights of fancy, and my general inability to focus ironically brought me to a place of fancy-less focus: the Federal Detention Center in Alexandria, Virginia. My lawyer grins Cheshirelike and insists we will win. No fear, he says, this will end soon, you will write a book, a movie deal will be in place and, years from now, you will look out over the veranda of your Hollywood Hills home, sipping chardonnay and laughing at this little adventure. Wake me up after the second coming, I tell him, when I'm in a good mood. Most days I tell him to shut up and give me whatever paper it is that I need to sign.

I wasn't always this surly. In fact, I'm *not* always this surly. I like to think of myself as personable. My fellow inmates seem to like me. They say things like "you ain't so bad (dramatic pause) for a white girl." And, when we are dancing around the cell block to entertain ourselves (my friend Galina in the neighboring cell can scat like she is channeling a Slavic version of Betty Carter), they tell me I move like a sista' and that I could easily have a starring role in a hip-hop video. I'm not sure if I'm flattered or not, but I think many of my outside peers would savor that as a compliment. The whiter you are, the more privileged your background, the more being "ghetto" is supposed to be a coveted commodity. I never understood this trend, the rich boarding school boys with droopy pants, walking with the lilt of a drug lord thug. Wispy wheat-haired lasses showing their palm and saying in a staccato cadence, "Talk to the hand." I appreciate the grit and flavor such mannerisms represent, but wouldn't it make more sense for people to want to mimic the rich and powerful? Of course, I'm not sure which would be more absurd, a prep-schooled, Ivy-educated, wavy-haired, nose-sculpted young woman like myself trying to talk jive (if jive is still spoken) or a middle-class, third generation mixed Eastern European young woman, also like myself, trying to act like a Vanderbilt.

Like I said, I digress. But that is actually not so off point. Because really, what got me here, into cell block six, had a lot to do with people (yours truly included) trying to appear like something they are not: morning television.

Dear *New Day USA*—

I watch your show everyday and have for years. But yesterday, I noticed that Faith had changed her hair style. I don't like it. She looks much better with a side part.
Sandy Franklin
Winona, WI

1

"Thirty seconds to air!" The stage manager skipped over the wires strewn about the floor and jumped behind the row of semi-robotic cameras.

"Shit!" The frail makeup artist rushed forward, armed with a powder puff, and dived for Ken Klark's shiny, pert nose. The white dust settled and she was gone, out of the shot.

"Ten seconds!"

Klark stroked his chiseled chin, smoothed back what there was to smooth of his ever so trendy, close-cropped, salt-and-pepper hair, and ran his tongue over his neon-white teeth. Four thousand dollars in caps right there. He had expensed them to the network, which did not contest.

"Five seconds!"

He tugged his dark blue blazer behind him once more and sat up cocksure.

"Three! Two!" On the unspoken count of "One" the stage manager mimed a gunshot at Klark, who smiled, leaned a bit forward, waiting a beat for the zooming camera lens to settle on him.

"Good morning, everyone! It's a New Day, USA!" he said. "Today is April 4th, and this is ZBC News. I'm Ken Klark."

"And I'm Faith Heide." A small, bobbed blonde in a fitted red sweater popped up on the screen, emitting a girl-next-door smile into eight point five million homes.

And I'm fucked, I thought as I ran into the control room behind the set, twenty minutes late. You are supposed to check your graphics and chyrons before the show, not when it's already live on the air.

The eyes of the executive producer were illuminated by the wall of monitors at the front of the darkened room, making it particularly intimidating as he turned them toward me for a brief moment, adding pressure to my dangerously undercaffeinated brain.

It was never a good thing to enter the control room without having had at least a sip of morning coffee, because even with the dimmed lights and hushed tones, the place was electrically charged. Figuratively, I mean. Of course it was literally, too. I often thought they turned down the lights not because it was easier for the director to focus on the monitors, since the darkness cuts down on the glare, but because sometimes it seemed the energy emitted by live television was too powerful to face front on. Think about it. For something to have enough energy to hold the attention of someone as far away as, say, Huntsville, Alabama, imagine the energy it has when up close and personal.

I tiptoed over to the row of graphics terminals.

"Maria," I whispered to the unionized (and therefore to be treated very nicely) woman whose job it was to hit the button to call up each title as the director asked for it. "Can I check my chyron list at the break?"

She didn't respond, but I knew she heard me. So I hovered,

counting down the seconds to the commercial interruption, at which point I knew, because we had been through this before, she would wordlessly, if slightly aggressively, punch up the titles on the computer so I could make sure that none of the characters in my piece would have a misspelled name show up underneath them on the screen. I did this because such an error is one of journalism's cardinal sins. No matter how moving, how well-crafted, well-researched, well-written, well-produced your piece, be it an article or a lower-third graphic for a segment of fluff, spelling someone's name wrong was as good for your career as if you got caught sleeping with the big boss's husband. Actually, that's a bad analogy. In network television, most of the big bosses have wives.

"It's P-u-r-n-e-l-l," I said. "Not P-e-r-n-e-l-l."

"That's what you sent us." She didn't turn to look at me when she said this.

"I know. That's why I'm here. We have to fix it." I was talking through my teeth, but trying to sound sweet and sympathetic all the same.

"Whatever," she said, typing in the correction one rigid finger at a time.

I exhaled. It was 7:12. That meant about eighteen more minutes for airing "important" stories, and twenty-three minutes until mine.

I went to the green room to steal some coffee. Technically, that pot was for the guests. But the mud they made for the staff was just plain offensive, and I'm sorry, I worked very hard and was entitled to something that was, at the very least, drinkable.

The green room was not actually green. Green rooms hardly ever are. When I worked at *Sunrise America,* the walls were blue. Here, our walls were a soothing, creamy yellow. If Franklin, the middle-aged man who considered himself the patron of the room, a man steeped in petty authority and indulgently expensive colognes, wasn't around, it was one of my favorite places to watch the show. The couch and chairs were upholstered in a soft, welcoming tweed, the monitors were tuned to every network, for comparison's sake, and there was an abundant spread of fresh fruit, cheese and pastries.

That day, a B-list movie star was holding court next to the latest reality game show reject, and I knew that Franklin wouldn't dare say anything to me in front of them. And by the time the show was over, he would have forgotten my trespass.

Or he would have if it weren't for the fact that as I turned to exit, carrying my hot, filled-to-the-brim cup of much needed coffee, I walked right into— Oh!

"Oh, my God, I am so sorry," I said as I put down my foam cup and grabbed for some paper napkins.

"Don't worry. It's just my shoe."

"No, but..." I bent down to mop up the brown liquid that was pooling at the front crease of this guy's tan suede Wallabies.

"It's really okay." And then he bent down just as I was looking up and...

"Ow." *Shit.* My head hit his chin.

"S'okay." And his tongue was bleeding.

This was worse than misspelling a name. I had now ruined the tongue of a man who, I assumed, was supposed to be a guest on our show. A speaking guest.

Franklin was already at the guest's side, ice water in hand, ushering him to the couch, fawning over him as if he were a damaged little bird.

I pulled myself up and started to apologize again.

"Wheelly," the guest said, tongue in cup, green eyes on me, "I wasn't wooking either."

Luckily, the B-list star and the reality guest had been too wrapped up in the accolades of their publicity entourages to notice what was going on. And before Franklin could chew me out, a barely postpubescent production intern appeared to say the guest named Mark was needed in makeup.

The tongueless guy stood up. "'At's me."

"Let me show you where to go," I said. "I promise it's safe now." He laughed and followed me down the hall.

I was never a morning person. I liked to think the fact that the bulk of my career was spent in the trenches of morning television was inexplicable. I'd started out my career assuming that by this point (the moment I spilled the coffee on the show, I mean, not right now, sitting here scribbling behind bars), almost ten years into it, I would be producing world-changing investigative reports and documentary-length profiles of the interesting and important. But aside from the fact that there wasn't much of an audience for such things, it turned out that getting a staff job at one of the few programs (most of them on public television) that did that sort of work required a kind of wake-up-and-smell-the-blood ambition I just didn't have. As already alluded to, when I woke up, I couldn't really do much until I smelled the coffee. And if you didn't wake up smelling blood, the rumor was that the only other way of getting one of those jobs was by waking up and smelling some suit's morning breath, if you know what I mean. Fortunately (or maybe unfortunately) that opportunity hadn't come my way.

Instead, I had developed a talent for turning out perfectly toned feel-good feature stories for the top-ranked national morning show. Wake-up-and-start-your-day-inspired stories. Have-a-good-chuckle-in-the-morning stories. Learn-how-to-improve-your-life-with-the-latest-soon-to-be-forgotten-exercise-trend stories. But sometimes, especially since the war, if I was lucky, I was able to sneak in an occasional learn-something-valuable-about-the-world-at-large story, and it was that sort of thing that kept me going. Like this day's story, for example.

"So, what do you do here?"

"Huh?"

"You work here, right?" said the man named Mark, tongue clearly improving, honey-brown hair being combed and teased. I was standing on the threshold of the fluorescent lit makeup room, waiting to escort him back to the green room once the face powder set, watching the artists work him up like a diva, slathering cover-up around his eyes as if looking like he was approaching his mid-thirties, which he did, was not entirely acceptable.

"Oh. Yeah." I twisted my ponytail around in my hand. My hair was long then, and I accidentally caught a strand in my mouth. I hated it when I did that.

I pulled it out, hoping he hadn't noticed. "Sorry. No coffee yet, you know? My brain isn't fully functional."

He laughed and playfully suggested I drink some off his shoe. Ha. Ha.

"I usually don't come to the studio," I said, explaining that I only did tape pieces, suggesting by my tone that I was somehow above the 6:00 a.m. call, like I was showing off. Which I suppose I was.

"So, why are you here today?"

"I heard one of our guests needed some coffee." He was looking at me via my reflection in the mirror, and I was deeply regretting hitting the snooze button earlier, not allowing myself enough time to put on any makeup. But, looking at my reddening cheeks, I knew I didn't need any blush.

He smiled. *Cute dimples,* I thought, which made me a little nervous. I glanced at my watch.

"We should get going."

The stylist sprayed Mark's (thick) hair one last time, trying unsuccessfully to tame a small cowlick on the right side of his head. He laughed (look at those dimples) and told her to leave it, that without it no one would know it was really him on TV.

I brought him to the sound check, where a lavaliere microphone was clipped to his tie, and then I left him with another nubile production assistant so I could get to the control room in time to watch my piece.

"Sorry again," I said over my shoulder.

"Don't apologize," he said. "I feel like I should buy you a coffee or something. I was the one who got in your way."

I emitted a shrill giggle (ugh!) and rushed down the hall. By the time I reached the control room, my cheeks were so flushed they hurt.

"What's wrong with you?" my friend Caitlin whispered as I sidled up next to her. Caitlin was another producer on the show, although she only did live bookings—politicians, pundits and their ilk. We'd worked together for years now, sharing late nights at work and many drinks at the corner bar afterward, and our friendship had long extended beyond the office. She was a friend I could call after a bad date or a bad haircut. I was a friend she would call for the same. Truth be told, for her the bad haircuts were pretty common. She had recently acquired an unflattering bob, streaked in brassy shades of red and yellow that seemed to change with each flicker of the monitor lights. She tried to tone it down by clipping it back with little baby barrettes, and the general visage was far from professional. Certainly, she looked odd as we stood in the control room, hovering in the back row where the segment producers waited to watch their pieces hit the airwaves. Apparently, I looked a little odd myself.

"Annie?" She tried again. "Your cheeks are like a clown's. What's going on?"

"Nothing," I said, my voice still sort of shrill.

"Whatever." She let out a quiet, knowing chuckle. "Thanks for babysitting my guest. I got here late."

"Mark?"

"Yeah. He goes on after your segment. Isn't he cute?"

"I didn't really notice."

She gave me a don't bullshit me kind of look. I glanced at the clock: 7:34.

"Excuse me, my piece is up." I went to stand next to the executive producer, the EP, which is what we producers did so we could gauge his reaction when our pieces were on. It was the only time to get feedback. The rest of the day, he was too busy planning for tomorrow. There is no such thing as retrospect in morning television. It's all present tense and tease the future.

"Take camera five! Cue music! Dissolve four." The director brought us safely out of commercial. "Take three!"

Faith Heide looked up.

"Welcome back to *New Day USA,*" she said with an engaging

smile, which quickly morphed into a furrowed, concerned-citizen look. "Later this hour, is the popular eggshell diet safe? And we'll talk to the stars of the hot new reality show *Who's Your Mama*. But first (pregnant pause), for this week's edition of our *American Ideals* series, I met a man whose free-market ingenuity is helping to improve the lives of some women who, until recently, didn't know what it meant to be free."

She turned her head to watch the video on the enormous plasma monitor to her left, and then the image went full screen.

I breathed in deeply. I always got a bit of a knot in my stomach when I heard the words I had written come out of an anchor's mouth. I never knew what they were going to do with them. And Faith, of late, had apparently decided she needed to be taken more seriously. Meaning she was constantly lowering her voice a few octaves and interjecting poignancy with per-ceptible sighs, trying, I suppose, to sound smarter. You could try to tell her to speak normally, but she wasn't one for taking direction. Her agent had recently negotiated to get her the largest salary in television history (with a decade-long job guar-antee), so she probably felt that she didn't really need to learn anything new.

"Douglas Purnell might not look like someone who would care much about mascara," Faith's narration began. I watched my work in the staccato reflections of light the monitor cast upon my boss's face. A flicker of emotion from him would be victorious. Call it compassion fatigue, but most television news professionals are in-tensely jaded. Once, I had produced a piece about a reunion of people who had grown up in a brutal orphanage. But the show was tight on time and something needed to go. "What do you think?" the director had asked the executive producer. The EP had turned to him and said, as if it was the most obvious thing, "Kill the orphans."

Anyway, the piece I had on that day had nothing to do with orphanages. It was a profile about this guy Doug Purnell who had set up a number of beauty parlors and cosmetics laboratories in Fardish refugee camps at the southern edge of the former Soviet Union, all run by women. We didn't shoot there, of course. There was no budget for international travel anymore, especially if it meant going to upsetting places where we'd once funded wars. All of the interviews were done stateside, in Purnell's D.C. office (an organization called Cosmetic Relief) except for a short pickup bit shot by one of the freelance crews the network retained in the region, and there was some amateur DV footage provided by Purnell himself. But it was clear, from the translated sound bites, that these women were immensely grateful to him. He was helping them become self-sufficient while building self-esteem in the process. And the story was as all-American as a network could ask for because a major American cosmetics company had loaned funds and supplies. It was the best story I had done in a while. The most interesting to me, anyway.

People always told me I had the coolest job. I traveled all over the country; I met loads of interesting, colorful people. Celebrities mostly bored me, they were so ubiquitous in my work. So, yes, I would say I had a cool job. But I also had a growing sadness about what I did. It was a feeling of constant loss. I would put in weeks and weeks researching, shooting, writing and editing hours of footage, building relationships with strangers and soothing their fears that they might be portrayed badly, and out of it came about three minutes, four if I was lucky, of a story that most people only half watched because they were chomping on their Cheerios as it played. And then it was gone. There might be an e-mail or two of follow-up, colleagues might say something like "nice piece" when I got back to the office, but that was basically that. The end of it, and on to the next one.

Besides, even if they did put down their Cheerios and watch, they would have no idea that you, the producer, had any hand in it, because someone like Faith would appear in a few shots and have her voice laid in. Some of the correspondents I worked with were more involved than others, and some were really great, but the truth was, in order to show up on the air every day, someone else had to be doing some of the lifting for you. With Faith, "some" really meant "all."

Sometimes I believed that she believed she had actually done the reporting. And why not? From beauty queen to weather girl to network wonder, Faith Heide always had a presence that caused people to take notice, and a voice that kept their attention. And that, in the end, is probably what matters: the personality of the person asking the questions and telling the tale, not who wrote the actual story. Or, rather, what matters is the viewer's *perception* of the personality of the person asking the questions and telling the tale.

I used to question the astronomic salary scales of our on-air talent, but after years in the business, traveling around, talking to our viewers, watching the mercurial dances of the ratings' shifts, I'm starting to think they deserve those big bucks. Their roles remind me of psychotherapy, with its theories of projection and all of that. It's morning, the audience is just waking up, and these faces on the screen, these players, are extensions of their dreams—people they know but not really, events they are familiar with but not entirely. It isn't actually news they are looking for when they turn on the TV; it is more of the same. And because of that, no story, no presentation of a story, can deviate too far from their expectations; it would be too disruptive, too jarring to their psyches. They would change the channel. But instead they had Faith. After all these years of appearing in people's bedrooms every morning, Faith seemed so familiar and so credible, that, well, she just had to be there. They stayed tuned.

"And for more information about my report, check out our Web site," she said, smiling. "Ken?"

His turn.

"Nice story, Faith," he said, as if he actually liked her, and then turned to a new camera angle. "Coming up—long-lasting lip sticks. Are they safe? And later, did she do it? Hollywood vixen Asia Sheraton is here to tell her side of the story. But first, he has been called the vice president's Prozac, the most trusted man on Pennsylvania Avenue, the brain of the millennium. And he's only thirty-five. People are saying that senior White House aide and speechwriter Mark Thurber is going to be a central player in Vice President Hacker's upcoming presidential bid. He's here with us this morning to give us an insider's perspective of what some say is the most secretive administration in history, and to discuss his new book, *The Scribe Inside: Memoirs of a White House Advisor.* Good morning, Mark. So nice to have you here."

"Good morning to you, Ken. It's nice to be here."

Oh my God. "That's Mark *Thurber?*" I asked Caitlin, who had come to stand between me and the EP (it was her turn to gauge his take on things). She didn't answer, though. She didn't have to.

"Are you enjoying your visit to New York?" said Ken. "It seems we hardly ever see members of the administration outside of D.C. these days." Cue large, fluorescent white smile.

Thurber laughed and said something about the terror threat being too high to allow high-ranking officials into the pubic eye. "But I'm glad I risked it today. I've quite enjoyed meeting some members of your staff," said the man *People* magazine had recently named Washington's Most Eligible Bachelor.

He looked different in person than he did in those airbrushed photos. A little more weathered and more, well, like a lot of guys I know: healthy, a bit on the thin side (I read somewhere that he was a marathon runner), dressed according to the preppy-chic suggestions of the latest J. Crew catalog. Job aside, I wouldn't say he was all that exceptional. Except look at that smile. Look at those dimples.

My cheeks started to burn. And at that moment, though of course I didn't know it at the time, the trajectory of my life was rerouted onto a different track.

Dear *New Day USA,*

I just want to thank Ken and Faith for being there for me each mourning (sic), bringing the important events of the world into my home. They are both so smart and well informt (sic) and Faith is so lovely and Ken is like the brother I never had. Would it be possible to have them send me autographt (sic) pictures? It would mean the world to me.

George Albridge
Allentown, PA

2

It sounded like a broken radiator, the almost deafening hiss that blasted through the Sweetwater, Texas Convention Center. And it was palpable, how the moist summer heat helped the noxious odor cling to my hair and my clothes. The smell was urinelike, and was particularly intense near the large pits in the center of the floor. Like at the pit I was standing next to as my correspondent, armed with freshly applied lipstick, protective gear and a poker, was learning how to extract the venom from a rattler who, unbeknownst to him (or maybe her), was on his way to the slaughter two pits down the way. I was in the depths of what a logical person might have thought to be the worst cliché of a Freudian nightmare imaginable. There were, in the space surrounding me, about five thousand live and very angry rattlesnakes. We were shooting a few interviews and some footage for a feature piece before we went out to participate in what was and probably still is the world's largest rattlesnake roundup. This wasn't exactly the place I would have liked to be when my phone rang—and the person calling was the guy who had become the subject of a more preferable variety of dreams. I probably wouldn't have even answered except I didn't know it was him because the caller ID was blocked.

"Hello? This is Annabelle," I said, sounding very serious. When I answered the phone on work time, my voice tended to drop a few octaves (sort of like Faith's, I suppose), something my friends ribbed me about to no end. My normal voice, my casual voice, was (and is) a bit on the high side; telemarketers often asked if my mother was home.

"Hello? Hello?" He didn't introduce himself, but having watched the tape of his appearance on our show too many times to count, I knew his voice. Mark Thurber's soft but masculine lyrics "I've enjoyed meeting your staff" had become the sonnet that lulled me to sleep at night. And, because Caitlin told me she had given him my number, I had been anxiously anticipating his call for the past few days.

"Hi!" My response got caught in the back of my throat and came out like a chirp.

"Hello?" he said again. "I'm sorry. I think we have a bad connection." Now he was almost yelling. "There is a loud hissing sound. I'll call back."

"It's just snakes!" I said, basically shrieking. He hung up anyway.

"What's next?" said my correspondent, who was gripping the neck of a fanged rattler with her manicured fingers, gripping it so he couldn't bite her and, understandably, at arm's length.

"Did you get a tight shot of the fangs?" I asked the cameraman. He glared at me as if it was a dumb question, because it was. I looked back at my correspondent. She was looking a little ashen under all the foundation and blush. She was, after all, standing in the middle of the pit, as opposed to standing comfortably on the other side of the wall with me. There were snakes trying to strike at her steel plated boots, and more snakes slithering between her feet.

"Drop it and get out," I said. And if that isn't power, I don't know what is.

The dynamic between producer and correspondent is a delicate one. On the one side you have an outwardly needy and demanding ego, and on the other, an inwardly needy and demanding ego. Sometimes it's hard to tell which is which. It can get incredibly tense, but without each other, we would both be unemployed; I look like a Muppet in front of the camera, and some of the correspondents I worked with couldn't write themselves out of, well, a rattlesnake pit. To be fair, not this correspondent. This one I liked. We might have covered a lot of really silly stories, but given the opportunity, she was a good journalist—and she could write. More importantly, she was a friend.

"Oh my, he called, didn't he?" Natasha said as she climbed out of the pit and landed safely on the snake-free cement floor.

"Huh? How did you know?"

"You are holding your phone the way I was holding that snake." It was true. I had the phone at arm's length, as if it might bite. "You look like you are channeling a signal from outer space," she said.

"Maybe that's what I need to do."

"Let me know if you get any reception."

So I held the phone higher, playing at the extraterrestrial idea, and as the antenna hit its apex, the phone rang again.

We both gave a start. I looked at the display. No caller ID.

"Do you think it's him?" I let it ring again.

"Answer it!"

I didn't. And it rang once more. Natasha grabbed the phone from me.

"Annabelle Kapner's phone... May I ask who is calling?" She looked at me, eyebrows up. "It's a Mr. Sage calling from Media-Aid."

Immediately deflated, I reached over to take the call.

"This is Annabelle."

I had no idea who Mr. Sage was, much less Media-Aid, and was quite prepared to send this call to the snakes, as it were.

"Ms. Kapner, we need to talk."

"I am sorry, I'm in the middle of a shoot. Would you mind calling back and leaving a message on my voice—"

"It's very important that we speak..." He had a slightly affected accent that I couldn't place.

"Sir, I'm sure it is important, but this is a really bad time for me to talk." Didn't he hear the hissing?

"Self-important bitch," he said, and hung up.

Stunned, I stared at the keypad, as if it could tell me something.

It wasn't the first time I had gotten an irate viewer call, assuming that was what this was. But no one had ever been quite so harsh. It felt as if one of the snakes had bitten me. Maybe it was the smell of the place, maybe it was the call, but my skin suddenly became cold and prickly, and I thought I might lose my balance, which is not something you want to do when standing near a rattlesnake pit. So I took a few deep breaths to still my nerves, put the phone into the back pocket of my jeans and walked away.

Natasha and the crew were already heading over to the concession area, where you could buy rattlesnake key chains, wallets and gall bladders (considered by the Japanese to be an aphrodisiac) among other things. I went to join them and distracted myself by stocking up on souvenirs, planning to expense them as props.

When I first started working in this business, a veteran field producer named John Mitchell had called me into his office and sat me down in a fatherly sort of way. Mitchell was a little creepy (rumor had it there were a number of harassment complaints filed against him), but he had promised to give me tips about how to succeed at the networks, so there I sat. He smiled, baring horribly crooked teeth, and told me that if I wanted to be a producer, which I did, I needed to learn to pad my expense reports. I started to ask about the ethics of doing such a thing, but he interrupted before I could finish the question. It's an unspoken honor system, he said. If every producer padded then it wouldn't be suspicious if something odd showed up. And odd things always showed up. Usually they were legitimate. Mitchell (multiple Emmy-winning, I should point out) told me he was once doing a live remote in an open field when a large cow got in the way of the shot. He asked the farmer to please move his cow, to which the farmer replied, "You wanna move her, you gotta buy her." So there it was, under "misc. expenses"—One Cow: $1,000.00.

"What do you think of this?" said Natasha, holding out a stuffed, coiled adult rattlesnake.

"I think you should have that on set when you introduce the piece," I declared, suddenly excited by this idea, happy to move on from the strange call. I imagined Faith having to confront a pile of dead, stuffed snakes on live TV, and I picked up another coiled one off the table, admiring the wide-open mouth, the pointy fangs up close and personal. A tiny bit of plastic dripped down from the tips, approximating venom.

Then my phone rang.

It rang again.

I was going to let it ring through to voice mail, but Natasha grabbed the antenna, and pulled the phone out of my pocket.

"Annabelle Kapner's office," she said, winking at me, mouthing, *"Maybe it's him?"*

And then she turned paler than she had been in the pit.

"They hung up," she said, and handed me the phone. "Annabelle, what was that story you had on last week?"

"About the Fardish beauty parlors?"

"Yeah, that one."

"Why?"

"I think it might have pissed someone off."

I looked at her blankly.

"Whoever that was just called you a few unspeakable terms, said something in some foreign language and then slammed down the phone."

I tend to be a fairly nonconfrontational person, or at least I was before I landed in jail, and one of the things I liked about morning television was that we hardly ever did the sort of stories that pissed people off. We stayed positive and hopeful because negativity is hard to stomach in the morning. Of course, it did happen upon occasion that people felt misrepresented (as I mentioned, we did get irate calls periodically), but usually that was because they felt they did not get enough airtime to promote whatever it was they were promoting, not because they felt personally slighted. And if a story was somehow critical, we did our darnedest to balance it to within an inch of its life, even if it was an unbalanced story to begin with. Often after my segments aired the subjects involved sent me flattering e-mails and even flowers. Once I got a cashmere scarf, but I had to return it because the network's news standards don't allow us to accept gifts worth more than seventy-five dollars. Of course, you could argue that the wholesale value of the scarf was less than that, which is why I did keep the matching hat.

"Annie?"

I had fainted. I must have been out for a while because when I opened my eyes, we were in a makeshift infirmary. The rattling sounded distant, but I knew we were in the convention center because the table across from me was lined with rows and rows of bottles of antivenom.

"Annabelle? Are you okay?" Natasha was sitting on a metal folding chair next to the stretcher I was lying on, patting a cool, damp cloth across my forehead.

"Where's the crew?"

"I sent them to shoot the snake hunt. Don't worry about it. Are you okay?"

"I think I fainted."

"You did."

A medic came over to check me out. He had greasy hair and was missing a front tooth, and I really didn't want him to touch me. I sat up.

"I'm okay. I must have overheated," I said, which was a stupid thing to say, because if anything the place was overly air-conditioned.

Natasha and the medic shared a knowing glance.

"I'm okay," I said again, and tried to stand. They both pushed me back down and told me to sit still for a while. The medic handed me a small paper cup filled with lukewarm water. I drank it down and handed it back to him. "It was probably the smell that knocked me out. Really, I'm okay."

"Why don't you relax for a few more minutes?"

"We need to keep shooting," I said. Never come back from a shoot without a story, that's the rule. Once, Natasha and I were doing a story about lobster fishing. Actually, it was about a lobsterman calendar. Anyway, it turned out that the Dramamine my cameraman had taken had expired two years earlier, and he spent the bulk of our boat ride tossing up over the side. But every few minutes he would wipe his mouth and take a few shots of Natasha helping the beefcake lobsterman bring in the traps, before he had to return to face the sea. The video wasn't his usual standard, but at least we had something to put on the air.

My phone rang again. I was resigned, and also by now a bit curious, so this time I answered on the first ring.

"This is Annabelle," I said tentatively.

"Hey. It's Mark Thurber."

I thought I might faint again, I was so relieved. And so nervous.

"Remember, we met on your show the other day?" he said.

"Sure," I said. "How are you doing?" As if his calling was the most normal thing in the world, as if we spoke every day, as if I hadn't just fainted from the combined shock of receiving two really odd phone calls and the hideous smell of thousands of rattlesnakes.

"Um, I was wondering. Well, I am going to be in New York next week..." (He said "um"! He was nervous, too!) "...and I was wondering if you might be around. Maybe I could treat you to that coffee we talked about."

What is that phrase, emotional whiplash? One second I am being harassed, the next I am being courted. I felt dizzy. Adrenaline was furiously racing through my body. I looked to Natasha for focus. She was making quizzical expressions, eyebrows up, forehead creased, desperate to know who I was talking to. *"It's Thurber,"* I mouthed, and she did a little dance, which made me smile.

"Yeah," I said. "I think I'm around. Let me just check my Palm." I counted to ten and then we made plans to meet after work on Tuesday.

The nice thing about being in jail, if one has to say something positive, is that it gives you plenty of space and time to appreciate honesty. More than appreciate it—recognize it. Or rather, recognize the bullshit. I am realizing that this is a very important skill to have, bullshit recognizing, and that it's one I sorely lacked before I got here.

Take my history with men. My last relationship, if I can call it that, had ended about six months before the phone calls in the rattlesnake pit. It had started online, and it pretty much ended there. The guy was nice enough, and apparently a number of other virtually sophisticated women agreed with me. We had been dating for a few months when we decided to take the next step; we took down our profiles from nicedate.com. But he was a lawyer, and a slippery one at that, so when a friend of mine discovered that he still had his profile up on ivyleaguedates.com, he defended himself by saying he had never agreed to take his profile off of *that* site. The ethical legacy of the Clinton era, I suppose. We lasted two more months. He was quite charming, and I was entering the age of the "why aren't you married yet" question, so I desperately tried to make it work. But when another friend discovered my beloved's profile on swingdate.com, well, let's just say I logged off of men for a while.

And now here I was, surrounded by thousands and thousands of very phallic creatures, being pursued by Mr. Too Good To Be True.

"Are you okay?" Natasha asked again, after we had completed our mandatory round of "Oh my God! That was him! Oh my God!"

"I feel fine."

"I mean about that other phone call. Before you fainted. What do you think that was?"

"I think," I said, suddenly bolstered by Mark's call and insanely energized, "I think I have no idea, but I'm ready to go find the crew now." She said okay, because she also knew the rules, and we hitched a ride on the back of a farmer's pickup truck, off to hunt some snakes.

To whom it may concern at *New Day USA:*

You had a story on this morning about a new facial yoga that helps to reduce wrinkles. Can you please tell me where I can find these classes?

Thank you,

Bonnie Eager

Fargo, ND

3

Tuesday.

We were supposed to meet at 7:00 p.m., but I was, as usual, running late. My senior supervising producer still hadn't signed off on the edit, promos was demanding more snake footage and my video editor was all bitchy because he only worked until six, per union rules, and he refused to do any overtime. And the piece aired tomorrow. It was 5:55 when the word came down that Carl was finally in his office, ready to screen. Carl Van Dunt—he was my supervisor. So up I went, tape in hand.

Many correspondents didn't have the time to sit through screenings, but Natasha took a pride of ownership in her work and tried to make a point of it, so I stopped by her office to grab her to come with me.

"Shh!" she said, vigorously waving for me to enter.

"What's up? We have to go to Carl's—"

"Shh! Listen."

Natasha's office was directly across from Tom Tatcher's, the

EP's. He had a corner window and she had no windows, but from a power perspective, it was a great place to be. The building was erected in the seventies, apparently a time when not a lot of attention was paid to soundproofing.

"He's in there with a team from legal."

This was weird. Legal hardly ever came up to our floor. Why would they? People don't regularly sue over diet fads and celebrity interviews.

We leaned forward intently. I couldn't hear much, but I was pretty sure I heard my name. Then they said their goodbyes.

The door opened and four men walked out. All in suits, Tom included. Down to the elevator bank and gone for the day.

"You heard my name, right?" I said, whispering.

"Don't be stupid. That wasn't you they were talking about."

"Do you know any other Annabelles here?"

"Maybe they said Isabel? You know, Isabel, the new girl?"

"She's an intern."

"So?"

"Well, what were they talking about?"

"I don't know. I just caught the tail end of it."

"Maybe I should talk to Tom, tell him about the calls?"

"What could he do? It's been almost a week and they haven't called back, and you have no idea what the story is, anyway. I'm sure he has other things to deal with."

Which was true. It was incredibly hard to get the attention of the boss, and you had to be judicious about it. Tom was a nice guy and tried to be welcoming, but his job was just too nuts. I used to think I wanted to climb the network ladder, perhaps run a show myself one day, but when I watched my supervisors, and especially the executive producers, I really started to question my career track. The stories, the guests, the competition, the overly ambitious young staffers, the hotheaded anchors, the egocentric correspondents, the late nights, the early mornings, the ratings, the marketing, the press, the promotion, the spin—it all fell on their heads, 24/7 (you can forget about a personal life), and the job security was as good as the weekly Nielsen Report. The American public could, essentially, vote you off the island on any given day, contracts be damned. We were the number one morning show, but only by a few ratings points. Should one of the other two network programs start creeping up (which they seemed to be doing), it was an invitation to a beheading.

"Let's go see Carl," I said. "My editor is about to bolt."

Neither of us liked Carl, and he didn't really like us, either. Carl was in the twilight of his career, recently fired from a big job at a different network, only to be hired by ours (word was he was golf buddies with the suits at the top). Carl had a big title for years and years over there, running one soon-to-be-canceled show after another, but the rumor was that for the past decade or so no one over there ever knew what he actually did. They said he spent so much time standing in the lobby, seeing and being seen, that everyone joked he should accept the dry cleaning deliveries so at least he would be of value.

Things didn't change much when he came to *New Day USA*. He had a big, beautiful office with big beautiful paintings, but most of the time he wasn't there; he was out in front of the building, modeling his stylish suits, which were decades too young for him, laughing loudly so everyone could see he was having a good time. He just seemed to be one of those people who kept fluffing his feathers and somehow charming the right people enough that he failed up and up.

The sad thing was, once upon a time, Carl was actually worth what they paid him. Word was that in the early days of his career, he was breaking stories right and left. He spent years covering war zones, telling stories that no one else would tell. But somewhere along the line, things changed. He started doing more and more pieces filled with style and less and less filled with substance. He was one of the first producers to mandate that every edit should be a dissolve, that more time should be spent worrying about the lighting and the correspondents' haircuts than about the questions they were asking.

Purists didn't like what Carl was doing, but the audience did. And as the ratings went up, so did Carl's stature in some parts (the money parts) of the industry. In fact, a lot of people credit Carl with the softening of the network news, but I think that might be a little too generous (or malicious, depending on your view of the world).

Anyway, you might think that someone who had been around so long would want to nurture younger staffers like us, maybe try to relive his proud and productive early years, but the truth was it often felt like he resented us. Understandably. We took up his time with our petty needs when he could otherwise be schmoozing with the people who actually could impact his career and his wallet. Never married, never really appearing all that happy, he had only his job and his authority, and in the end, there was no security in that.

Word was, after years of him doing pretty much nothing, the suits in our front office had seen the light and were now trying to push him out, make room for some younger, less wrinkled, less expensive blood, and Carl was holding on for dear life, making dealings with him more uncomfortable than ever. Up front he was as charming as all get-out, but he routinely took credit for other people's work, gossiped incessantly (well, we all did that) and, worse, liked to change our pieces just to put his fingerprints on them. In fact, he was sort of a tyrant; he enjoyed tearing producers (and especially associate producers) to shreds. He would never raise his voice, but would say things like "this makes absolutely no sense" and "who wrote this shit?" and "how did you ever get a job at a network, anyway?" Usually he was comparably easy on me, but not always; he was the first and only person ever to make me cry at work.

But he was a sucker for celebrity.

"Annie has a date with Mark Thurber tonight," Natasha said before we even sat down.

I should have been pissed, but I knew Carl would be impressed (I was a bit impressed with myself, after all), and, more importantly, I knew that he would be nice to me in the hopes that I would return with good gossip tomorrow. And, hope of all hopes, he probably figured if a relationship took root and Mark and I became an "it" couple, he could claim us as friends, one of whom was in a very powerful place.

Carl spoke to us while simultaneously consulting his Black-Berry, periodically typing a few things, putting it down, picking it back up again, as if to remind us of his importance, acting disinterested while inquiring about how Mark and I met, where we were going, what I thought might happen.

I stifled a sneeze. Carl's office was saturated with a musky male cologne (I could have sworn he shared it with Franklin); the scent trailed Carl wherever he went. It was so strong that some people would take the stairs if they saw him waiting for the elevator. It was weird, and made me wonder if smelling sensitivity toughens with age.

"Excuse mc," I said, and grabbed a tissue off his desk before offering up a little more information, just enough that we got the desired response.

"Did you make the changes we discussed earlier?" Carl asked, referring to his meddling with our snake piece.

"Of course." I blew my nose.

"Then I don't need to see it again. It's fine. Have fun tonight." He grabbed his remote and turned toward the monitor opposite his desk to watch the feeds of the evening news packages.

And that was that.

For now.

Dear *New Day USA*,

I am what some might call a news-junky. I am always very impressed with Ken's hard-hitting interview style and just wanted to say that I wish there were more newsmen like him. His recent interview with the White House spokesman Mark Thurber was very insightful, really pounding out the truth of our administration. Do you know if Mr. Thurber is single? Can you please give him my address and phone number? I have included it below.

Robin Fayer

Orlando, Florida

4

We met at Mecca, a Middle Eastern–themed bar on the roof of the new Scheherazade Hotel, the latest hot spot in town. Normally, as a regular gal, I wouldn't have been able to get past the red velvet rope (unless I wanted to risk waiting in the line that snaked through the lobby, leading up to a metal detector and an armed guard blocking the elevator bank). I suppose I could have shown my network news ID and claimed press privileges, which usually worked, but I was pretty sure my date's credentials were enough to merit VIP status.

"I'm meeting Mark Thurber," I said to the Armani-clad, steel-shouldered bouncer behind the rope. I could hear a few girls in the line behind me rustle when I said the name.

The bouncer looked at his list, asked to see my driver's license and unhooked the latch. "Twenty-ninth floor, take a right."

And there I went. Clop, clop, clop down the marbled hall and into the elevator.

And there he was, sitting at a small corner table, surrounded by candles and dark velvet cushions, wearing a little stubble and a dark gray shirt. I tried to take a good look at him, to take him in, in the flesh, without the studio makeup or the unreal glare of television lighting.

Sitting there, back straight, chin up, eyes searching around, Mark reminded me of the guys in high school that I had been too terrified to talk to, the thin, chiseled waspy ones that had landed at my progressive private school only after being expelled from a string of blue blood boarding schools or Upper East Side preps. He had floppy, straight brown hair, an aristocratic profile and a slightly smug countenance reminiscent of a British movie star. Totally out of my league. But then again, sometimes guys like that actually liked girls like me—thinking girls like me (with small bones, light olive skin, oversize eyes and the surgically altered residue of a prominent nose) to be somewhat exotic. Mark was trying to push down his cowlick when he looked up and saw me. He smiled (those dimples!).

"Hi," I said as I walked over to him, grateful that the Persian carpet snuffed out the graceless clop-clop of my high-heeled shoes. "I hope you haven't been waiting too long." I was only a few minutes late, but I hate when people aren't punctual. It's the producer in me—time sensitive and tightly scheduled.

"Just got here," he said, but he was probably lying. He was already halfway through whatever it was he was drinking. "Coffee?" he said, holding up what appeared to be a tube leading to a hookah pipe.

"That's coffee?"

"It actually is. Some strange coffee martini they make here. These are actually straws. Try it. It's good."

"Odd." I sat down and took a sip. "And clever."

Basically, the bowl was made to look like one of those Egyptian water pipes, but the proprietors had created a way to drink from them instead.

We bantered. We sipped our alcoholic coffee through straws.

It was like a lot of first dates, the kind where you talk and talk to avoid any awkward silences. Until the inevitable.

"So."

"So."

Silence.

"How about we order another one?" he said.

"Okay," I said.

I was surprised to find that I wasn't self-conscious and squirming next to a guy like him, but there I was, comfortably slouching into the pillows, gently touching Mark's arm after he accidentally spilled a little of the drink on the table and tried to mop it up with his sleeve without my noticing. I had noticed and I thought it sweet.

He told me about working in the White House, about how every day he had to pinch himself because he couldn't believe he was actually there, in the most powerful place on earth.

"What's he like?" I asked.

"Who?"

"The president, silly."

Mark laughed and said that, because I was a member of the press, he couldn't really give me a straightforward answer. And anyway, he said, he worked more directly with the vice president. So I asked about him.

"Off the record?" He gave an exaggerated snarl and then held up our now empty hookah. "Waiter! Can we have another one?"

Hookah or no hookah, Mark did not need much lubrication to

tell me that the VP was an ass. It was common knowledge that he was a screamer, a phone thrower, a man in dire need of mood stabilizers but too macho to take any. At one of his first press conferences (not that there were many), the VP took off his shoe and banged it on the podium in a manner reminiscent of a certain Soviet leader circa 1960. In fact, that was the perception—that the VP fancied the savior of America would come in the form of an iron-fisted, quasi-totalitarian, Sovietlike regime, just with a nice capitalist overtone. Since Mark was about as far as you could get from a gray, bland, perfunctory Soviet apparatchik, they didn't really get along on a personal level. That said, the vice president was preparing to run in the next presidential election, and Mark did have issues of professional longevity to consider.

"I figure I don't have to like him. And he doesn't have to like me," he said. The waiter returned and Mark leaned forward to take a sip from our refreshed bowl of caffeinated elixir. "As long as he likes what I write."

"But do you believe in what you write? I mean, do you believe in his policies?"

"His policies are based on the polls. So there isn't much to believe in. It's like that with any politician."

"That's ridiculous."

"I didn't say I respect it."

I sat back and crossed my arms, like a disappointed schoolteacher. "How can you live with yourself, working for something you don't respect?"

"Oh come on, people have lived with a lot worse. Especially in Washington. You just have to learn not to personalize the political."

"But that's not why you got into the business, is it? Just to rub elbows with power? I mean, you could have done a lot of things, I imagine. Why work in politics if you don't really think you're doing some good?"

"I didn't say we weren't doing any good. We are doing some good."

"Like what?" I said, and then immediately hated myself for being so argumentative.

Mark laughed. "You just can't suppress that hard-hitting reporter inside you, huh?"

"Yeah, right," I said, hiding the fact that I was blushing by sucking up some more of our drink. "But seriously, I'm sorry. I didn't mean it like that. I mean, I'm just curious about what it is about your work that moves you, you know, gets you out of bed in the morning?"

He fumbled with his straw. "I know it sounds clichéd, but I guess a lot of what we do is just simply better than the alternative. It's not that anything is so great, but we could be doing a lot worse. It probably sounds like moral gymnastics or defensive reasoning, but I do believe that." He took another sip. "At least I like to believe that I believe that," he said, looking up from the hookah with a full dimpled grin.

"What a mental menace," I said, citing the words Mark had in-famously coined referring to the Fardish president before he was, also Mark's words, effectively eviscerated.

He smiled again.

"You like those alliterations, don't you?" I said.

"This is a luxurious libation, don't you think?" he said, changing the subject with a wink.

An ambrosial aphrodisiac, I thought to myself as I lifted the straw to my mouth once again. And that, basically, is how, a couple of

hours later, I wound up in the hotel suite of a *People* magazine cer-
tified eligible bachelor.

And that's where he leaned forward across the plush velvet
couch and gave me a soft, gentle kiss on my mouth. He had soft,
full lips, warm and, oh…this is hard for me to write, even now.
One doesn't get many kisses like that behind bars.

"I should go," I said, not really wanting to, but proud of myself
for saying so.

"It's okay," he said, "we can just talk if you want."

I wanted to kiss him. "It's just, well, I don't want to do
anything stupid, and you are one of the most coveted guys in the
country and I really don't want to be another conquest and…"
I went on like this for a bit too long, embarrassing myself more
and more with each word. I grabbed a water bottle from the
coffee table and finished it off, because if I was drinking I
couldn't talk.

Mark laughed. His eyes closed when he laughed. It was incredibly sweet.

"You know the stupid thing?" he said, sitting back into the
cushions, away from me. "Because of that *People* article, sure I can
get laid, but no woman will trust me enough to take me seriously."

I shot him an impish grin. "Poor you."

"No. Seriously. I really like you, Annie. And I know it sounds
like a line, but I would really like to get to know you. See what
happens." He crossed his arms, giving himself an uneasy little hug.
"Is that okay?"

"Okay," I said, wanting to believe him. I told him that if we really
wanted to get to know each other, he had to trust that I understood that everything he said was off the record, and that made

him smile, as if there was a lot he wanted to tell me, which, of course (I later found out) there was.

We didn't kiss again that night. We just talked and talked until the sun started to rise, and then we both fell asleep on the bed, fully dressed.

When I woke up, there were two pink peonies on my pillow. Mark was in his hotel-issued, white terry-cloth bathrobe, watching me.

"I stole them from the breakfast spread," he said, pointing his chin at the flowers.

There was a cart with coffee and pastries at the foot of the bed. He poured me a cup and sat down next to me. I sat up to take it.

"Peonies are my favorite," I said. "And lilacs."

He smiled.

I smiled.

It was a little awkward again. And there was no alcohol in this brew.

"You have beautiful hair." He gently touched my brown tangled nest.

I worried about my morning breath.

"What time is it?" I said, looking for the television remote. Found it. I turned on my show. "I have a piece on at 7:44."

"Cool." Mark looked at his watch. "We have thirty seconds." He put his arm around my shoulder, giving me a quick squeeze, causing me to spill a bit of the coffee on the sheet.

It is an odd thing to watch someone watching your work, especially when it's someone you have a crush on. And, if I could have chosen it, this certainly wasn't the first piece I wanted Mark to see.

"Wow," he said when the story was over and Natasha was showing Faith and Ken some of our purchases. "That was totally disgusting."

"You don't like snakes?"

"Remember, I work in Washington."

I laughed. "It was pretty gross. The place smelled like a subway toilet."

"I think I might have fainted if I got anywhere near one of those pits."

"I did faint," I said, quickly regretting admitting that.

"You did? From the smell?"

"No, I...I don't really know why."

"You don't know?"

"Well, I had gotten a disturbing call, and it kind of made me unbalanced. And maybe that, with the smell, I don't know..."

Mark looked at me as if I was nuts. But in a sweet way. And I don't know why, but I guess I needed to talk about it with someone, so I told him the story. About the piece, about the calls.

"Wow," he said again. "I saw that story. I was there the day it aired, remember? It was a really nice piece, but what's the big deal?"

"I know. But Natasha said that the second caller specifically mentioned it when calling me all sorts of horrible things."

"Like what?"

It was too embarrassing for me to spell out how he had phrased in hideously derogatory terms that I was a weak journalist, a lazy hack, that reporting like mine was part of the problem, and that I might as well be producing Nazi propaganda and working for Leni Riefenstahl at the rate I was going. It had really hit a nerve.

"He just said stuff about the story being totally wrong and misleading, and basically blamed me for the downfall of society," I said. "There were some threats about needing to get it right, or else."

It sounded funny when I summed it up like that. Now I wasn't even so sure why I had gotten so upset.

"Or else?"

"Or else. I'm not really sure what."

"Well, who do you think it could be?"

"Honestly? My best guess is that it was some whack-job viewer. We do have a few, and they do make strange phone calls from time to time. But the weird thing is that I don't know how they would have my cell number. Unless some idiot intern forwarded the call. I suppose that could happen. But it was still upsetting."

"And they haven't called again?"

"No."

"Will you let me know if they do?"

"Okay," I said, relieved that I could talk about this with someone, that he didn't seem to think I had overreacted.

And then we got up because I had to rush home to shower and change, and Mark, well, he had a country to help run.

Dear Faith and Ken,

I have been watching your show for over five years, but after your interview with the family of the runaway, I am turning the dial. It was completely distasteful to harass the parents in such a way. At least on *Sunrise America* they just spoke to the siblings.

Disdainfully,

A Disappointed Viewer

5

Every Wednesday at 10:00 a.m. we had our weekly staff meeting. It was usually a fairly staid affair in which we would pile into the conference room (walls decorated with the ever-present mosaic of monitors and posters from our network's sitcoms and reality shows). We crowded around the ferry boat–sized conference table, coffee in hand, sometimes a bagel, stragglers standing in the back. Tom would read off the previous week's ratings, usually getting overly enthusiastic if he had anything positive to say about ours, which was becoming rare. The staff would give tentative feedback (the grumbling happened out of Tom's earshot), and then we went on to tear apart the competition:

"June and Jack looked like they were about to hit each other yesterday, did anyone notice that?"

"I know! It's so obvious they hate each other!"

or

"How stupid was that segment on *Sunrise* about the toe therapy? They are really getting desperate, aren't they?"

Of course, what no one ever said is that, as we all knew, our own Ken and Faith were so jealous of each other they wouldn't even speak to one another unless the camera was rolling. Or that we had done a similar toe therapy segment the week before.

But the best part of the meetings was when the bookers regaled us with their latest war stories from the field. Not travel bookers, guest bookers—the people who line up all of the live talking heads you see on the shows—the Elizabeth Smarts, the families of infants who fell down wells, the best friends of the latest soldier to die (especially if the soldier had an interesting story to tell, that is, like if he were previously a famous baseball star). People loved this stuff, and that was why morning shows made more money for their respective networks than any other news program that aired. No one under the age of sixty was watching the evening news-casts anymore, and morning was the only growth market on the dial, so the pressure was on. But because morning shows fell under the news divisions, there were rules. Of gravest impor-tance: no one was allowed to pay for interviews. But no one ever said anything about offering overnights at five-star hotels and tickets to Broadway shows. Or mind games. Most bookings were made over the phone, with our (mostly female) bookers sweet talking the intended guests into believing that by coming on our show, their lives would improve dramatically. But if the story was big enough, armies of bookers would descend upon the home of, say, some teenage girl from Arkansas who had miraculously escaped a traumatic weeklong kidnapping. Scores of New York City bookers would camp out at the Holiday Inn closest to her small, rural town, each one striving to become the family's new best friend, convincing them that by going on her show (as opposed to the other shows), it would be therapeutic, inspiring to others, good for the girl. And fun, so much fun. Bookers had been known to take such girls shopping in the mall, out for ice cream, and give her all sorts of candy (never money!) so that she would pick, say, *Sunrise America* and not *New Day USA* for her first interview. Of course, while said girl might give one show the first interview, she would more often than not appear on all the other shows a few minutes later. Often, the cameras would be lined up outside her house, with a slightly different angle for each program. As soon as she finished talking to, say, Faith (via remote), she would be escorted a few feet to talk to, say, Sally.

Sometimes bookers were known to lie outright, claiming to be from a show they were not, telling the guest the interview was canceled or moved. Tom forbade our staff doing that and generally asked us to toe an ethical line, to make sure we could all face the mirror in the morning. And that might be why our ratings were slipping a bit. Joe Public was getting savvy, and potential guests would ask things of our bookers that we wouldn't, but other shows sometimes would, provide.

I was lucky. I sometimes considered listing it on my résumé, under relevant skills: "digital editing, digital photography, French proficiency and luck." I had somehow convinced the powers that be that I was a horrible booker, and so happily avoided the so-called booking wars that were the backbone of morning television. Well, I shouldn't say *somehow*. The truth was that I *was* a terrible booker. On the one occasion that I was asked to do what we called a "door knock," I basically fled the crime scene faster than the criminals. It was a few years back, up near Niagara Falls, in the dead of winter. But it wasn't dead at all. The world seemed very alive that day, with forty-mile-an-hour gusts of piercing wind and the kind of temperatures that cause your nose hairs to freeze.

It was around this point in my career that the romance of all the travel had started to wear thin. In the earlier days, I was so thrilled to be hopping on planes and in and out of cars that it didn't matter if I was going to stay at the Mansion on Turtle Creek in Dallas, or at some no-name motel in a polygamous hill town in Montana (though, that's actually one story I never did that I always wanted to do—an exploration into polygamy in the Mountain West. Unfortunately, unless one of the polygamous patriarchs had murdered three of his eight wives, we weren't interested).

Anyway, up in Niagara Falls, the story was that three young children, all from the same family, had jumped into the rapids together, in the dead of winter, involving what was either a suicide pact or an insidious push by a psychotic mother, who had witnessed the whole thing. The mother hadn't been charged yet, but was currently at the hospital under a suicide watch herself. My job? Knock on the door and ask the poor father how he felt—and if he would like to share his story with millions of viewers, because it would be cathartic and possibly help another family from suffering the same loss. And I had to do so before the other two network fists beat me to the door.

I had been up in that neck of the woods anyway, working on a story about family-friendly casinos, when my pager went off. My pager almost never went off, so if it did, I knew I was in for something unpleasant. For a self-proclaimed newsperson, I was rather skittish of breaking stories. I didn't look at my pager. Then my cameraman's cell phone started to vibrate, and he was a much better newsman than I was. So we left the overlit casino where we had been shooting some footage, piled into the crew car (a fortified SUV with a gated rear door, darkened one-way windows, and more locks and bolts than a drug trafficker's Humvee), crossed back over the bridge to the American side of the falls, and drove up to a bland one-story redbrick house, with children's toys and bikes scattered about the yard, covered with a few inches of snow, clearly untouched for some time.

My cameraman practically had to push me out of the passenger seat, I was so reluctant to do what I had to do. But I did it. I zipped up my puffy black parka, pulled my thick wool ZBC News ski hat down over my ears (briefly catching one of my chandelier earrings in the knitting), took a deep breath and cut a path to the front door.

I could tell we were there first. No other press in sight. No trodden down, muddied up snow on the walkway. Just a few footprints of varying sizes going to and fro. The freshest ones looked like they were going fro, and I took that to be a good sign. Such a good sign, in fact, that I knocked just once on the door, and when no one answered, I slipped my crisp white business card under the door (with a short note scribbled on the back telling the sad dad to call if he wanted to share his story), turned around, announced to the crew that no one was home, and we returned to the casino to continue the other shoot.

That didn't go over so well when, the next morning, the father of the dead kids, husband to the suicidal suspect, appeared as an exclusive on *Sunrise America* in tears and sobs and oh, so compelling. He was even holding his one remaining child, an infant son (postpartum psychosis was the lay diagnosis of the mother's state), in his arms. *Sunrise* beat us in the ratings that morning and I almost lost my job, which was saved only because the date coincided with the announcements for the Emmy nominations, and a piece I had produced a year prior was listed as a candidate (it didn't win, but still).

My luck got even better when, a few days later, it was revealed that the *Sunrise* booker had basically bought the father off by giving him the use of a new car for a two-year period in exchange for appearing on their air, which he had been understandably reluctant to do. That producer did get fired (though the father kept the car), and suddenly my work was being held up in press releases as the ethical standard to match (though my name was never mentioned—it just said something along the lines of "a producer from *New Day USA* was first on the scene, but understanding the sensitivity of the story and the pain of the family, she made the journalistically appropriate call to give the father some space and time.").

Since then, I avoided guest booking at all costs and was very happy that Tom liked the *American Ideals* series, because they were my favorite pieces to produce. The stories were heartwarming, caught your attention, and we didn't have to worry about competing for guests. These weren't front page tabloid sensation stories, they were just good stories, pure and simple. And they rated well.

"Nice piece, Annabelle," he said, when we had moved on to the housekeeping portion of the meeting. This was a bit odd because he rarely singled out praise.

I was a little taken aback. "Oh! The snakes? Thanks."

"No, the Fardish thing. Last week's *Ideal*. Nice job. We've been getting a good response on it."

"Oh. OK. Thanks." I uselessly tried to will my cheeks not to flush.

"We want to do a follow-up. Come talk to me about it after the meeting."

"Oh, that's great," said Carl, who was sitting, as always, to Tom's right. "We really worked hard on that piece." Like he had anything to do with it.

Tom's office was not a subtle place. The shelves on the sidewall overflowed with Emmy statues, and the wall behind his desk was covered with pictures of him in just about every place on earth, shaking hands with every luminary imaginable. A number of awards and honor plaques and paperweights lined the windowsill. A whole slew of things still needing to be hung were stacked in a corner.

Tom was fairly young (pushing forty) to have achieved so much, but clearly he had impressed the right people—impressed them so much that less than six months earlier they had poached him from a different network's evening news program and named him head of our breakfast fare. As Tom liked to say, morning television was a whole new universe, Edward R. Murrow be damned.

"Hi." I meekly knocked on the door, which was already open. Tom was on the phone, so he motioned me to take a seat in front of the bloated mahogany desk. The chairs were large and leather and I felt very small. I counted three pictures of him shaking hands with the president. Two with the vice president. Tom towered over both of them. He was ridiculously tall, a fact that I am sure did not hurt his career.

After a few minutes, he hung up and we awkwardly exchanged a few niceties.

"So," he said, "I hear you are dating Mark Thurber." Even in this gossipy business, this was weird. I mean, it hadn't been three hours since the date ended. I immediately turned red and was, needless to say, a bit upset.

"Um," I said. Brilliant response.

"Carl told me." Of course. "And it was on Page Six."

He opened up Page Six, the gossip page of the *New York Post*. There was a small paragraph at the bottom right:

Which Hollywood starlet was seen at Rocco's last night, sitting *thisclose* with her latest—married—director? And which action star is reported to have cried when turned away from Mecca? And speaking of Mecca, which hot young D.C. insider was seen canoodling with an unidentified petite brunette at that hot spot late into the evening?

My cheeks felt swollen, they were so hot. "Uh, well, we just went out for a drink. Is that a problem?" I wanted to protest the canoodling bit, but decided it best not to go there. Anyway, there was hope for canoodling in the future.

Tom said that if people figured out who I was and where I worked, it could be a perceived conflict of interest, and that if things progressed, it was important to disclose these matters and so forth.

"It was just one date," I said. "Anyway, I don't cover politics." And, wait a minute, wasn't it a conflict of interest that our network (with its stock-holding news division employees) was owned by Corpcom, a corporation whose interests included just about everything we covered: movies, books, oil companies, chemical companies, fast-food chains, amusement parks, an airline...the list of conflicts went on and on. I didn't say that, of course.

"Right, right," he said, shaking his head a bit as if, oops, he had forgotten what it was that I reported on—which was mostly innocuous and soft. And then he apologized for meddling in my personal life, but he just wanted to protect me, and...whatever.

"Didn't you want to discuss the *Ideals* piece?" I was anxious to change the subject.

"Of course."

His barely postcollegiate assistant stuck her blond head in the door. "Max is on line one," she said.

"Hold on," Tom said to me. He picked up the phone. "Yup, uh-huh, yup, yup. Okay, I'll let you know." He hung up.

"A really strong piece," he said, as if it were a continuation of a sentence. "Rated well. Max wants a follow-up."

"Max?" The rumor was he hardly ever watched the show. Too early.

"Yes. Max Meyer. He liked your work. You should feel proud."

I did. But I was confused.

"There's not much else to say, though," I said.

"Figure something out." Tom turned to his computer and started answering e-mails, which I took as my cue to leave.

When I was little, I loved watching the monkeys at the zoo, the way they climbed all over the place and each other, periodically stopping to pick at each other's scalp. That's what our newsroom was like. Everybody was into everybody else's business. But the funny thing was, so many publicists sent us so many flowers so often, that when an enormous bouquet of lilacs and peonies landed on my desk, no one took any notice.

I felt faint again, but in a very good way, and sat down in my ergonomically correct chair to open the little note that was attached to the basket.

There's some good coffee in D.C. Perhaps you could come do a story about it.
Mark.

And so, after thorough consideration (and a fair amount of squealing to Natasha), I decided it was only logical to start the *Ideals* follow-up with Doug Purnell's Washington office.

Dear *New Day USA*,

I am writing to register a complaint. Last week, we came all the way from Florida to stand outside your studio window with Weather Mike. Mike was very kind to us during the commercial breaks, but our friends and family said that the only glimpse they caught of us was a quick shot of my husband's arm. If people are going to travel this far to stand outside your window, you should make the effort to show all of them.

Sincerely,

Donna Clemente

Tempe, AZ

P.S. Could you please send us some *New Day USA* coffee mugs to the address below. It is the least you can do.

6

Perhaps I should step back a bit, explain how the whole refugee cosmetics story fell in my lap in the first place. It was a little different from our typical fare, because, typically, unless a piece had already been covered by, say, the *New York Herald,* we would not consider doing it. Seriously. A huge number of the stories we produced were stolen from a newspaper story, wire copy or magazine article. Or, sometimes, from a noncompetitive television program, like something that aired on CNN or MSNBC, or, on rare occasions, from public radio. Our senior staff, especially Carl, were very reluctant to approve an unproved entity. But the best way to have an idea okayed? Tell the seniors that the other morning shows were hot on it already. Which is why, when Carl handed me a press release from Cosmetic Relief, I was fairly surprised that there were no supporting articles or transcripts to go with it, much less outside interest.

"We want you to produce this," he said, coming up from behind me, putting a single sheet of paper on top of my keyboard. "It will be a Faith piece. Don't fuck it up. It came from Max's office." Max

Meyer. He was above Tom. He was above us all. He was the CEO of Corpcom.

"Max's office?" This was a first. This would be like Bill Gates telling a junior software programmer that he had a suggestion for some code.

"Yes. Max's office."

I took a quick glance at the pitch. "Why was this sent to him?"

"Annabelle, I have no idea, but it's here now, on your desk. I e-mailed it to you as well." He was clearly exasperated by me (this was already more work than he usually did) and started to walk away.

"So, can I go over there, to this refugee camp?" This was a very exciting prospect; I had never been sent abroad for work.

"What do you think?" he said, turning back toward me, glaring as if that was the stupidest question in the world. "Of course not. Just coordinate with the foreign desk for the pickups. And apparently Cosmetic Relief has some footage we can use."

Years ago, almost a decade, when I was in journalism school, all green and idealistic and out to save the world, we had a class on ethics. The class was supposed to be pragmatic, sort of a guide for us innocents for when we went out into the big scary world of modern media. But what the aging, Ivy-shielded professor failed to mention—and what we would all find out way too soon—was that there were two sides to the ethics camp, especially for those of us who wound up working in television. On one side, you could make a living, perhaps a decent one, so what if you had to compromise a little? And on the other? Well, most of us had student loans to pay. So, if my boss told me to put together a story using footage provided by the very people I was doing a story about, who was I to argue? And of course we would credit it on the screen so the cereal-eating, coffee-sipping, lunch-box-packing viewer would have full disclosure.

"Okay," I said, "I'll get right on it." And I did. And, apparently, I did a good job.

But now, to follow it up, I really wasn't sure what, beyond perhaps another interview with Purnell, I could throw together. So I called him in the hope that there were some new developments—particularly some that would bring me to Washington.

"Annabelle!" he said, once I got him on the phone, "I've been meaning to call. We absolutely loved the story!" Purnell had a very feminine voice for a man, and it took a minute to register that it was him speaking and not, say, his secretary.

I thanked him for the compliment and told him about my plight, and he said he was of course thrilled to get more publicity for his cause and was happy to help. In fact, he told me, it just so happened that a rather big story was about to break. Vanity, the cosmetics company that was funding his venture, had decided to start using some of the Fards as models for their new line of lipsticks and lip gloss. A delegation of select refugees was coming to Washington to kick off the campaign.

"Why didn't you tell me this before?" I said, because Lord knows that would have been a great way for Faith to wrap up the story the first time around.

"The deal just got finalized last week, after the piece aired."

To me, that new information really only meant one thing: it was a good excuse to travel to D.C. sooner rather than later. It meant I might find time for that cup of coffee right away.

"Why don't I come down," I said. "We could discuss this more in person."

"On camera?"

"Well, yes, but not immediately. I mean, we will need to do another interview on camera, but first maybe I should just come down to talk."

Purnell hesitated. Then he cleared his throat, sounding like a jungle bird doing a mating call. I moved my phone's headset off my ear for a moment.

"Are you there?" he said.

"I'm here. So, how about it? I could come down one day later this week."

He exhaled loudly. "Well, at this point, Annie, I would love to see you, but I wouldn't want you to make a wasted trip. There's not much more I can say in person that I couldn't tell you over the phone."

"Well, is there anyone else I can meet? What about those refugee models? Are any in D.C. yet? Maybe it would be good for me to meet them once before we put them on camera?"

"I would need to check on it."

"I won't take a lot of your time," I said, meaning it. He wasn't the person I really wanted to see, anyway. "And it would be easier to discuss how to proceed with the follow-up segment if I could meet some of the other people involved. It's really important that I do the best job possible on this story. Even our CEO, Max Meyer, is interested in this, so you should feel pretty good about it, Mr. Purnell."

"Call me Doug."

"Doug."

Usually, people responded to a request from a network news producer as if it were a request from the president—rolling out the red carpets, bending over left, front and backward to accommodate. I've had people cancel school, surgical appointments, work, you name it, just for the chance to be on TV. Apparently, Douglas Purnell just wasn't that impressionable.

"Well," he continued, "I am not sure they are available yet. Hold on, though. Let me look at my schedule. For my old pal Max Meyer, maybe I can squeeze you in."

"You know Max?"

"Figure of speech. Just met him at a conference once. A long time ago. Anyway, I'm leaving town later in the week." I could hear him tapping at his keyboard. "Schedule's pretty packed," he said. "How about lunch today?"

"Today?"

"Sure, why not?"

Because I'd only had about three hours of sleep, that's why. "How about tomorrow?"

"I have meetings all day tomorrow. I'm free this evening, though. How about dinner?"

Well, I figured, that would mean I would have to overnight in D.C., which would mean more time for coffee. I could always nap on the plane. If I left the office now, I'd have time to go home to grab some clothing, some perfume, and drop off a key for my doorman so he could stop in to feed Margarita, my cat.

"Okay," I said, "I'll meet you at your office around five."

I called travel to book the ticket and hotel, confident that Carl would approve the expense.

From: akapner@riseandshine.com
To: Mark.Thurber@whitehouse.gov
Re: Coffee
Not sure about you, but I didn't sleep much last night. I could really use a cup of joe. And, guess what? They want a follow-up on that *Ideals* story. I am going to be in D.C. in a few hours. —Annabelle
P.S. The flowers are stunning.

Dear *New Day USA,*

I am not the sort of person who writes letters to television programs, but I just wanted to write and say that I love your *American Ideals* series. In times like these, it is so important for us to highlight what is good about America.

Bless you all.

Jim Merit

Sterling, VA

7

I always felt there was something momentous about flying into Washington, D.C. Partly because they made you stay in your seat for the full half hour prior to landing, which was often the point when you needed to use the facilities. But mostly it seemed momentous because from high above, the nation's capital looked like a very promising place. With its elegant memorials lining the banks of the Potomac and the Washington Monument proudly reaching to the sky, from just below cloud level Washington was one of the prettiest cities on earth. It was a pity that the drive downtown quickly shattered that illusion.

Purnell's office was in Logan Circle. It was an area that just a few years prior had practically been a no-man's land. Now it held some of the most prestigious and coveted properties in town. Like Tribeca in the nineties. Except, of course, this was not New York, so pretty much the only people wearing black were the ones heading to funerals. Anyway, while prestigious, the neighborhood was still transitional, and not three blocks from Purnell's office it was fairly easy to find a crack house, should you want to. But that is neither here nor there. Crack has no part in this story. Like a lot of stories that take place in Washington, we will simply avoid discussing or acknowledging the fact that the capital of the richest country on earth is practically third world, what with the intense division between rich and poor, the horrendous state of local corruption, the pathetic public works and insanely high crime rate. Violent crime, I mean. Other types of crime, white-collar crimes, the sinister sort of crimes where you never see your victims so you don't have to feel guilty, well, they do play a part in this story.

The Cosmetic Relief office was very much in the style of a New York City loft, all airy pretense and boasting with space, making it the envy of nonprofits and NGOs everywhere. I couldn't help but think that the money spent on rent might have put a number of inner city kids through college, or, more to the point, feed a few hundred Fardish families for a year. But then there were the mural-size photos that lined the entrance walls, pictures of refugees happily putting on lip gloss, of little Fardish girls learning to apply eyeliner. If these were the models, they were worth a lot. Their lacquered smiles said it all.

"Annabelle!"

Purnell met me up at reception, open-armed, squeaking. He startled me.

"Oh! Hi." I had been sitting on a tightly stuffed orange armchair, and when I started to stand I knocked a few magazines off the circular glass table in front of me. "Sorry," I said, leaning forward to pick them up, belatedly aware that at that angle he might be able to see down my wrap dress. I quickly stood.

"Thank you so much for taking the time to meet with me," I said.

"No worries, Annabelle. No worries," he replied. He was a

bit creepy. His body did not fit his voice. While he spoke like
an adolescent girl, or, to be fair, a young boy whose voice still
hadn't exited the developmental stage, his body was a bit more
well formed—like a big, goofy uncle figure, a Santa Claus or a
Buddha. A mass of white-gray hair connected to a well-
trimmed but full beard, completing a circle around his head,
causing his face to look like the pit in the middle of a halved
fleshy fruit. He had a lot of extra insulation; when we had done
the first round of interviews it took my crew a full hour to light
him because sweat kept breaking through, creating too much
shine on his forehead and nose no matter how much powder
we applied.

"So…" I so eloquently murmured, trying to move our conversation forward.

"So," he said, "are you hungry? Ready to eat? We have a reservation at Casablanca."

This surprised me, as well. Casablanca was a new restaurant, so
busy it was almost impossible to get a reservation there. And it was
cavernous and loud, not the typical place for an intimate business
meal. I would have much preferred the Oval Room or the Palm.

How did I know so much about D.C.? Full disclosure: Karen,
my best friend from college, was a scientist at the National Institutes of Health and I spent a lot of time visiting her. Soon, I was
going to want her to be spending a lot of time visiting me.

Anyway, I liked D.C. Many people don't, but for me, a native
New Yorker, I found it calming and almost provincial. And actually
quite interesting. Karen once told me that she thought D.C. was
a bit like L.A.; if you picked up the industry types and held them
in the air, underneath you would find some fascinating signs of life.

"Sounds good," I said to Purnell. "I've heard they have great calamari."

We piled into the Town Car that was waiting out front, and I text messaged Mark that he should meet me at Casablanca at seven to celebrate the one-day anniversary of our first date.

"So, tell me," I said, once I had swallowed a few calamari. They were quite delicious. "You've dragged me down to D.C. This had better be good." I said it with a flirtatious air, admittedly a little full of myself (and a martini), knowing full well that no one had dragged me down but me.

Purnell laughed. Or, I should say, he giggled. "He he he." Like that. He told me basically what he had already told me on the phone—that Vanity was going to be using Fardish makeup and models for their new line, and that the presentation would be happening very soon. He wasn't sure he could introduce me to any of the Fards just yet, but he did expand on the story a little. He said the products would be marketed at the "tweenager" market—girls between the ages of eight and twelve. And the really exciting thing, he said, was that the products had special ingredients that would help the young girls grow into adolescence with less acne and fuller lips.

It wasn't really information I needed to come all the way down to D.C. for, to be sure. Most of our shoots were set up from the office. Unlike the prime-time, big budget magazine programs, we rarely scouted locations or pre-interviewed in person. But this time, well, my phone started to vibrate. It was a text message from Mark. He was on his way.

"So," I said to Purnell, trying to sound like I deeply cared about the story, which, now that I was about to see my Adonis, I really didn't. "Those models... You never told me if I could meet any while I am in town?" But before Purnell could answer, my phone started to vibrate again. Now it was a call, but with no caller ID.

"Excuse me," I said, and answered it. "This is Annabelle."

"Ask him about the tests," said a male voice, weirdly accented but now a little bit familiar.

"Who is this?"

"Just ask him." The man hung up.

Purnell was looking at me quizzically, and I wasn't sure what to say.

"Wrong number, I think." I took a large sip from my second martini and ate the olive. I was trying hard to buy my own it's-probably-just-a-crazy-viewer story, the martinis hazing my line of inquiry, allowing me to completely ignore the fact that whoever called seemed to know where I was and who I was with. But journalistic integrity demanded I ask something. "Um. Do you know anything about some sort of test?"

"What kind of test?" A small ball of sweat ran down his cheek and into his beard.

I didn't really know what kind of test, so I took a stab. "The makeup. Is it tested?"

He giggled again. "Of course it is. Totally safe. This is a top-notch product, Annabelle. Vanity wouldn't have considered selling it otherwise." The bead of sweat was jiggling at the base of his beard now, ready to hit the table any second.

I glanced at my watch. It was almost seven. I couldn't think of another test to ask about.

"Okay," I said, trying just to look at his eyes, not his beard or the table below it. "So when does this all start? Who can I interview? Do the refugee models speak any English? When can I meet them?"

"Annie," he squeaked. "Can I ask you something?"

"Sure." I sat back, quizzical.

"You are just doing a follow-up, right? A simple little story?"

"Right."

"Like, three to four minutes?"

"Uh-huh." I had no idea what he was getting at.

"So, you don't really need to shoot a lot, right?"

"Not much. An interview or two, the models…it depends."

"Okay, I just needed to make sure we were both on the same page here."

"We are."

"To Max Meyer," he said, and, I think, attempted to wink, although both eyes twitched closed for a second, so maybe he was just squinting. He raised his near-empty martini glass. And although I wasn't really sure what he was talking about, I met his glass with mine.

We discussed the logistics of when and where and what I could shoot, and though a little disturbed about the strange man on the phone, I was satisfied that I would be able to put a nice story together, one that would be good for Faith and make the big boss proud, easily justifying a few trips down to D.C., which truly was all I cared about.

We ordered dessert.

We talked about having some of the models live on the set for a makeup demonstration.

We discussed which shades might work best for Faith's complexion.

We had some port.

My head was spinning and it was 7:50, and Purnell was calling for the check.

There were no text messages on my phone and Mark was most certainly not in the room. He was almost an hour late. Being stood up, even just the suspicion that you are being stood up, can deflate pretty much anyone, even a stylishly dressed New Yorker.

"Can I give you a ride to your hotel?" Purnell said.

It felt as if a calamari was lodged in my throat.

I looked at my watch again. I thought about waiting longer, but did I want to look like some desperate wench, waiting around for him with nothing better to do? I slowly nodded at Purnell and, as if to change the subject, brushed a few crumbs off my dress. Marc Jacobs. Simple, black and tremendously flattering to the figure. I had recently bought it at a sample sale and had been very excited to take it out on the town. Now it occurred to me that maybe the dress was a bad luck omen, payback because I had grabbed the last one off the rack, out from under the grasp of another eager shopper. Karma, if you believe in it. I did. The black suede boots weren't helping the matter. I had taken them from an old roommate's closet without asking, and hadn't ever returned them.

"Are you okay?" Purnell asked, his voice sounding more and more like my mother's. I had to look at him to make sure she wasn't actually there.

"Boy trouble." I was never very good at keeping my personal life out of my professional, and, as stated, I was a little drunk.

"That's ridiculous. How could a young lady as lovely as you have boy trouble? Ridiculous." He reminded me at this moment of Tweedledee. Or perhaps Tweedledum.

"Yeah, right," I said. I just about started to tear up.

"You know what? Let's get out of here. I can show you some things that will take your mind off this jerk."

"It's okay," I said, trying to inconspicuously wipe away the tear I felt forming. "I should just go to the hotel. I could use a good night's sleep anyway."

"Oh, this is pathetic," Purnell said. "Come on. We're in this together." He had, at this point, placed his hand on top of mine, on top of the table. It felt soft and a bit sweaty. I gently removed my hand from under his. "You want to meet some of those models. Sure, why not. I can introduce you to a couple of them right now. Plus a few of my Fardish friends," he said.

"I thought you said they weren't available."

"Most of them aren't. But a couple might be."

It sounded interesting, but I must have looked hesitant (or just plan pitiable) because now Purnell was acting as if he was trying to prop me up.

"I might even be able to scare up a few lip gloss samples for you to take back to New York," he said.

For a moment, in my inebriated state, that seemed to me like as good a reason to go as any. I did have better things to do than wait around for a disrespectful guy. I could meet the models tonight. I could find out more about the Fardish makeup. I could sample it. Usually, there was no need for us to investigate very deeply into our stories. They were simple and formulaic, and most of the reporting had already been done in the newspapers. But there I was, and my subject was willing to give me more time and more access. Maybe I would even think of another test to ask about. At the very least, I would get some free makeup. I could

give it to Carl to pass on to whatever up-and-coming local correspondent he was dating, and he wouldn't give me any grief about
the expense of my coming down here. People in television loved
freebies, no matter how big their salaries.

But I really didn't feel like going. I felt like crawling underneath the king-size bed in my nonsmoking hotel room and never
coming out again.

"Annie," Purnell squawked, grabbing my shoulder with his
inflated hand, pulling me back so I stopped slumping. "I don't
know much about dating, but I do know something about power,
and it seems to me that you are giving too much of it over to this
boy toy of yours." I looked at him. I was about to take dating advice
from a damp, bulbous, thoroughly unattractive, much older man.
Because you know what? He might be right.

And so, check paid, we made for the door and had the valet call
our car around.

"Where are we going?" I said, once I hazily realized that we had
crossed the 14th Street Bridge and were headed into Virginia.

"Don't worry so much, Annie." Purnell patted my bare knee
with his chubby hand, making me start to regret this trip. I moved
closer to the window and checked my phone again, just in case I
had somehow missed Mark's call. Nothing.

We turned off at the Crystal City exit, passing Costco and the
Fashion City Mall before turning into one of those bland, cookie
cutter town house complexes built in the mid-1970s, probably
around the same time as my office.

We got out at the last unit, number 15. The front light wasn't
on and I tripped on the first step leading up to the door, giving

Purnell the opportunity to grab my arm with his puffy hand to help steady me. He had a key and opened the door, and that's how we went inside—arm in arm.

It looked like Mecca. The bar, I mean, the one I had been at with Mark the night before. Lots of velvet cushions and hookah pipes. Except these ones didn't have alcohol inside, these ones were real. Five men (each of a sun-weathered, indiscernible age) were sitting around, spilled out over the carpet, lounging on the pillows, puffing the pipes, filling the air with a thick smog and a strange cinnamonlike scent. There were no women in the room.

Upon seeing us, the men cried out in unison, *"Cow!"*

That's what they said: *Cow.* There being no cows among us, I figured that was how they said hello. When Purnell said something like *cow* in response, they went back to smoking their pipes.

"These are my Fardish friends," he said, motioning for me to take a seat on a large, uninhabited purple cushion pushed up against a carpet-covered wall. "They are helping us with the project."

I sat down and out from nowhere a little girl rushed up, offering each of us a cup of tea. Purnell held his up as if to make another toast. "Here's to *New Day USA* and Vanity Cosmetics!" he said, knocking his against the cup now in my hand.

The girl curtsied and quietly scampered off, but I couldn't fail to notice her absolutely radiant skin and full, movie star-like mouth.

"She looks nice, doesn't she?" Purnell said, having caught me staring at the child. "Fida's a big fan of the products."

"Fida?"

"The girl. She's going to be one of the presenters next week. Others are coming in a few days." Purnell, now seated next to me, took a puff from one of the pipes. "Fida and her sister are the prettiest, I think." He looked to the door Fida had run behind. "Fida! Lida!" He said something in Fardish. At least I think it was Fardish. He was clearly fluent in whatever language it was.

Fida came back into the room, accompanied by a smaller and fuller-lipped girl who couldn't have been older than eight. Maybe ten for Fida. Maybe.

Eyes glued on the floor, the two sisters approached us. Purnell said something that sounded reproachful and they both squatted down, placing their round, beautiful, flawless faces at eye level with me—so I could get a good look. And, actually, under closer inspection, they looked a bit weird. The lips were too large for their Kewpie-doll faces. They didn't look real. For a feel-good story, this was starting to feel a lot less so.

None of the men seemed to be paying us much mind. I think they were all stoned on whatever it was they were smoking. That Purnell was smoking, too, for that matter. "This is off the record," he said, giving me another blinking wink. I said sure, because without a camera, everything is off the record in TV land. Then he offered me a pipe, but I declined.

"Hi." I turned to the girls, speaking very clearly. "You look very pretty." It seemed the right thing to say. Purnell translated, his sounds slurring, and the girls curtsied a bit and then he shoed them away.

"We are trying to teach them English, but it doesn't seem to be taking." He sounded as if he were underwater. "Weee rrrr trrry-ingggg…" Whatever was in that pipe was obviously potent.

My phone rang again. I looked at the LCD display.

"The boy?" said Purnell. Or rather, "deee boooya?" It was. So, both angry and relieved, I excused myself, stood up and went into the other room to answer it.

"Hello?"

Fida and Lida were sitting on a cheap, plastic-covered floral couch, watching a video of what looked like it might be Disney's *Snow White*. I sat down between them. They stared straight ahead.

"Annie?" Mark sounded a bit breathless. "Where are you?"

"What do you mean?" I leaned back on the couch, noticing that in front of me, spread out on a glass coffee table, were dozens of lip glosses, still in the packaging. I picked one up. "Are you at Casablanca?" I asked. Pink Passion. That's what the shade was called.

"Yeah, I've been here for about twenty minutes. Are you in here somewhere?"

I most definitely wasn't. I looked at the package some more. Under the plastic wrap, a clear tube of bubblegum-pink lip gloss lay on top of a very sultry looking photo of a girl who looked a lot like Fida. Or maybe Lida. "We were supposed to meet over an hour ago. I left."

"Oh, shit. I'm sorry. I couldn't call. I was pulled into a meeting on my way out."

Yeah, right. Who has meetings at seven o'clock on a Wednesday night?

"The vice president needed to speak to me about something."

Oh. "I think I'm in Alexandria."

"Alexandria?"

"At some Fardish hookah party, actually. Near the Fashion City Mall. Everyone is stoned out of their gourds." I started to put the lip gloss back down, but then gave it a second thought and kept it in my hand.

Mark laughed. "Well, that sounds interesting."

"And there seem to be some party gifts here. Lipstick for the Barbie doll set."

"Now I am getting jealous."

"You want to get really jealous," I said. "Check this out." I held up my phone in front of me to take a quick picture of the scene, me sandwiched between these two beautiful little girls, sitting on the plastic floral couch. "Aren't they stunning?"

"I like the one in the middle." What a charmer, huh?

"I'd ask if I could invite you to join us, but I don't speak Fard." We were both giggling now, because it was kind of funny, that he was there, in a trendy faux Middle Eastern hot spot, and I was here, in a decidedly untrendy Middle Eastern spot that, come to think of it, was kind of hot. The plastic couch covering was sticking to the back of my thighs.

"Can you come back to town? I'll call you a cab. Just go outside and tell me the street address."

I thought about it for a moment, about whether I should stay and try to figure out this strange scene or, figuring I would have more opportunities to powwow with Purnell now that he was all chummy with me, if I should forgive Mark and take up the offer. I peeked into the other room and immediately started coughing from the smoke that was seeping out. From the looks of it, I doubted I would be able to get any information from Purnell at this point. I was, of course, curious, but this wasn't a long investigative story I was working on. This was supposed to be an *American Ideals* profile, albeit one that was quickly seeming less than ideal. Chances were that if I told my supervisors about the bongs, the story would be dead before I finished the sentence. This was morning television, after all. But I wasn't sure I should tell them just yet. I mean, the story was funding my romantic life; just a few miles away, there was a cute boy waiting for me.

"Come on," said Mark. "I promise I'll make it worth your while."

"Worth my while?" I could feel my cheeks heating up again.

"I know, I know. I screwed up. But I really want to see you again." With words like that, he could have pretty much asked me to do anything.

"I'll bring you a party favor," I said, grabbing what looked like a piece of scrap paper, a page torn from a spiral notebook, filled with what I assumed to be Fardish scribble. I wrapped the lip gloss inside and then held my little package up as if to ask Fida and Lida if it was okay that I take it. But they seemed oblivious to my kleptomaniacal action. So I grabbed a few more samples and put them in my purse. Which is when I realized I didn't have enough cash to get back into town.

"Doug?" I said, gently nudging Purnell with my foot. "Doug?"

He didn't respond, so I knelt down and took his wallet out of his jacket pocket. It was an icky thing to do because I had to get so close to him. I almost started choking from the aftershave. Of course, I wasn't just going to take the money and run. I wrote across a taxi receipt I found in my pocket "IOU $20—ANNIE" and then folded it up and put it where the money had been.

Then I left Purnell, who by the time I walked out seemed to be quite content. I don't think he even noticed I was gone.

Dear *New Day USA* and Chef Joe,

Could you please post some more recipes for the eggshell diet on your Web site. The pudding was surprisingly taste-less, so I would like to try something else. I have successfully lost a few pounds on the diet and since my high school re-union is just around the corner, I would like to keep going.

Sincerely,

A. Kramer

Concord, New Hampshire

8

Like most people, before I was afforded the starker look at my own life that imprisonment has provided me, I defined myself by my inadequacies. And, like most people, my inadequacies were mostly defined by the failures of my personal life. So, given that I, a wannabe newsperson of importance, more regularly tuned in to my own program when affairs of the heart were being discussed than when we aired stories about international affairs, it wasn't too surprising that most of the network's foreign correspondents were axed and replaced by numerous lifestyle experts, including our own senior dating editor, Candy Curlish. Candy had made a name for herself by writing a book about how women could understand a man's commitment level by studying his simple daily habits, such as the way he brushed his teeth or how he tied his shoes. We had her on the show a number of times to discuss her book, and she rated so high we hired her full time. Now she had a weekly feature called *Dating News* that aired not only on our program, but on our venerable nightly newscast, as well.

It was a definite low point in both my personal and professional life when, after having produced a few segments of *Dating News*, I was told that Candy felt my approach to the subject was stale and juvenile and not very successful, and recommended that I stick to the stories I was good at. I quickly got my professional life back on track with some nice *Ideals* and other feel-good stuff, but it would take a lot more than Candy Curlish's advice to help sort out my personal life. That said, as my cab pulled up to the curb, I found myself recalling some of Candy's tools. My favorite? Handwriting analysis. "If he writes the letter *X* like two back-to-back Cs," she warned, "run away fast and furious." According to Candy, there was no surer sign of commitment-phobia. Curved lines were a sure signal of a wishy-washy sensibility. She said to look for a man who wrote his *X*s with two straight, deliberate lines. If a guy was focused, she said, it stood to reason that his letters should be, too. How I could inconspicuously get Mark to write a word like *excellent* or *xylophone* was beyond me, but thinking about it calmed me down.

Second dates always made me more nervous than first ones. It was no longer just a question of basic attraction or the "it can't hurt to have a drink with him" barometer. On a second date there is a lot more going on, including the open possibility of a third. I'm not sure that meeting at night in the shadows of the luminescent Lincoln Memorial should qualify as a date (it seemed more like a location out of a spy thriller), but as the car drove up to the curb where Mark was waiting (hands in the pockets of his light brown cords, casting a long shadow because of his height and the angular light, looking a bit nervous himself), the butterflies were slapping against my stomach and my heart was in my throat.

He held the door open for me as I stepped out.

"Hi."

"Hi."

Flash back to awkward junior high dates and school dances. The memories never leave you, no matter how old you are. The weird halogen glow of the streetlamps even reminded me a bit of the hokey disco lights we would string around the gym on the afternoon before the dance, and how they cast shadows under everyone's eyes, giving us all a slightly terrified, but slightly older, countenance. I also knew there were shadows forming under my eyes, present tense, and was glad when Mark took my hand and led me over to the memorial, where the light was not so top-heavy.

"Sorry about missing you at the restaurant," he said as we walked up the stairs toward Abe.

"That's okay. If you had been on time, I wouldn't have made it to the Fardish hookah party." We sat down on one of the steps halfway up. "My God, was that bizarre." I gingerly arranged the skirt of my dress so that it covered my thighs, and then told him about the stoned *cow*-callers and the spaced out little Kewpie dolls named Fida and Lida.

"Kewpie dolls?"

"Like Kewpie dolls on smack," I said, not knowing exactly what a Kewpie doll on smack would look like, but it sounded cool to say it.

"How did you even wind up there? That doesn't seem like a place for a nice girl like you." Mark nudged me in a manner again reminiscent of the awkward, hormonally choreographed gestures of adolescence.

"What makes you think I'm so nice?" I nudged him back in a similar fashion. And then I flashed back to my thirty-year-old self and told him about the rest of my evening with Purnell, about how he'd wined and dined me, about how he'd kept touching my knee when we were in the car.

"Like this?" said Mark, putting his palm on my knee. I laughed and let him keep it there. He had nice hands. They looked strong, but not scary strong. Just solid and trustworthy, the kind that send signals of respect when you shake them. I liked having his hand on my knee.

"Man, that guy must creep you out," he said. "He creeps me out."

"Yeah, he is a bit of a creepy man."

"An American Ideal." Mark said this sarcastically, referring, of course, to the profile I had done about Purnell. Mark meant it to be funny, but it wasn't. The residue of the evening's drinks evaporated and suddenly I was feeling tremendously sober.

"I got another phone call."

"Oh," he said. "That's not good."

"No," I said, "it's not." I told him about what the caller had said and about my growing concerns about my "just another crazy viewer" theory, which I was starting to realize had a few holes.

"Man." Mark took his hand off my knee and rubbed the light evening shadow that had once again formed along his chin.

"It's odd, right?" I said, wrapping my arms around myself, swaying back and forth a bit as if I was davening, like an old Jewish man praying at the Wailing Wall.

Mark nodded and bit his lower lip.

We watched silently as another couple climbed up the steps, past where we were sitting.

"Maybe you should tell someone at work about this," he said, once they were well beyond us and up by Lincoln's feet. "Maybe there is a very simple answer to what's going on."

It was starting to seem ludicrous that there might be a simple answer, what with the calls and the cows, but the more I thought about it, the more it seemed that there wasn't much I could do. With the edict from the front office and all, I was now thinking it best to just produce the story and lie low. As I've said, you can't go out on a story and come back with nothing, and I had already spent enough money on this one trip alone. I had to produce something aside from fodder for the gossip columns. Carl and Max were salivating.

You tell the president that you can't finish a speech because you have some questions about the policy, I wanted to say.

Instead I said that it might be best for me to just keep my mouth shut and do my job.

"Isn't your job to get to the bottom of things and tell the truth?" he said, more inquisitively than aggressively. "Isn't that what journalists are supposed to do?"

"Sometimes I'm not sure if I can call myself a journalist anymore," I said. "Not really."

Mark sighed.

"What?"

"No, it's just that I get it. I mean, I get what you mean. I don't often think of myself as a public servant anymore, either."

We sat quietly for a moment, staring down at the reflecting pool below us.

"Are you going to be okay?" Mark asked, putting his hand back on my knee.

"Actually," I said, "I'm a little scared." How's that for second date vulnerability?

He put his arm around me and gave me a hug. He smelled of soap. It reminded me of home, this feeling of being held and smelling what must have been Ivory, and it was pretty much what I needed. I sighed perceptibly. He kissed my forehead.

"Annie," he said, after thinking for a moment, lips pressed to my bangs, "what do you know about this Purnell guy? I mean, aside from this lipstick business?"

"What do you mean?" I leaned back and looked at him square on. I had Purnell's bio, of course. His assistant had e-mailed it to me when I had started doing the story. Three years of the Peace Corps right out of college. A master's degree from the London School of Economics. After a number of years at the World Bank, he'd started up his consulting firm. Etcetera, etcetera. It was pretty standard stuff for a development guy.

"Well, at this point, my guess is that he's the only one you know who would know anything about those phone calls."

"I can't ask him about them!"

"Of course not. I'm just thinking out loud."

Then Mark reached into the inside pocket of his sports jacket and took out his BlackBerry.

"What are you doing?"

"Research," he said. "I am going to have my assistant do a little background search on Purnell. Is that cool?"

I nodded, feeling mildly stupid, as if I probably should have thought of that a while ago.

"Trying to impress me, Mr. Thurber?" I said flirtatiously, trying to cover my embarrassment at not having done the research myself.

"Hey, if it helps," Mark laughed. But we both knew, it was obvious, that he didn't need to impress me with his access to information. "Seriously," he said, "I'd like to help. I mean, if you're comfortable with it."

I was, at least as far as I was concerned. "Do you think it's okay, though? I mean, isn't your assistant going to wonder why you're asking?"

"She knows better than to ask. Anyway, she owes me a number of favors."

"For what?"

"Well, for starters, I hired her. And then there is the fact that I walked in on her making out with the vice president's daughter after the last White House Christmas party, and this is the first time I've mentioned that to anyone."

I laughed. "Well, I suppose that is valuable information. But isn't it a bit late to be asking her to do work tonight?"

"It's just an e-mail. She'll get it when she gets it."

Mark typed a few lines and then put the BlackBerry back in his pocket, but his expression changed to one of concern as he did it. Thick, furrowed brows and all that. Or maybe he was just tired. It was almost eleven and the stone steps were cold. Yes, it was a romantic place to meet, but the air was getting brisk and there was nothing to cushion the sit bones.

"What?" I said, noticing a number of crinkly lines extending from Mark's eyes, the kind that could be construed as cheerful or decrepit, depending on one's outlook. To me, Mark looked like a happy guy. Except for right now. Right now he was frowning.

And it was getting cold and our legs were falling asleep.

I leaned against him and he held me again in his warm, familiar-smelling arms.

"So, what do you think?" I said to his chest, getting a bit of wool lint in my mouth from his sweater.

"About what?"

"About what we should do."

"Do about what?" he said, but he knew what I was asking.

He stood up and reached for my hand.

"I should probably get back to my hotel," I said as he pulled me up. "There isn't too much I can do about any of this right now, anyway." I did have to catch an early shuttle back to New York, after all.

Mark smiled. And then he leaned over to kiss me.

"I'm so glad you don't have Fardishly enhanced lips," he said.

"Oh, this is for you," I said, pulling out the notebook-paper-wrapped lip gloss gift. He tore off the paper and laughed when he saw what was inside.

"Mind if I try it on later?" Smiling, he put the whole wad into his pocket.

"Not at all," I said, deftly pulling some lint off my tongue, and kissed him back.

"Hi."

"Hi."

There he was, Mark Thurber, lying next to me on a king-size bed in the Jefferson Hotel, once again easing the painfulness of waking up at daybreak after not enough sleep. But this time, instead of flowers on my pillow, it was just him, morning breath and all. It was wonderful. It was one of those sun-saturated moments that sticks in your memory, the kind of moment that makes you believe in Hallmark cards. Life diffused. You try to hold on to it, dreamily gazing into the eyes of your new lover, gently welcoming the day.

He smiled at me, dimple forming, a little nocturnal crust in his eyes. It was the kind of smile women often fantasize about, the one that says, "Hey, I'm here, and there is no other place I'd rather be."

I smiled back. Take that, Candy Curlish.

Then the newspaper was shoved under the door, and because it was a professional compulsion, we both tossed off the sheets and jumped up to get it, divvying up the sections, Front, Metro and Style to me, Sports and Business to him, and crawled back onto the disheveled bed, covering our naked bodies with newsprint.

We read and waited for room service to deliver our coffee.

"Annie?" Mark said after we had been skimming the pages for a few minutes. "Did you see this?" He placed the Business Section in front of me. There it was, over on the right, below the fold.

Corpcom Gets A Makeover

Media Giant Adds Global Cosmetics Company to Its Holdings
New York—In an unanticipated move, the board of Corp-com (CPC) announced on Wednesday that it was purchasing Vanity, a privately held cosmetics interest with assets estimated around 500 million dollars...

"Holy cow," I said. Like with dating, shock tended to set me back a couple of decades in diction.

"Looks like you've got yourself into something," Mark said, brows furrowed, lip bit.

"Looks like Fred Friendly would be turning in his grave."

Mark looked at me quizzically.

"Fred Friendly?" I said. "One of the fathers of broadcast journalism? He did a number of ground-breaking documentaries with Edward R. Murrow? Produced for Walter Cronkite? Set the standard in broadcast ethics? The icon of the golden age of television news?"

Mark shrugged.

"Nevermind."

"So, you can't do the story now, right?"

"Are you kidding? Now there is no way out of it. The only question is how much of it I can actually tell." I pushed the papers off of my lap and went to take a shower in an attempt to clear my head.

It felt like I had sent my mind onto one of those whirly-rides at amusement parks—the ones where they drop the floor out from under you, the g-force sucking you safely up against the wall, the spinning making you want to vomit. Did Tom know about this? Did Stan? Obviously someone from the front office wanted me to do the follow-up for the promotional value, but why not just tell me? And what about the calls? Were the calls somehow connected to this weird corporate conquest? It was possible, I suppose. A disgruntled investor, a rogue employee. But, no, that still didn't make any sense. I scrubbed the shampoo hard into my scalp, trying to gain control of things, bubbles erupting all over the place.

"Annie?" Mark called through the door.

"Out in a minute!" I yelled, just like I did back in high school when I was calling to my mother. I started to rinse.

"I have to show you something!" Mark opened the door. "My assistant e-mailed me back."

"What?" I stepped out of the shower, grabbed the robe on the door (why is it always embarrassing to be naked in front of someone you had just been intertwined with. Really, it makes no sense.), and turban-twisted an oversized white towel around my head.

"Here." Mark handed me his BlackBerry. "You might want to sit down." He gestured toward the toilet.

I didn't want to sit down. Certainly not there. So, I stood there in the threshold of the bathroom as I read the message:

Mark—I looked at social security and did classified search... found no listing of a Douglas Purnell. Don't forget 9 am briefing. —Clair

"Where is the coffee?" I said, handing it back to Mark. "I really need some." And then I called in sick.

Dear *New Day USA,*

I think it is a disservice to your viewers that you don't list the designers of Faith's clothing. I loved what she was wearing yesterday, and would like to know where to find such a sweater.

Jill Sibley

Huntsville, AL

Dear *New Day USA,* I am just writing to thank you for your heartfelt anchor background series. I felt so much closer to Faith and Ken after learning about their first jobs and their big fears. I loved the story about how Faith learned to overcome her childhood fear of crowds by spending time in department stores. I really could relate to that. Thank you again,

Sally Sultash

Syracuse, New York

Dear *New Day USA.*

Last week you did a story about a girl with new brests (sic) and how they changed her life. Please help make my dream come true. I pray to God and Jesus everyday for a new pair of brests (sic). I pray the Lord will impress upon *New Day USA* to see this through.

God Bless you all,

Kathy Sanders

Omaha, NB

9

We had drunk our coffee, eaten some eggs, and left the hotel. Mark had to go off to the White House, but I wasn't ready to jump on the shuttle back to New York. So Mark gave me a nice kiss and an encouraging hug and then dropped me at his Woodley Park town house, where, having successfully located a handwriting sample in the form of a shopping list that included Rice Chex (and milk, orange juice and butter), and satisfied with the sturdy committed lines of Mark's letter *X,* I was now sitting at a large wooden desk in front of a sun-splashed bay window, logged on from my laptop, wearing a way too big for me pair of Mark's sweatpants and one of his T-shirts, suffering from a pounding headache and unclear on how to proceed. Instead, I culled through my e-mails—noticing some fan mail that got sent to the show.

Dear *New Day USA,*
Your story about the rattlesnake roundup that aired the other day was a complete outrage. Rattlesnakes are God's creatures and your portrayal suggested that the concentration

camp-like conditions to which they were subjected is acceptable. How can you all look at yourselves in the mirror
each morning?
S. Vito, San Francisco

That one was forwarded directly to me, but not knowing how
I should respond, if at all, I scrolled down my overflowing in-box
some more, deleting messages from publicists, reading some of
the other fan mail that had been sent to the whole staff, skimming
through some of the mass missives from Tom.

We weren't supposed to open attachments from unknown
senders, but when I saw the subject line "Vanity Kills," I couldn't
help myself.

There was no message, just a JPEG file. I double clicked.

My screen filled up with a very pixilated, unidentifiable image.
Then I realized the "view" was set to 500%. I changed it to fit
my monitor.

It wasn't pretty.

A young girl, maybe about fourteen, give or take a day, looking
a bit like Fida and Lida, lay on a floor, looking vacantly into the
camera, oblivious, it seemed, to the complete absence of her lips.
She had no lips at all. Just raw, blistered scabs where lips should
be. Underneath was a caption. "Pretty?" was all it said.

I looked around, as if there was someone else in the room to
confirm what I was seeing. As if someone was standing there who
could explain this to me.

"Shit," I said out loud. I was going to have to figure this out myself.

I closed the image and hit reply.

Who are you? I typed. I can't do anything unless you let me know.

I hit Send.

Two seconds later, my message came back, recipient unknown.

This certainly wasn't morning show fodder. This was more like a *60 Minutes* investigation. Or beyond. It was like I had my own Deep Throat. Someone was leaking me information. Someone was pulling me into a story. A real story. The phone calls, the e-mail... I felt like Brenda Starr.

Years ago, I think I must have been in seventh or eighth grade, I had an assignment for English class. "Write a profile of someone you admire," the teacher told us. "Pretend you are a reporter, and find out what makes this person tick." Well, she probably didn't say "tick," but that's how I remember it. I chose as my subject a friend of my parents, not because I admired him, but because he was visiting from Paris and was staying at our house. He was a journalist. The first real journalist I'd ever met. He told me how he had been one of the earliest Western reporters to uncover some of the atrocities being committed in Vietnam. And after explaining to me what "atrocity" meant, he described a series of articles he had done that brought down a corrupt politician. He said his favorite story he had ever done was an investigation into the mistreatment of young children in a foster care system.

"How did you do all of that?" I'd asked him, eyes saucer-wide with amazement.

"I did it," he'd said, "by asking an insufferable amount of questions and pissing a lot of people off."

I'd like to say it was at that moment that I decided I wanted to be a journalist. It wasn't. My plan to be a journalist actually started as something of a joke. At one point during my senior year of college, a friend and I were trying to figure out a career path that would allow for lots of world travel and a touch of do-gooder-ship while affording me expensive clothing.

"How about network news?" he'd said. And, since the movie *Broadcast News* starring Holly Hunter was the extent of my knowledge of the industry, it sounded realistic to me. Soon, I picked up some books on Edward R. Murrow, and with growing visions of looking good while producing impactful documentaries and bringing down governments, I applied to graduate school. World travel never made it into the budget line, much less the couture, but it suddenly hit me, sitting there in Mark's sweatpants and staring at this disturbing image, that this might in fact be my first opportunity to actually do some of the real reporting I was ostensibly trained for.

I dumped the samples of lipsticks and glosses out of my purse and called over to the National Institutes of Health.

"Karen Jamison." Karen answered her phone in that somber professional tone that always makes old friends laugh. Friends who had known each other as insecure college freshmen who ate too much ice cream after midnight and who had slept through not one but three final exams.

"Hey. It's me," I said.

"Hey?" she said, more like a question than anything else. I never called her at work. "Are you okay?" Karen was always the more mature of the two of us, even back in college. From freshman year on, we'd shared a dorm room. She was the one who worried, the one who sat up waiting for me into the wee hours if I didn't come home from a date. She was the one I turned to when I needed

advice, help or assistance in soul searching. She was also the one
who kept the room clean.

"I have a favor to ask you," I said.

She asked what it was, and I was about to tell her that I wanted
her to run some tests on some lipsticks at her lab, but I thought
better of it. Perhaps I had seen too many movies, but what with
strange callers and weird e-mails and odd men smoking Lord
knows what, it occurred to me (and, I have to admit, kind of
excited me) that my cell phone might be tapped. Instead I asked
if she could meet me for lunch.

Karen laughed (she hadn't even known I was in town), but of
course she said yes. It was an easy favor to grant. So I got dressed,
packed up my stuff and flagged down a taxi for the very expensive ride to Bethesda, a ride I was sure I wouldn't be able to
expense.

10

There are days when I think jail really isn't so bad. Kind of like my online dating days, I'm meeting a lot of interesting people that I never would have met in my real life, my life before I was accused of being the cover girl for a terrorist organization and an enemy of the state. I maintain my innocence, by the way, even though, yes, I did manage to get into the Cosmetic Relief headquarters after the lights went out, and yes, the documents in question weren't exactly mine to have. But everyone maintains their innocence here. And, in many cases, the crimes were in fact innocent. Is it a crime to shoot your husband when he comes after you with a gold-coated fist? Is it wrong to rob a convenience store when your kids are going hungry at home? Okay, well, maybe the whole stick-up thing was a bit over the top, and yes, there are such things as soup kitchens, but extreme situations often force extreme measures.

In my case, I suppose I could have crawled into my parents' attic and dug out my old spiral-bound notebook from my decade-past Investigative Reporting 101 before embarking on my own personal Watergate. But my Deep Throat had been silent of late and I was anxious to understand something about Karen's mysterious findings of trace amounts of hemotoxic stiletto viper venom (snakes!), among other things, in the innocent looking tube of Bubblegum Pink.

Bottom line, I couldn't really help myself when the opportunity fell on my foot.

It had taken Karen a few days to get back to me. She was hesitant at first, because research is highly monitored over there. But then, having applied some of the colors to her own lips (stunning in and of itself because she never wore makeup) and, soon after admiring herself in the mirror (the Plum Passion brought out a rich brown in her eyes, which she was surprised to find she quite liked), feeling an odd tingling sensation, she had a hunch about what it might be, or at least the general ballpark, and realized she could pocket a few chemical testing strips (stuff with names I can't pronounce) and sample the products at home.

And now a week had passed since the JPEG incident, and I was back in D.C., set up at the Cosmetic Relief headquarters, ready to interview for part two the man who was calling himself Purnell. He hadn't mentioned Fida or Lida or the stoned Fards, and there didn't seem to be a comfortable moment for me to ask. I certainly didn't mention my trip to the NIH, especially not any concerns I had about Bubblegum Pink.

"I'm sure she'll be here very soon." I looked down at my watch and then back at this so-called Purnell. He was starting to sweat again under the heat of the lights.

For a second time we had taken over Purnell's boardroom, moved aside the bulky furniture and lit the space to look like a sun-dappled parlor, if you could ignore the three cameras, the six crew members and the miles of cable and cords snaking all over the rug. I hadn't seen a setup like this in years. Since the war, our budgets had been slashed, and typically, I would be lucky to have a soundman to adjust microphones and modulate the audio so it didn't seem as if we were underwater. More often than not, it was just me and the shooter, bare bones and overtaxed. And since union rules forbade me from helping to carry or touch anything, we kept the production to a minimum.

This time, though, Faith was doing the interview. She had decided it would be good for her to be more involved with the story, and when an anchor was on the scene our budget went from public access to Hollywood. The crew even dressed the part. I was wearing a fitted black pantsuit, something I had blown a whole week's salary on. And the crew guys were all wearing khakis or cords—a step up from the usual denim uniforms.

"Why don't we cut the lights until she arrives," I said to Tony, the lead cameraman. Like many of the shooters at the network, he had been shooting since the Vietnam War, back when they used film stock instead of video, and network news was supposed to be a service, not turn a profit. Like most of the guys, he had given up fighting for the journalism a long time ago, and was just holding on for a few more years to guarantee a good pension, hoping for maybe one or two more decent stories along the way, something he could feel proud of before hanging up his press pass.

Under my breath I told him this could be a while. Faith was already a half hour late, and she wasn't responding to my page.

I turned back to Purnell. I wanted to ask about Fida and Lida and the stoned Fards, but instead I just acted like this was any old interview. I didn't want things to go wrong before the cameras started to roll.

"Oh," I said. "I owe you twenty dollars." I reached down for my purse, which was sitting on the floor next to one of the light stands.

"For what?"

"The other week? I borrowed money for a cab?"

"I have no idea what you are talking about, Annie."

Tony laughed. "What, are you trying to pay him off? Twenty bucks for a good sound bite?"

"Ha, ha," I said. "Very funny. No, really, Doug, didn't you get my IOU?"

He shrugged, refusing to take the bill I was trying to hand him.

"Okay," I said. "I'll mail you a check later. You can do what you want with it."

"Well, if we have to wait much longer, maybe you can buy me something to read? Like *War and Peace?*" He laughed that cackling, horrible laugh. We all politely giggled back.

"I am sorry about this wait," I said. "If you want to go back to your office, we can call you—"

"No, no. I was just kidding. I cleared my afternoon. No worries." A ball of sweat was about to take a dive from the tip of his globular nose. A nosedive, you might call it. Not wanting to look at him much longer, I offered to make a run to the Starbucks downstairs. I said I would use the money for the drinks, and Purnell agreed. So, orders taken for an Earl Grey tea with honey for Tony (who had a bad cold), a tall drip no milk, two tall lattes, a grande mochachino no foam, and a venti half-caf double chocolate chip frappuccino blended crème with an extra shot, the latter for Purnell, I headed to the elevator bank, reciting the caffeinated list to memory.

The coffee shop linguistics developed at the end of the twentieth century reminded me of schoolyard jump rope games. I could easily imagine a group of ten-year-olds doing double Dutch, chanting a rap of beverages, perhaps giggling when they hit into the precocious syrup category. I was thinking about this when the elevator door laboriously opened, allowing Faith's perfume to seep out before her.

"Oh, Annie," she said, once the doors gave way. She said it as if she was expecting me to be standing there, patiently awaiting her arrival. So much for the beverages.

"Is there a room for us?" Faith motioned her statically coiffed, highlighted head toward Sarah, the makeup artist she toted around like a lapdog. There were rumors about eyelifts and facial implants, but I had seen Faith without makeup and I thought those rumors were false. It was Sarah who could sculpt the transformative magic. Sarah hardly wore any makeup herself, and looked rather beleaguered and drawn and mouselike. I wondered if she made herself up on the weekends—kind of a role reversal. And I wondered what Faith did on the weekends, when Sarah was at home.

"The shuttle was overheated and I need some touching up," said Faith.

I knew she had arrived the night before, anchoring the show from D.C. that morning (an interview with the First Lady about her puppy play initiative), and had probably just been having lunch with her latest conquest at the Four Seasons, but I let it pass.

"Over here," I said, and they followed me to an empty office Purnell had set aside for us. Sarah opened up her oversize satchel and spread out her tools and palettes across the desk. Faith settled into a chair next to her.

Normally, our correspondents didn't travel with an entourage, but Faith was Faith. In fact, it was odd that she hadn't brought along a stylist and a hairdresser, as well. She had packed light. Maybe it was part of her strategy to be taken seriously.

"I read the questions you wrote up," she said, while Sarah applied another layer of cover-up under her eyes. "So, what's the signal?"

"The signal?"

"You know, so I know when you get the bite you need, and I can get out of here."

Of course.

I asked if there was anything in particular that she thought we should focus on, and she said she hadn't read the background material I had prepared, giggling conspiratorially like a kid who hadn't done her homework, as if it was bad in a cool way. Then she changed the subject.

"I hear the Neiman Marcus here just put out their new inventory. I think they're only open until five." She said this like we were girlfriends and I would fully want to help connive to get her out of the interview as quickly as possible.

"Oh," I said, as if interested, playing along with the girlfriend game, aware that if Faith didn't like me, she just had to bat an eye and my career would be over.

"How about you cough when you think we're set?" she said, closing her eyes so Sarah could apply a deep purple eye shadow. She painted delicately, with tiny stokes, as if Faith's lids were an oil painting in progress.

I said fine, knowing it wouldn't happen. I'd be lucky if she even got through half of the questions, and I wasn't about to short shrift the interview on account of Gucci.

I had spent the better part of the week constructing a line of questioning I had hoped would get Purnell to unwittingly reveal intimate details of what was clearly a pernicious enterprise, but I was well aware that the first order of business was for Faith to butter him up. Faith was no Mike Wallace, to be sure, but one thing I had to hand her was that she could soften even the toughest of men.

"I just love the shades of the lip gloss line," she said to Purnell as she settled into the chair opposite him, and Larry the audio engineer adjusted the microphone on her Chanel lapel. "If I were a twelve-year-old girl, why, I would just be drooling all over them." Sometimes Faith affected a slight Georgian (the state, not the country) accent, even though she actually hailed from Ohio.

Purnell, in what I suppose was an attempt to be flirtatious, suggested that she looked so young she could pass for twelve if she wanted to.

"Oh, you are too, too much," said Faith, gently touching one of Purnell's billowy knees with her bejeweled right hand.

"Ready?" said Tony. He sounded terrible, and I felt badly that I hadn't gotten him his tea.

"We're rolling," I said. I was sitting in a chair next to Tony, whose camera was facing Purnell, so that I could see Purnell but he didn't have me in his direct line of sight. I had a monitor to refer to, but Sarah insisted we kept it switched to Faith's camera so she could make sure not a hair fell out of place.

"Okay," said Faith, reading the first of the questions I had typed up. We started with a softball. "Since we last spoke, can you just give me a brief update of what has happened to Cosmetic Relief?"

"Hold on!" said Sarah, jumping up to fix one of Faith's hairs, which I guess to her eyes actually had fallen out of place. And then she applied some more powder to Faith's nose.

I rolled my eyes at Tony. He nodded in agreement. This was going to be a long day.

"All set?" Tony said when Sarah had settled back down.

"All set," I said, which was the cue for Faith to continue. Which she did, asking a few more Pollyanna-ish questions and getting a few more Pollyanna-ish answers, as planned. My heart started racing because I knew she was nearing the good stuff—like an SAT test, the questions would get increasingly difficult, both for her and for him. I was counting on the fact that Faith wouldn't give much thought to what she asked, that she would read my questions like she would a teleprompter.

She started to ask the next question. "It was recently reported that a main source of your funding actually comes from Vanity Cosmetics, which is partly owned by Corpcom, the parent company of—" She stopped. "Annie?" she said, not looking at me. "I am going to skip this one. Maybe we can come back to it later."

But Purnell knew he was in friendly hands. "No, no. It's okay," he said. "No reason we can't discuss that." He gave a nice do-gooder answer about the value of corporate America backing morally responsible development.

Faith smiled.

And then Tony coughed. "Excuse me," he said.

Faith looked at me. I shook my head, as if to say, *No. No, that wasn't me coughing. That was Tony.* But it was too late. Before I could say bubblegum pink, Faith had unclipped her microphone, shaken Purnell's puffy palm and spun out the door, tossing me an air kiss and a wink as she went.

"No, no," I meekly shouted after her. "Everyone, please stay. We aren't done." I ran down the hall.

"So, you got what you needed?" said Faith, as she pressed the elevator button. Sarah was carrying both of their bags. "That was clever, that coughing thing. Do you want to come with me to Neiman's?"

I just stood there dumbfounded, mouth agape. How could she possibly think the interview was finished after not even five minutes of questioning? But how could I stop her? Clearly, she was dead set on her expedition. And maybe, I thought, I would be better off without her.

The elevator doors opened, and away she went.

"Faith, your mike!" I yelled down the shaft, noticing that she had forgotten to remove the microphone and its receiver.

And this was it. This was my chance. I went back to the conference room and sat down in Faith's chair, telling Guy and David to turn off their cameras. Only Tony's, which was focused on Purnell, was still running. Edit out my voice, and Faith would never be missed.

Purnell looked at me. I looked at him. I apologized for the confusion. "Talent, you know," I said. And he laughed complicitly, because anyone who reads the gossip pages does in fact know.

The problem, however, was that I was not Mike Wallace, either. I didn't have the clout or the weight to pull off what I wanted to pull off, to ask the questions Karen had pressed me to ask. And so, after a few more softballs, when I asked Purnell, point-blank, if any dangerous substances were used in the cosmetics, he just coughed.

"Annie," he said, unclipping his mike with his swollen but manicured fingers, and standing up to leave. "I thought we were on the same page. And we already discussed testing. I really need to get back to work now."

"No, wait!" I said.

"I think you've gotten enough for your piece, Annabelle," he squeaked. "And I think you might now know enough to realize that you had better be careful. We are working for the same people, you and I."

He stood up and made for the door.

But the thing about large bulbous men like Purnell is that graceful exits are hard to come by. As he attempted to storm out of the room, he skidded across one of the cables on the floor, right next to my chair, and fell onto his sizable behind. It took all three cameramen to pull him back up. This all happened very fast, but not so fast that I didn't notice that during this turbulence, something had fallen onto my foot. And since the guys were busy propping up this mirror image of Tweedledum, they failed to notice as I grabbed the set of keys off my toes and slid them into my jacket pocket.

11

Clearly, I wasn't thinking straight. I don't know what universe I thought I was in, assuming it would be so simple. I really did. I honestly thought that, key in hand, I could just waltz into Purnell's office, rummage through some files, find some miraculously synthesizing document, and be done with it. What I would do with that synthesized information, I had no idea. What that information would be, I had no idea. I don't know—maybe deep down I thought I was some sort of holy crusader, out to save those poor lip-scarred girls, do some good for the world, something beyond disseminating diet advice and dating tips (not that such things don't have their place and need). Maybe. Or maybe I was just too caught up in my Nancy Drew moment to think clearly. To think, *Hey silly girl, just because you have a key doesn't mean it's a legal trespass.* Or to consider, when I actually did find the classified government file, that by opening it I was playing in a league so beyond me I didn't even know what it was.

I'm digressing again. Let me back up.

It was dark when I let myself into the Cosmetic Relief headquarters that evening, but the bottom of the walls were lined with tiny glow lights, like the ones in the corridor of an airplane, perfectly spaced so you don't trip on your way to the bathroom. My eyes quickly adjusted and I could make out the smiling faces of the pretty young girls on the posters, their eyes watching as I walked down the hall to Purnell's office. It was easy. In fact, it was too easy. The office itself was unlocked, but on the key chain there was one particularly small key that obviously opened either a suitcase or a filing cabinet. Being that I wasn't exactly in a tourist destination, it was pretty clear which one it would be.

I turned the lock. I felt so smug, so proud of myself, so filled with a sense of, well, smartness. What a schmuck. My friend Galina in the cell next door teases me relentlessly about this. Lately, whenever she wants to get my goat, she's been calling me Ms. Holmes, or sometimes just Sherlocka.

Galina's in for a much brainier screwup than mine. She was just a bank teller with a bad Virtual Shopping Network habit, but in order to fund it, she got caught up in some sort of document falsification and embezzlement ring that it would take a Harvard MBA to understand. Some of the people she was involved with are still out, and with nicknames like Sledge and Stungun, you might think Galina hung out with a rather thickheaded and seedy crowd, and that she might be rather seedy herself. But she isn't. The thing about Galina is that even though her face reminds me of any number of the Slavic supermodels that have washed up on our shores in the past decade or so (mile-high cheekbones; catlike eyes; full, pouty lips), she is smart as hell. She claims she has the equivalent of a Ph.D. in comparative literature from her native Russia, but that outside of Moscow, no one gives a damn.

Normally I am intimidated by such striking looking women, but prison light can have an equalizing effect, and Galina and I hit it off from day one, right after being processed. We carried our beige jail-issued jumpsuits back to our cell block together. Along the way, Galina made a comment about how she was impressed with the quality of the cotton. It wasn't what she had expected, she said; it was thicker. I noticed her accent, and when she told me she was from Russia, I told her that my cat was named Margarita, from *The Master and Margarita* by Mikhail Bulgakov, because that was my favorite book in college. She said she was impressed that an American would know anything about Russian literature, aside from the obvious tomes by Tolstoy and Dostoevsky. I said that was ridiculous, and anyway, if pressed, she probably didn't know much about American authors, at which point she started rattling off everyone from Philip Roth to Danielle Steele. Of course, Galina isn't as smart as she puts on. After all, she got caught, too. So maybe she should just keep her mouth shut.

Anyway, there I was, hovering over a metal filing cabinet I shouldn't have been hovering over, straining to make out the labels in the dim light. And there it was, so comically obvious I wouldn't even believe me if I told the story to myself. But I swear. The files were flawlessly alphabetized, and right smack in the middle of the Cs was a stiff manila folder with a label titled Cosmetic Relief. And right inside that folder was another folder, this one slightly faded with age and stamped with the most unsubtle red letters possible: "CLASSIFIED CIA DOCUMENT." I should have stopped there. But I didn't. No one in my place would have. It was my own personal apple (though if that office was Eden, I suppose it would be a sad state of affairs).

"Holy shit," I said to no one, and pulled it out. And then? And then I was stumped. The documents were too thick to think about reading right there, and the paper was too thin and delicate to flip through quickly. The file was clearly a few decades old. *Do I take the folder and run,* I wondered, *or do I, because I am thoughtful like that, go look for the Xerox machine down the hall so that I can make myself a copy and then put it back where it belongs?* Or, because of my clearly pathological need to brag about what I thought was my shining moment, do I decide right then and there to call Mark? Where was Candy Curlish when I needed her?

Mark was already on my speed dial.

"You're where?" he said, sounding like I had just stunned him out of a good sleep, which apparently I had.

"I told you I was coming here."

"I thought you were joking."

I didn't answer.

"Annie, are you seriously in Purnell's office?"

"Yes. And you won't believe it. There's this old classified folder here, and—"

"Annie, leave right now. Get the hell out of there. Fuck."

"Mark, I—"

"You have no idea… I just found out… Shit. Just get out of there."

"But—"

"I'll explain later. Just leave. Now." He hung up.

So much for impressing the boy.

I looked at the stack of paper in my hand. I was paralyzed. *Do I go? Do I stay?*

I didn't get to choose.

Just as I was putting my phone back into my purse, the lights went on. All of them, florescent and glaring. I would have looked guilty even if I wasn't.

"Homeland Security," one of the dark-suited men said, flashing his ID much too quickly for me to actually read it. His partner stood near the door, as if on lookout.

I am sure I seemed more like a kid caught with my hand in a cookie jar than any kind of professional, news-based, criminal, or otherwise. But, hell, I thought, if the press pass could get me across police barriers, maybe it could get me out of one.

"I'm with ZBC News," I said.

"You're in trouble is what you are," said the officer, taking my left hand to meet my right behind my back and then fastening them together with a hard plastic band that cut slightly into my wrists. Then he told me I was under arrest for a violation of the Espionage Act, that I was misappropriating state secrets as well as associating with foreign nationals believed to be a security risk to the United States, and that I had the right to remain silent, and that anything I said could be used against me in a court of law and so forth. Which is why I figured it best not to ask right then why I wasn't being arrested for illegal trespass, which, as cause for arrest goes, would have made a lot more sense.

My perp walk was embarrassing. It had taken a good sixteen hours to process me before my arraignment, and of course there was no shower, no brush, no comb. With my mascara now rimming my eyes like dark coffee cup stains on a newspaper, and my hair frizzing up as if I had been electrocuted, I looked so crazy I probably could have argued insanity and been done with it. I am not exaggerating. I saw the photo in the *New York Star* the next day.

They brought it to me in my cell to celebrate my celebrity. Apparently, by the time I was escorted into the courthouse, the word was out that a young, female media type was embroiled in an allegedly treasonous plot. And, apparently, we media types eat our young. It was a paparazzi circus, with cameramen and reporters yelling my name and flashing bulbs blinding me. But this was no red carpet fantasy. The defense attorney held me close under the cover of his crisp trench coat, helping me navigate a straight line and keep my knees from buckling as we walked the hundred or so feet from car to court. I was exhausted, terrified and profoundly confused. The thing that shook me the most, though, the thing that really made me panic, was hearing my name being called by a familiar sounding voice. I turned and there was Miranda Weiss, a booking producer who had left our show to go to *Sunrise America*. Then I looked to her right. There stood a crew from *American Breakfast*. Next to them was a crew from my show, and Caitlin, my booker friend from work. All of them were jockeying for my attention.

I didn't know it then, but soon one thing would be clear: morning television was my shot at salvation.

PART TWO

When the politicians complain that TV turns the proceedings into a circus, it should be made clear that the circus was already there, and that TV has merely demonstrated that not all the performers are well trained.

—Edward R. Murrow

12

"Thirty seconds to air!" The stage manager skips over the wires strewn about the floor and jumps behind the row of semirobotic cameras. And then, in a scene with which we are familiar, the same one that happens every morning, a frail makeup artist rushes forward, armed with a powder puff, and dives for the host's shiny, pert nose. The white dust settles and she is gone, out of the shot.

"Ten seconds!"

Multiple cameras are posed, like gunmen at an execution, ready to shoot. The red lights on top of each lens, the ones that indicate the cameras are recording, are flashing with admonition.

The theme music kicks in, adding a softly uplifting and melodic instrumental soundtrack to the pan shot of the gathered crowds outside, the people with the hand-painted signs wishing this uncle or that aunt a happy birthday, the ones jumping up and down to get the camera to settle on them, to grant them their three seconds of fame.

"Roll camera A!" shouts the director, pointing a decisive finger at a single monitor amid the wall of monitors in front of him, and suddenly a very attractive and very groomed dark-haired man and a very attractive and very groomed light-haired woman, each with perfectly symmetrical features and wide and welcoming toothy smiles, enter your living room, your kitchen, your bathroom—whichever room you happen to be in when eating your cereal or brushing your teeth.

"Good morning," says the woman, looking awfully resplendent considering she's been at work since 3:00 a.m. prepping for the day's show. "Welcome to *Sunrise America*. Second to coffee, we're America's favorite way to wake up. I'm June Lacey."

The man guffaws at June's little joke. Last night's numbers showed that for the first time in three years, *Sunrise America* had finally beaten *New Day USA,* their main competition, and they were enjoying every second of it. "And I'm Jack Strands," he says, suppressing his smile as he launches into the teases, promising that if you stay tuned past the headlines, if you keep watching into the morning, you will be entertained, amused and informed. An interview with the star of the latest blockbuster, great new tips for the grilling season, and, stay with us, an update on "Gloss-gate"—the Annabelle Kapner story, with more new exclusive coverage. Stay tuned for shocking details!

Across the street and a few blocks closer to Times Square, Tom Tatcher watches Jack Strands out of the corner of his eye and cringes from the back of his control room as he listens to Ken Klark recite *his* show's less than stellar rundown; as he watches, as it were, his show's Neilsen ratings (and possibly his own career) spiral into a downward vortex. Sure, since the story broke, *New Day USA* has been there—Caitlin Donohue, their ace booking producer, has been on location, gathering video at the perp walk, collecting exterior shots of the jail and sound bites from press conferences, trying to convince people in the know to go on the show. Meanwhile Natasha Spark, with little information to go on and even fewer people to interview, sews slight packages together, looking perhaps a little sad and distracted in her stand-ups, clearly not her usual tenacious self. During the midshow anchor chats, Faith banters daily about how shocked she is, shocked, because Annie always seemed so professional ("although we can't make any judgments just yet," she is always sure to add), Purnell seemed so decent, and the colors of the Cosmetic Relief lip glosses are so vibrant. Even former *New York Herald* reporter and former first amendment warrior Janet Muller arrived on set to discuss the conditions of the detention center, the same one she toiled at before she resigned herself, as it were, to reveal some sources a few years prior.

But as things develop, and they rapidly are, the story is becoming more and more awkward for Tatcher and his team to touch; how do you report on a scandal involving your own parent company, even if only associatively? Nowhere in the ZBC Guide to News Standards and Practices is it discussed how to cover a story like this. If ZBC News is owned by Corpcom and Corpcom owns Vanity, and Vanity funded Cosmetic Relief, and something fishy is going on at Cosmetic Relief that may or may not include an employee of ZBC, what is an executive producer to do? It would be like a news division owned by a company owned by, say, Disney, investigating allegations of bigamy against Mickey Mouse.

Sure, there was a press release from Max Meyer, claiming horror, dismay and ignorance, announcing the immediate sale of all of Corpcom's Vanity holdings (which they somehow managed to do without suffering a loss—the name recognition initially sent Vanity stock into the ether). Otherwise there is just silence from the front office. It is a loud silence, one that says to Tom that all of those photos of him standing tall with presidents, all of those awards and accolades, are only as good as the current show he is producing; embarrass headquarters and they will be as forgotten as the star of a sitcom pilot that never ran past episode two. Tom's staff cover the story, but they cover it tentatively, with hands tied. Anyway, at this point, they couldn't cover it well if they tried; even if *New Day USA* wanted to be all over this Kapner thing, none of the pundits want to be affiliated with *New Day*, because *New Day* is now affiliated with an anchor whose own role in the story is a little questionable (seeing as she is a major shareholder herself) and an allegedly treasonous producer, and in this day and age, who knows what that means.

Tom pops two Zantacs and turns back to watch Faith on the middle monitor as she attempts to scramble an egg under the guidance of Chef Fromage, Faith's own frustration with her slipping Q rating (the industry measure of name recognition and general appeal) worked out in the slightly too frothy soufflé.

"Glossgate!" screamed the headlines of the *New York Star* the morning after Annie's arraignment. "Lips Locked Up!" splashed across the cover of the *Daily Views*. But the scoop of all scoops is scooped up by *Stellar* magazine—not so much with words, but with grainy surveillance photos taken a few weeks prior, when allegedly treasonous Annie swapped straws at Mecca with White House hunk Mark Thurber. The first to have a viewing? The audience of *Sunrise America,* fortunate in that their program of choice is run on a network that owns the publishing company that prints *Stellar,* and that the editor of the magazine is a regular contributor, usually with movie star gossip, this time with a video clip purchased from the security guard for an undisclosed sum.

With a parade of high school classmates, former lovers, college professors and childhood babysitters, *Sunrise* positively owns the Annabelle Kapner story. Keep it safe and spin the show on *Sunrise,* follow up with an appearance on the lower-rated *American Breakfast,* the guests silently agree, and quickly a new army of pundits emerges, new careers are made, as they traipse across 24-hour news channels, Al-Jazeera, the blogosphere, even materializing on the Virtual Shopping Network (one reporter's 72-hour turnaround book, *Producing Treason: Inside the Annabelle Kapner Story,* is first sold in an exclusive televised offer before hitting the shelves of Barnes and Noble). Even the venerable *New York Herald* succumbs, initially tucking Glossgate reports deep inside section A (maintaining a certain aloofness while hiding behind the veneer of the media beat, while more gossipy tidbits were safe from infringing on the *Herald's* credibility because they appeared in Sunday's *Style*) but steadily moving it closer and closer to the front page.

Having the desire to be famous is arguably the defining characteristic of what it means to be an American at the beginning of the twenty-first century. What someone wants to be famous for is irrelevant. Most often, they don't even know themselves. I've produced tons of stories about kids (in high schools, elementary schools, colleges, even nursery schools), and across the board, the most common answer to the "what do you want to be when you grow up" question is "famous." "Really rich" comes in a close second. Our aspirations are limited. No one says "I want to fly to Mars" or "I want to develop the cure for cancer" or "I want to broker world peace."

I suppose the kids are on to something, because without being famous a person probably wouldn't even get the opportunity to do any of the above. Well, at least the opportunity wouldn't come easily. Now, if he or she were a movie star or, better yet, a beloved reality show contestant, I am sure NASA would happily consider an invitation. Funding for cancer research? No problem. Just declare it the cool new trend in your interview with *Star Weekly* and in minutes the phone lines to the Lymphoma Society are clogged. World peace? Well, it wouldn't be shocking if Angelina Jolie was invited to the next summit. In America, celebrity is the most valuable currency of all.

Of course, that's not what I am initially thinking as I watch "Annabelle Kapner" become a household name. Even the vice president mentions me on the campaign trail, something about the slippery slope between press coverage and enemy fodder, and how the likes of me are good examples of the fourth estate playing with fire. I do wonder how this has all affected Mark's job, and I feel sick when I consider the possibility that Mark might even have something to do with these speeches, but then the president himself chimes in on his Sunday radio address, so I just hope that maybe the media/Annie bashing directive is coming from the Oval Office and not from Mark's much smaller domain in the executive building. Still, it doesn't seem like he is doing anything to stop it.

Anyway, some people charged with crimes would probably get excited about such exposure, but as Galina and I sit here on the cold metal folding chairs in the jail's recreation room, watching my fame build (and my reputation tarnish) across the morning newscasts, it takes extreme effort on my part not to toss up my breakfast (lukewarm cream of wheat and watery coffee with a painfully negligible amount of caffeine) or run looking for some rope (or I suppose a bunch of tied together sheets) to hang from.

It's been a few weeks now that the Federal Detention Center in Alexandria, Virginia (ironically, just a few miles from that Fardish den of iniquity) has become my home. The government is busily building an espionage case against me, there has been no mention whatsoever about the maltreatment of little Fardish girls, and my bail was set at five million dollars. No one is setting up a fund to raise it, not even my parents. I comfort myself by trying to trust that my friends and family believe my protestations of innocence against the charges brought, that they are sympathetic when I try to explain my actions, but in this day and age it would be a risky personal venture to publicly align oneself with someone who is perceived to be an enemy of the state. I understand.

What I don't fully understand is how I got here in the first place. Yes, I should probably have thought twice before entering Purnell's office, but honestly, I didn't think it would be illegal if I had his keys. Well, I knew it was probably illegal, but I thought it would be less illegal. It doesn't matter, anyway. That isn't even one of the charges against me. So here I am, searching desperately for what is left of a nail to bite, sitting cross-legged on my paper-thin mattress, a mattress that is probably older than I am (when I want to calm my mind of the present turmoil, instead of counting sheep at night, I lie awake wondering about this mattress's inmates from the past—there must have been hundreds).

There really is no other word for it, I am miserable.

I am thirty years old, about to turn thirty-one, and my biggest concerns should be about procreation and vocation, not about the state of the mattress I am probably doomed to sleep on the rest of my life. I should be worrying about my weight, whether my new haircut looks good, who I am going to date on Saturday night, who I am going to marry. It's certainly not like Mark and I are going to be setting a date anytime soon. Even if he hadn't completely run out on me, even if he wasn't a totally duplicitous a-hole (my latest theory—they change hourly), even if he was here every day, bringing me flowers in reception, powwowing with my lawyers and pulling all of his strings, it wouldn't matter. People have been held for years without trial on charges less than mine, so right now my biggest fantasy is to be able to have my old neurotic concerns back. A dateless night curled up on a couch with my cat and some Ben & Jerry's sounds downright dreamy.

"Annie, get off your *zhopa*. It almost seven."

"*Zhopa?*" I say.

"The rear, the ass." Galina taps her butt to clarify.

"Oh."

She is standing at the door to my cell, backlit. I can see only her silhouette: a tall, thin woman with short but not insubstantial hair (which if she wasn't silhouetted you could see is a shocking shade of peroxide blond), one hand at the top of the doorpost, the other now resting on her behind. She steps in, grabbing my wrist, pulling me up to my feet and out the door, dragging me down the hallway to the recreation room, a dim space illuminated only by light coming through the dusty old windows up near the ceilings, crisscrossed with bars. She drops me onto one of the only empty metal folding chairs, the one that was reserved for me, and then, pushing through the other women who are congregating about the room, arrives at the television set, manually flipping through the channels (no remote controls here) while I nervously smooth out the wrinkles on the leg of my (extremely unflattering) beige jumpsuit.

Every inmate here has a story to tell, but my story is televised, and I guess that makes me the most respected inmate of all. My status comes in handy at mealtimes and during chores, but the real value comes now, in the morning. Normally the television is set to Telemundo or the Soap Opera Network, but due to my now infamous case, the other inmates kindly defer to me in the post-breakfast hours, allowing me to watch the morning news programs instead of their usual fare.

Galina sits down next to me, as she has every morning over the previous few weeks, cradling my shoulders for support, pulling me into the comforting warmth of her long, sinewy arms, while everyone else settles in around us, packing the cement-floored room with a titillating sense of excitement as if we were watching the Academy Awards.

We fix our gazes on the boxy old television set chained to the shelf in front of us, and the show bumps out of commercial, a little peppy music fading up and then away as the host looks up and out of the screen.

"It is the story we've all been watching," says June Lacey, drool almost visible at the side of her plump but neutrally painted mouth. "A promising young journalist allegedly embroiled in a terrorist plot. Did she use the platform of her prestigious network news job to help generate funds for a dangerous organization? Were there drugs involved? And where is her White House boyfriend in all of this? Was he in fact her boyfriend? What did he know? The plot gets thicker. *Sunrise America*'s Valerie Valdes is in Arlington, Virginia with the latest. Good morning, Valerie."

"Good morning, June," says the woman standing in front of a redbrick town house, her long dark hair tied back into a serious looking knot, as if she was working too hard getting the scoop to have it styled. Her tailored brown blazer is buttoned snuggly against her chest, a simple pearl strand resting just below her clavicle. The conservative studiousness of the look doesn't hide her glee; of all the correspondents at the show, she was the one to get this assignment, an assignment that guaranteed her more exposure and story count than any contract her agent could ever negotiate.

"June," she says, seeming relaxed, as if she were about to speak off the cuff, as if her words were ad-libbed, though in fact she probably wrote them last night and then recited them repeatedly until they were stamped into her memory. "This is a case that has celebrity watchers, industry insiders and government agents all salivating to get more information. And it seems it might have all started here, in this seemingly ordinary suburban home." She gestures to the brick building behind her. "Behind these doors, authorities say, there was activity that was far from ordinary—and they say embroiled *New Day USA* producer Annabelle Kapner was at the heart of the strange goings-on."

The screen cuts to video of the interior of the house, complete with pillows strewn about on the floor and the plastic-covered floral couch that once held young Fida and Lida. Valerie's voice continues to narrate.

VALDES NARRATION: Authorities say that it was from the comfort of this house that Annabelle Kapner may have been helping to funnel money—from here (camera reveals a pile of lipstick on top of the coffee table)...to here (cut to a grainy, almost indecipherable shot of some figures running around in formation in the middle of a desert).

UNIDENTIFIED MAN IN FRONT OF A PRESS CON-FERENCE: We have been watching so-called "Cosmetic Relief" for two years now, and we have evidence to show that the Fardish cosmetics program may have been a front for a trafficking operation that supported terrorist groups.

VALDES NARRATION: John Roe is a spokesperson for Homeland Security.

MAN NOW IDENTIFIED AS HOMELAND SECURITY SPOKESPERSON JOHN ROE: Recent tests show that a number of the items collected from what we believe to be a command center for Cosmetic Relief contain trace amounts of an undisclosed narcotic substance.

VALDES NARRATION: It is a stunning new allegation... and one that Roe says could lead them to the man at the center of the scandal, Douglas Purnell, the CEO of Cosmetic Relief. But there is a small problem (file video of Purnell from when he first appeared on the competing *New Day USA* broadcast, ZBC's icon obliterated by a large *Sunrise America* graphic).

HOMELAND SECURITY SPOKESPERSON JOHN ROE: Douglas Purnell is believed to have left the country on the night of the break-in. We believe Annabelle Kapner is the most solid lead to his whereabouts (replay of the perp walk shot, looking just as bedraggled as she did the last time it aired, and the time before that, and the time before that...). Ms. Kapner's fingerprints taken from illegally appropriated classified documents found at the CR headquarters match perfectly with the prints on these lipstick cases we collected in a raid of the CR storage facility yesterday (he holds up a few pink lipstick cases, each sealed in its own Ziploc bag). Additionally, we have found documentation to prove that on the night of April 15th, Douglas Purnell gave Kapner a cash payment of unknown quantity.

VALDES NARRATION: Authorities now believe that Kapner was paid off to promote the positive side of CR and deflect from its possibly seedy underbelly. Kapner's lawyer, Ron Ruby, maintains that she was just reporting a story.

RON RUBY, ANNIE'S LAWYER (a broad, tall man in a form-fitting designer suit speaking through a jungle of microphones as he pushes his way out of his car and into his office building): Annabelle may have made some mistakes, but they were mistakes in her reporting process, nothing else. If she is guilty of anything, it is of trying to do her job just a little too hard.

UNIDENTIFIED MAN (bald, with jacket and tie, sitting at a desk): I have to say, that's a ridiculous statement.

VALDES NARRATION: Alexander Churn is the media critic for the *New York Spectator* and a consultant to *Sunrise*

America (shot of Churn walking through his paper's news-room, trying to act nonchalant, as if he always saunters through the space while being followed by a camera crew).

BALD MAN NOW IDENTIFIED AS ALEXANDER CHURN, MEDIA CRITIC FOR THE *NEW YORK SPECTA-TOR* AND CONSULTANT TO *SUNRISE AMERICA* (again at his desk): I mean, who ever heard of a morning show pro-ducer doing the kind of investigative reporting Kapner's lawyers are suggesting? Sure, I'd welcome it, but come on. This girl has produced nothing but light features for five years. Suddenly she's an overzealous Christiane Amanpour? Please.

VALDES NARRATION: And that would be a very odd twist. The program Kapner works for, our competitor *New Day USA,* is owned by Corpcom. Corpcom recently pur-chased and then promptly sold an ownership stake of Van-ity Cosmetics, the company that had been planning to start distributing the makeup in question to Wal-Marts and Tar-gets across America (montage of the headquarters and logos of each of the aforementioned concerns).

ALEXANDER CHURN, MEDIA CRITIC FOR THE *NEW YORK SPECTATOR,* CONSULTANT TO *SUNRISE AMERICA*: Anyway, if miraculously *New Day USA* had decided to start competing with *Frontline,* and Annabelle Kapner was trying to become an investigative producer, why in God's name would she start by investigating her own company? It's an ab-surd proposition.

VALDES NARRATION: But perhaps the biggest question—
where is Mark Thurber, Kapner's White House insider boyfriend in all of this? (file footage of Mark getting into a Town
Car outside of the White House, dated a year prior). The
White House maintains Thurber and Kapner were just passing acquaintances, but acknowledges that he recently left for
an extended European vacation.

DANIEL SPINNER, WHITE HOUSE SPOKESMAN: We
feel that Mark's involvement doesn't go beyond the fact that
Annabelle Kapner, like so many women, had a crush on him.
End of story.

Valdes reappears front and center on the screen, standing
exactly where she was two minutes prior. "But, as you know, June,
the story is far from over."

June thanks Valerie and then introduces her next guest, the
aforementioned Alexander Churn, here to discuss more details
about the story. And joining him? Bobbie Lesser, the afore-
aforementioned editor of *Stellar* magazine, here to put the White
House spokesman to shame.

"What an ass," says Galina (pronouncing "ass" like the letter *s*)
as we listen to Alexander Churn and friends denigrate the history
of my entire career, and although I am much more preoccupied
with other, more pressing concerns, I have to agree with her. I
mean, sure, maybe I've never done reporting that brought down
dictators or changed industries, but I have to believe that at least
some of what I have done, from the inspirational to the devota-
tional, has some value. I know it does. I've seen the e-mails. I've

been on the receiving end of the effusive gratitude. And really, isn't there more value in, say, encouraging people to dream, to take risks, to, I don't know, start their own business or lose a hundred unwanted pounds than, say, sit on your butt as if it were a high horse and pick out the failings of the rest of the press as if you, Mr. Churn, are somehow above it?

"Can you believe this guy?" Galina continues as Churn pontificates about what he calls the shallow morality of morning television, even though he himself is pontificating from the set of a morning television show. "I gamble he think he pee tea water. What a—what you call it—a schmuck?" She is speaking in a tone more hopeful than pissed off, as if the fact that Churn is an asshole should be soothing, and maybe the whole freaking country will recognize his asshole-ishness and sympathize with me, which is, unfortunately, completely unlikely. Nothing works better on television than a belligerent but charismatic asshole. Nothing is more appealing. Just look at history—Tony Soprano, Simon Cowell, Joan Rivers once upon a time. I am sure they are paying Churn nice money to offer his opinions on *Sunrise America*. It is a funny thing, because though they can't pay for interviews, they can put a covetable character on their payroll. It is irritating, but ultimately Churn isn't the focus of my attention. I am way too upset about something else.

"I can't believe he left the country," I say, completely demoralized.

"Purnell?"

"No, you idiot. Mark."

Galina pulls her arm from my shoulders. "Don't you talk to me this way. I am your friend. Friend is most important."

"Sorry," I say, now even more demoralized, sinking into the

cold, hard back of my chair. I put my face in my hands and try to suppress the tears threatening to flood out of my eyes. Galina immediately softens.

"It okay, my little *zaichick*," she says, putting her arm around me again. She gets up to turn the channel to *New Day*, where we see Faith aggressively chopping onions.

"*Zaichick?*" I sniffle when she returns to her chair.

"Bunny. Little bunny. It just nice word, mean, like, 'sweetie.'"

I repeat it again, *zaichick*, and let myself be comforted for a moment. A very brief moment. Because before I can wallow in it as I really want to, the other inmates start peppering me with the usual questions, like they do every morning, wanting to know not so much about my case, but about what Faith Heide is like in real life (harmless), if I have ever met Brad Pitt (no), if Ken Klark is single (he is, but ex-model ex-wife and outings with arm-candy aside, he is also rumored to be gay).

And then, at nine o'clock, the show is over. Galina offers me a hand to pull me out of the seat, and we all make our way to our own centers of purgatory, teasing our own futures in our heads as we wait to see which lawyer, which bit of news, which fleeting glimmer of hope (or the opposite) would befall us today. Bump to commercial.

13

A lie gets halfway around the world before the truth has a chance to get its pants on.

—Sir Winston Churchill

During the time I've been in jail, I have become intractably superstitious. In my panicked, despondent desperation, I have to cling to something. I turned my flimsy graying mattress to face south, walk in the yard when it is raining, and pick up any penny I can find (they are understandably few and far between). Without Internet or e-mail, aside from the time I spend with Galina, my only salvation is my limited telephone privilege and the thirty minutes daily when I am allowed to receive guests other than my attorneys. So, when I walk into the reception room and see Caitlin, my booker friend from work, sitting on one of the white plastic chairs in the reception room, my heart skips a beat and I count my blessings. In the three weeks I've been in Alexandria, the only people I've seen are my parents and my lawyers. Karen wrote once, but only to say that although she wanted to speak with me, she was a bit afraid to do so. That was it. Honestly, while I believe in my heart of hearts that Karen would be here if she could be, sometimes it is hard to know who your friends are when none of them show up. And sometimes you really need them. So when the warden asked me if I would accept a visit from Caitlin Donohue, I almost started to cry.

Caitlin looks a little malapropos among the husbands and boyfriends and grandmothers, most of them trying to keep the squirmy little sons and daughters of my fellow inmates sitting still, trying to stop them from running to the rusty vending machines as they impatiently wait for their mother, girlfriend, aunt, to materialize through the door in the back. Caitlin is dressed simply, in a high-necked black cotton sweater and loose fitting pants, apparently having studied the long list of dos and do nots for our visitors: no tight fitting, revealing clothing. No stretch jeans. No tank tops. No halter tops. Skirts must be no more than three inches above the knee. No fatigues. No sweatpants. No multiple clothing layers. Hats and religious headwear allowed, but they will be searched. No jewelry. No pens.

We hug awkwardly and then I pull up one of the plastic chairs and sit at a table, motioning for her to join me. You have to get close here, because given the shrieking kids, the crying lovers and the endless buzzing of the fluorescent lights, it can be difficult to hear anything. My forehead is practically touching Caitlin's. I can feel the heat coming off of her, but the tension is so thick there may as well be a glass divider between us, two clunky beige receivers our way to communicate, like you might see in an old Mafia film.

"I like your haircut," I tell her, straining to think of something to say. Caitlin gently pats the perimeter of the layered pixie do, a style that makes her seem younger than her thirty-two years and does nothing to draw down her severely upturned nose.

She laughs nervously. "You look skinny," she says, clearly straining to make conversation. It's not as if she could tell me I look anything near good. But at this point I will take whatever compliments come my way.

"Thanks," I say, and joke that if they are still in style when I get out of here, I'll finally be able to wear those size zero designer jeans I mistakenly bought on eBay a few months back, too excited by the cheap price to notice that the last time I would have fit into them was when I was in eighth grade.

Then we do what most people do when they don't know what to talk about: we talk about someone else.

"Faith looks a bit like she's about to blow," I say, commenting on this morning's overly energetic frothing of the eggs.

"Yeah, it's pretty bad. We've fallen behind *American Morning.*" Caitlin leans in and whispers, as if this is a huge secret, "Actually, word is that this week's rating might even have us behind *all* the cables."

"Wow," I say with a laugh. "If I had known I had such an impact on the ratings I would have negotiated for a better contract." That, of course, puts us directly on the topic of me and only serves to make both of us even more ill at ease.

Caitlin's eyes shift toward the floor.

I sigh. "So," I say.

"Yeah." Caitlin is struggling to look me.

"What?"

"I just thought you should know that Tatcher has decided to try to refocus on the story, your story. To try to get some of the ratings back. To try to prove that we can be a credible news program."

"And?"

"I just thought you should know."

"Are they going to help fight my case, help prove my innocence?" I am getting excited, despite myself.

Caitlin doesn't say anything.

"Do you think there is any way I can get them to investigate the real story, the real reason I wound up here?" I am about to tell her about the e-mail, the photograph of the little girl and the testing, but I quickly realize I would be wasting my breath. "I guess that wouldn't be very good for the ratings, now would it?" I say. "Not nearly as sexy, right? And it would make them look even worse."

Caitlin is still staring at the floor, silent for what feels like an eternity. Finally, she focuses her gray eyes on me. "I heard from Mark."

My mouth drops open slightly. She looks away again.

"You know, from when I had him on the show? We had each other's cell numbers and stuff. He asked if I could get a message to you."

"Excuse me?"

This is weird. Mark and Caitlin had no relationship beyond that one appearance. There were a million other ways he could have contacted me. Like directly, for starters. Why would he go through her? But since he has, I have a million questions. Like why *hasn't* he contacted me? Where is he? What does he know? Does he miss me? Does he think I am a total idiot?

I don't ask anything.

"He said I should tell you that he's sorry," she says softly, slowly turning her gaze toward me again as she finishes the sentence, looking, I suppose, for my reaction.

"Sorry?" I raise my eyebrows. "What are you, his mole? Well, if he is so sorry, than why has he fallen off the face of the earth? Where the hell is he?"

"I couldn't tell where he was." She looks straight at me and furrows her eyebrows. I can't tell if she is registering with a small degree of horror that I clearly don't have tweezers in here, or something else. "He was on his cell," she continues. "It sounded far away. He just said, 'Please tell Annie that I'm sorry.'"

"And that's it? You came all the way here from New York to give me a scoop on *TV Guide* and to tell me that?"

"Not just that."

"Not just that?" Despite myself, I say this a little excitedly.

"No. I mean, actually, they have me temporarily based in D.C. Just in case. I'm staying at the Jefferson."

"In case of what?" Now I am raising my voice. What the hell does she think is going to happen? What the fuck does she think I am going to be able to do? What kind of friend is she, anyway?

Let me just say that my usual MO is to passively absorb whatever negativity is at hand and put it on myself, if that makes any sense. Over the years my therapists have loved to focus on this concern, trying to chalk it up to some trauma I faced as a kid, something I don't even remember myself. But it is a problem. Since I've been here I've been more acquiescent than enraged, and that can make a person like me get fairly depressed. But now that the truth is revealing itself all over Caitlin's face, it is hitting me that I am truly, completely on my own, and short of Galina I have no idea who my friends are. Karen's been silent. Mark is gone. No one aside from paid lawyers, blood relations and sycophants has come to visit me. I have no friends or face to lose anymore. And that's freedom, isn't it? Maybe that's why I am feeling this now, this sense of, I don't know, anger. I am totally pissed off.

I kind of like it.

"Caitlin, what the hell?" I say with my voice lowered and chin down. "Who sent you here? Carl? Tatcher? Is this some sick booking trick? Butter Annie up and maybe she'll grant us the first exclusive when, or should I say *if,* she gets out? Annie ruined our ratings, so maybe she'll feel like she owes it to us to bring them back?"

Caitlin just sort of nods at me. I can't tell if I am scaring her or not.

"Well, they're wasting your time and their money," I say, whinier than the threatening tone I am striving for. "It doesn't look like I am about to make bail anytime soon."

She shrugs slightly, as if she's a freaking mute.

"And anyway," I say, leaning in closer to her, lowering my voice, "even if I did make bail, at this point I don't owe the show anything. It doesn't sound like Tom is exactly planning to help me out here. Or Faith, for that matter. Why would I bother..." But before I finish the question, something hits me. This thing about Mark is total crap. It was just a way to butter me up.

I sit back and stare at her. "Did he really call you? Or are you just bullshitting me about that, too? Isn't he supposed to be out of the country? Fallen off the face of the earth?"

"No, Annie," she says, finding her voice. "I really spoke to him. He sounded sad."

"But did *he* call *you?* You called him, didn't you? You had his number from when you had him on the show. You called him." And then it hit me. Even if it were true that she had even tried to call, it didn't make any sense that she would have reached him. "No one in the world knows where he is, Caitlin. The only phone he actually might answer is his private cell number, a number he only gives out to close friends and family. So you are telling me that you actually had that number and called him on it to see if you could book him, win major brownie points with Tatcher, and that he actually answered the phone? Don't bullshit me."

Caitlin's complexion is now growing so pale it's practically transparent. She is barely audible when she tells me that Mark gave her his private number that day he was on the show so that she could give it to me (which, now that she mentions it, I remember she did). She is even less audible when she asks me why it matters who called whom, and I am incredibly audible when I tell her that she has played her cards badly. If she thinks she can use Mark as some sort of carrot to get me to commit to the show, then she is producing like an amateur.

We sit in silence.

I desperately want to tell her to get lost, but I also want desperately for her to tell me something, anything, to make me believe that she actually did speak to him, anything that could give me a hint about where Mark is and what he is thinking, and, as if it were even fathomable, what he knows and if he can help me. And she, well, I know what she wants. She wants to be able to call Tom with the reassurance that, even though they've taken me off payroll, even though they are doing this much short of nothing to help my case, that as soon as I have the opportunity to talk to the media, my first impulse will be to return to the proverbial womb.

None of these things are going to happen.

"Excuse me," I say, and turn to the guard to ask if I can go get a sip of water. And then, once my thirst is sated and I've calmed down, I return to the chair, its legs seeming to buckle slightly under my now insignificant weight. Caitlin says she is going, but that she brought me some stuff to read and might as well give it to me. She hands me a small stack of newspapers and magazines, all dated today, Friday the 13th.

14

I do not mean to be the slightest bit critical of TV newspeople, who do a superb job, considering that they operate under severe time constraints and have the intellectual depth of hamsters. But TV news can only present the "bare bones" of a story; it takes a newspaper, with its capability to present vast amounts of information, to render the story truly boring.

—Dave Barry

The *Wall Street Eagle*
Corpcom Stock Sinks As Network Tumbles: Nothing Can Shake The Vanity Connection
Investor Confidence Falls as Allegations of Producer Pay-Off Build.

The *Los Angeles Examiner*
Terror TV
VP Hacker Alleges Media Abuses: "It Is Impossible to Trust the Agenda of the Press."

The *New York Spectator*
Morning Gory
In Midst of Kapner Scandal, the Once Number One *New Day USA* Takes a Tumble as Booking Becomes Blood Sport
By Alexander Churn
New York Spectator Media Critic

New York—It's a rare moment in TV land when one of networks' biggest money-making ships sinks fast enough to rival the *Titanic.* Yet that appears to be just what has happened to ZBC News's once beloved *New Day USA,* home to the erstwhile queen of the morning, Faith Heide.

In less than a month, *New Day's* market share has dropped from seemingly unreachable heights, with ratings once rivaling prime-time shows like *ER* and *CSI* in their heydays, to knee-skinning lows, with numbers that look more public access than big budget network. We are talking a plummet from 8.5 to, I kid you not, ladies and gentlemen, a 1.6 ratings share. One point six. In less than a month. That's right, *New Day,* once America's breakfast champion, is now showing numbers that are more likely to be reflections of folks having forgotten to turn off the tube the night before than people actually tuning in.

The iceberg that sunk the boat in question is of course the Cosmetic Relief scandal, or "Glossgate" as my colleagues at the *New York Star* so aptly termed it. The bumblings of *New Day* segment producer and probable love interest of MIA White House hunk Mark Thurber, Annabelle Kapner, brought the situation to light when she inadvertently exposed herself, and possibly Thurber, to the feds, but equally concerning is ZBC's own corporate tie to Cosmetic Relief by virtue of a shared parent company.

None of this looks good for Faith Heide, who did herself no favors when she proclaimed on air that she had nothing to do with the story, even though it was her face on the screen doing the so-called reporting, and even though, given the number of Corpcom shares she owns, she stood to make a nice chunk of change off of the success of Vanity Cosmetics. Prominent media blogs like the "Dirge Report" and the "Puffing Post" are calling for boycotts of *New Day USA,* and it appears the public is taking note.

"For twenty-five million dollars a year, you would think Faith Heide could take a little responsibility for her work," Oxana Puffy posted on her popular blog last week, and her tirade received thousands of responses, mostly from disillusioned Heide fans. "It's like finding out that all your grandmother's home-cooked meals are really takeout," posted one reader. "It's absolutely crushing."

"I find it heartening, actually," said Sal Franks, dean of the Columbia University Graduate School of Journalism. "In this day and age, it seems credibility still matters. *New Day* is suffering from a serious credibility gap."

The public might be turning away from *New Day* in droves, but the thirst for the story that is causing it to sink seems to be unquenchable. The other network morning shows, and *Sunrise America* (on which, I must disclose, I periodically appear as a consultant) in particular, show enormous ratings hikes surrounding the segments covering this scandal and the

Kapner-Thurber story in particular. Now, the heat is on to get the scoop, and according to *Sunrise America's* executive producer, Sally Animus, this booking war could be a bloody one. "I am exceedingly proud of my staff for all of the stellar guests we have booked around this story on *Sunrise*," she said yesterday. "We are all waiting with bated breath for the White House to deliver Thurber, but everyone knows that the booking to end all bookings will be Annabelle Kapner, if she is ever in a position to speak to the press. And one of these days, she will be."

The ratings shift and the booking lust have created a situation no one could have predicted. ZBC's money-making warhorse has become their Trojan horse. And as that ship sinks, what happens to that woman who is the highest paid female anchor in history? The one who was the face of Kapner's stories on Cosmetic Relief. Faith...who? The Schadenfreude troops are forming.

15

"Did you see this one?" I hold up *Newsweek,* opened to show Galina the grainy, outdated and not particularly flattering photograph of me on page 13. It was obviously acquired from one of my graduate school peers (I wonder how much they got paid for it). My hair is cropped short, pushed back from my forehead with a wide black band. My chin is propped in my hand as I fight sleep in front of a bulky old ASCII text-filled computer monitor.

Galina and I are sitting together on her bunk, the now well-thumbed-through newspapers and magazines spread between us to catch the dust as I read and she pathetically attempts to file her nails with the worn, soft emery board one of the guards allowed us to have. For the past day I have been reading and rereading each article, each sentence. Galina's been humoring my obsession, although she makes no attempt to hide her disdain.

"Ridiculous!" she likes to say as she skims the headlines and then plunges into long monologues about how insane it all is, how absurd this insatiable appetite for a story about what? About a silly little girl (who just so happened to be dating a White House hottie) getting into trouble. She's counted it up. In the print publications alone, for every mention of Purnell or Corpcom stock, or even the funding of terrorist organizations, there are like five or six mentions of me—everything from my high school prom to where I used to buy my lunch to how Mark and I first met.

I, of course, tend to get defensive, even if I do on some level agree with her.

"It's probably a lot easier for people to grasp, and in some ways a welcome relief from yet another story about why we should care that yet another man of foreign descent with an unpronounceable name is doing indescribable things in a foreign place," I tell her. "Unfortunately for me, it's a much sexier story to have a home-grown terrorist who looks like the girl next door. And, even better, who has dated someone famous and who worked for the most popular show on television and basically brought down its star. Of course they're eating it up."

I always feel bad for people who grew up not watching TV. They have no cultural reference. It is sort of like that for Galina, I think. She can't comprehend the American news media because she grew up without the concept of a market-driven press, love it or hate it.

"But they miss, how you call it, the large picture. No one asking about why just you, and why that Cosmetic office. I mean, why those Homeland guys wait there in first time."

"In the first place."

"*Da.*"

"No, I mean, the phrase is 'in the first place,' not 'in first time.'" Galina rolls her eyes because clearly that isn't her point.

"It's been covered, Galina," I say in an exasperated tone. "They were watching Purnell for suspicious activity and they found me, and they figure that I am part of whatever the hell it is that he is actually up to."

"*Nyet. Nyet,*"she says, putting the emery board down as if for emphasis. "No one ask the government why watching, not one ask the big question. The Homeland people say it is big deal, so the news says, okay, we agree. But no one is saying, hey, you wait, why this big deal? Why we care about this Annabelle so much? She just little person, why we care? We need to look at bigger story. All they say is Annie this, Annie that. Who care?"

"They care because I was connected to someone famous and I worked for an important show, Galina," I say, exhausted by the obviousness of it. "They care because it is selling papers and enhancing ratings."

Galina shakes her head disapprovingly. "You Americans, you have free press and you just piss (she says it like 'peas') on it."

"It's hardly free," I say, "and it's pronounced 'piss' not 'peas.'"

"What you mean?" says Galina, ignoring my English lesson.

"Oh, come on. When all the major news organizations are profit driven, don't you think that kind of impacts what the reporters and editors decide they have to cover? That's not exactly free."

"Bull-sheet." Galina stands up and I brace myself, because I know I'm in for another one of her floor-pacing monologues. And I'm right. From the pulpit of the cement cell block floor, she rants about how we take our freedoms for granted, about how American reporters are lazy, about how if they wanted to, they could go after the big story, but it is easier to just say, oh, no, we have to worry about the big boss, we have to worry about the profit line, we'll just cover what we think we know the audience will want.

"You think audience just want fun, want entertainment," she

says, stopping midstride and turning to me. "You no trust the audience. For big story, real story, they will come. I think American press think people are dumb. But they are maybe not so dumb all the time."

"But aren't they?" I say. "I mean, it's not like mass media forces them to watch these shows and buy these magazines, is it? If people wanted to, they could be watching public television documentaries in droves, but they aren't."

"Maybe they just not tell it right," says Galina. "Maybe they not make the important interesting enough. Maybe you all just lazy."

But I don't think I would call the people who have culled together all of these photos and background information about me lazy. I mean, there is no question that the reporters and researchers and (most likely) interns have been working hard, at least as far as getting pictures of me is concerned. From the collection in front of me, you might think that my life had been as photographed as Princess Diana's.

Anyway, I am a little too tired to continue this debate. We've had it so many times at this point that it seems self-defeating. And, really, right now what I care about is in fact that they are focused on me, that my entire life is being curated through the pages of newspapers and glossy magazines. My entire life, in fact, has become so public that it no longer feels like it's mine. It feels like the person in all of these articles and photographs isn't me at all, but rather some character from a fictional realm or a dream. Or maybe, if I can humor myself a little, an overly exposed Hollywood starlet.

It is so surreal to see oneself in this light that at a certain point, you just have to laugh. I guess for me that point is now.

I stop paying attention to Galina's rant and look at this photograph again, the one on page 13, and I chuckle. You can see I've been typing something on the computer screen, but you can't make out what it says. It looks like gibberish, and fittingly, the caption underneath says I studied numerous languages in graduate school, including Fardish, which is patently untrue. They didn't even offer foreign language courses at my J-school.

"Don't they have fact checkers?" I say. "Aside from English, the only other language I speak is pig Latin."

Galina seems happy to change the subject and, sitting back down on the cot, takes another look at the photo. She snorts. "Annie. You already showed me this picture, and you told me the same."

I roll up the magazine and smack her playfully over her head. She grabs it from me and starts to laugh.

"Look at your hairstyle," she says. "It looks like you no wash the hairs in weeks."

"I probably hadn't," I say, taking another look.

I remember that night, working hard on my final project, exhausted from three overnight editing sessions in a row. If you could blow up the picture you would see the language on the screen wasn't foreign, it was television. I was hard at work on my script for the documentary I had shot about formerly corrupt cops seeking redemption. I had convinced one of New York's finest, just out after a ten-year term, to talk to me about what had pushed him down that slippery slope. He then introduced me to a few more, and it turned out to be a pretty good piece, winning me an honorable mention at our graduation ceremony a few weeks later. So, amusing though it is (what with the bad haircut, the stupid caption, the smudged mascara), more than anything this photograph makes me nostalgic. It reminds me of a time when I actually believed in all of this: my profession, my career, myself.

Earlier that year, back in graduate school, I had an internship at a major network newsmagazine, the kind that did long-form features on things like unsolved murders and eating disorders, profiles of the latest batch of Oscar nominees, occasionally an investigative report into the hidden risks of outlet shopping or stove tipping dangers or something like that. But as straightforward as the story choice might have sometimes seemed, the production that went into each report was tremendous. Back then, magazine shows were all the rage. They were cheaper than your typical prime-time drama show, but drew ratings just as high. The networks could afford to throw money at the productions, and they did. Dolly shots, animations, multiple location scouts, months to research and cast a story—you name it. The producers called the shots, and I wanted to be one of them. It was still early in my career (not even the real start of it). I knew I had a long road of dues paying before I could become a member of that club, so I did the next closest thing: I dated one. It's like living in a foreign country, I figured. The best way to learn the language is to get romantically involved with a local.

Jake was sweet, in an older, pedagogical, receding hairline sort of way. And at thirty-one (eight years older than I was at the time) he seemed downright venerable to me. On our first date we met at the multiplex on West 23rd Street, all set to see the latest blockbuster on opening night. Not surprisingly, just as we got to the front of the tediously long line and the couple in front of us finished paying for their tickets, the Sold Out sign lit up. I was all ready to just go grab a latte at Big Cup around the corner, but Jake was not one to throw in the towel.

"You want to be a producer, right?" he said.

I vigorously nodded my head. Yes. Yes.

"Well, why don't you try to produce our way in?" So, never shy of trying to impress, I told the teenager behind the counter that we wanted two passes to a different (and unpopular) film, gave the tickets to the ticket taker, told Jake to go to the men's room, wait five minutes and then meet me in front of the popcorn stand.

We had no problem getting in, much less getting good seats. It wasn't the most original method of sneaking into a show, I suppose, but it worked.

"I'd hire you," he said, once we'd settled in, center aisle, ten rows back.

Galina laughs as I finish telling the story. "And this is why you become a producer?" she says. "You wanted to be a producer because some daddy man told you that you may be good at it?"

"No," I say, gently hitting her hand with the emery board (which is as good as hitting her with wet spaghetti). "That was when *I* understood that I might be good at it."

"At manipulating peoples, you mean?"

"Ha, ha. No. I mean at shaping stories, at setting things in motion."

"You think you will want return to this work when you get out?"

"When I get out? That's almost funny. They are holding me as a possible enemy of the state. You know as well as I do that these days I'd be lucky to get a trial, much less get off."

Galina puts her nail file down on top of the *Daily Views* (Headline: Duplicitous Lips Sink Morning Ship!). Then she takes my shoulders and gives me a hard shake, like she's trying to get me to breathe or something.

"Get grip, Annabelle," she says, although when she says my full name it comes out more like "Anna-beel.""You keep think this way and you can forget this."

"You sound like my lawyer," I say, once my head settles back into place.

"What I sound, my little *zaichick,* is as woman who has seen some things. And what I see *seichas,* right now, is no good."

I grin sheepishly at her. "I assume you are referring to my eyebrows?" I say, snorting at my little attempt at levity. Galina doesn't find me amusing, however. She takes one long-fingered hand, and with the force of a major league pitcher, smacks it across my face.

"Ow! What the f...?"

"You want to talk about eyebrows, Annie? You are seeing, what? Thirty years to death in prison? For a crime you had zero to do with. *Oy, bozhe moy,* oh my God. This is what interest you? Your eyebrows? Well, I will tell you a thing. Right now, they are so—" she forgets the word she wants and instead scrunches her fingers up, shoving them into my face "—so like this, that crack between them is getting so deep that no amount of that, what do you call it, this disease juice, Botox? No amount of this could ever help you. That crack..."

"You mean crease," I say wearily.

"Crack, crease. Whatever. It is like Great Canyon. This moment your eyebrows framing your shot with blood eyes, eyes that telling me, as you have been telling me, that you are in trueness angry as hell. Well, stop boo hoo and do something about it."

I am caressing my flaming cheek. No one has ever hit me before. It's funny, though; the pain isn't as bad as I would have imagined, even with the strength of someone like Galina behind the blow. I mean, it hurts and all, but I am still very much here. More here than I was a minute ago, actually.

I look at Galina, not sure if I should hit her back or thank her.

As I have mentioned, anger hasn't been a familiar emotion to me. My therapist would probably be proud of me for the small strides I have taken in the past couple of days; that instead of beating myself up for doing stupid things that got me into this stupid situation, I've finally been able to turn it outward. I've spent long hours sitting on my useless mattress, old school style pen and pad in hand, writing letters (all unsent, now crumpled up, sitting in my wastebasket) to almost everyone I know, letters that are blaming, accusing and dismissing: *Dear Karen, I know it might not be fair of me, but I am hurt that you haven't made it out here or at least written again. I could really use your support right now, but I guess after all of these years our friendship doesn't count for as much as I thought.... Dear Faith, I can't say I am sorry to see you fall.... Dear Caitlin, I lied—your new haircut looks terrible. You look like a wannabe Cathy Rigby.... Dear Mark, you are a pathetic excuse for a man....* That sort of thing. Not very productive, I suppose, and not entirely rational, but it felt good to write it all down. But Galina is right. I know she is. Anger has motivated much greater causes than mine, and sometimes with good results: the end of apartheid, better conditions for grape farmers, less cosmetics testing on bunny rabbits, *zaichicks,* whatever she calls them.

"Oh my God!" I say. "I am such an idiot." It's not that I had forgotten about the lip gloss testing, about those little girls they were testing it on, that horrible photo, it's that I had given up thinking there was anything I could do about it. But I just realized something: whatever it was in that folder I found, I am sure it had something to do with whatever it was they were testing on those girls, and it's obviously something someone doesn't want the world to know about.

"Tell me new thing."

"Okay," I say, ignoring Galina's latest comment. "You want to know the first thing I want to do when they drop these ridiculous espionage charges and I get out of here?"

Galina nods, smiling a self-congratulatory smile, because she realizes that her slap has stunned me out of my stupor.

"I want to finish reporting on this damn story."

If I reported the real story, the lip gloss story, if I could get to the bottom of what all of this was really about—if anyone could— I suddenly realize, it would clear my name and empower the Fidas and Lidas of the world in one fell swoop.

Galina nods slightly, bobblehead-doll-like, and says, "Hmm."

"What?"

"Well, my little *zaichick*," she says, green eyes looking skyward the way eyes tend to do when someone is having an imaginative moment, "is there any way that from here you can try to do some of this reporting?"

At which point I start laughing, more out of nerves than humor, until, smack! Galina slaps me again.

"Okay. Don't report," she says, as if she knows all about the media business. "Produce."

16

Journalism is the ability to meet the challenge of filling space.
—Rebecca West

There are times in morning television when you flip from channel to channel and back again but nothing changes. You see the same story on the screen. Try as they might to differentiate themselves, the competing shows all look exactly alike. An interview with, say, Annabelle's lawyer might be live on one program, but it is pretaped on the others, and they all run at once. Since he doesn't deviate from his script, if you can change the dial fast enough, you could probably string his sentences together to sound exactly like they would if your dial had stayed in one place. There are differences, of course, but they can be very, very subtle. The graphics at the top of the screen, the news bar running across the bottom. Or, and perhaps most importantly, the personality of the person asking the questions or telling the tale.

Catapulted from green room to green room, Lincoln Town Car to Lincoln Town Car, Ron Ruby finally arrives at *New Day USA,* sitting larger than life in a faux living room setting (plush arm-chairs, teak coffee table), opposite Ken Klark, for his third, last, but only live, interview of the morning.

"Ron Ruby," says Ken Klark in a deeply important sounding baritone. Ken has lowered his voice and sharpened his directness of late, as if approximating the profundity of a Larry King; he is acting like a man who believes he can fill the shoes of a departing eight hundred pound gorilla, or, more accurately, a man who has a rare opportunity to completely hog his network's morning air. With Faith increasingly out of the picture, mostly relegated to appearing only in cooking segments and fashion demonstrations while Tom Tatcher and the company suits figure out how best to handle her, the show is becoming Ken's and Ken's alone, jolly weatherman be damned. Not that many people (just a couple of million now, down from the stratosphere) are watching anymore, but no matter.

"Tell me," Ken says, leaning forward so far his forehead seems at risk of hitting Ron Ruby's, and causing Ruby to push himself backward as if avoiding Ken's coffee breath and not just his encroaching face. "You've worked on some of the most high profile cases of our times. Football players, corporate raiders, you name it. If a trial was headline news, your name was attached. So why take up this case, Ron? Did Ms. Kapner come to you?"

"That is between me and Ms. Kapner, Ken. But Annie is no fool. She knows a quality lawyer when she sees one," Ron Ruby says, though the truth, of course, is that Ron knew a media opportunity when he saw one, and as soon as he heard about Annie's case, he hightailed it down to the District. Before Annie could even ask to make her one call from the city jail, Ruby was knocking at her cell bars. It was a choice between him or a court-appointed, pimply-faced attorney, and it wasn't much of a choice to make.

"For the past few weeks, Ron, you have essentially been silent on this Kapner affair."

"So have you guys."

"Well, we are covering it now."

"Desperate times, huh? Well, Ken, had you been covering it all along, I believe you would know that I have said a couple of words here and there."

"I believe those words were 'no comment,'" says Ken Klark, ignoring the comment about the coverage.

They both laugh in an insidery, wink, wink kind of way.

"But why now?" Ken Klark says, attempting to take charge. "Why the sudden media blitz, Ron?"

We watch the studied, momentary silence on set, but 240 miles south of Manhattan my fellow inmates cheer and whistle; they know why the sudden blitz. They know who produced it.

"You go, girl!" they shout at me, their enthusiastic support filling the recreation room and flowing down the halls of the jail for anyone else to hear. But everyone is here, even the guards, even the warden, surrounding me, watching TV.

"Shh." I motion with my hands (nails untouched since last week's attempt at a manicure) that this is the time to be quiet. I sit up straight on the hard metal chair and quickly glance over my shoulder. Galina is across the room, across from the crowds gathered with me to watch *New Day,* so she can monitor the Ruby interview on *Sunrise* on the old black-and-white set one of the guards kindly brought in. She raises two crossed fingers in the air and I smile. Then we both turn back to watch the respective shows, attention focused.

This is the point of the program, as it is the point of the other two programs in the interviews that are airing right now, that everything hinges on. But on this program, my alma mater as it were, it hinges that much more.

I anxiously watch as Ron Ruby, my millionaire celebrity defense attorney to the notorious and vainglorious, a man of ample size, skill and self-import, anxiously clears his throat. Though he has been through this routine twice already this morning, it is probably an awkward moment for him. As he was clear to point out to me when we had our consultation about all of this yesterday, he might be a showman, but he is no actor. But he said he would do this because, he said, he knows that there is a good chance I am leading us down the right path. The court of law could take a while, but it is time for us to start fighting this case in the court of public opinion. And what better place to start than where it all started. Especially since, given their ratings, *New Day* really had nothing to lose by finally trying to cover the story, by putting him on.

The camera pushes slightly into his face, and even though I am hardly the religious type, I say a little prayer.

"I am here, Ken, because my client, Annabelle Kapner, is getting a little tired of watching from the sidelines as your colleagues covering this story talk about her as if she were the love child of Monica Lewinsky and Osama Bin Laden."

"Pardon me, but I think that's a little—"

Ron holds up his hand, palm to Ken like a stop signal. "Would you like me to explain, or would you like to fill six minutes of dead airtime?"

Ken sits back.

Faith, off camera at the anchor desk across the studio, is trying hard to look calm and confident, just in case anyone is looking at her, which they aren't. She shuffles through her thin stack of papers, pretending to review her upcoming segment on how to wear the new platform espadrilles that are the season's rage. She crosses and uncrosses her legs. She twirls a small strand of her newly darkened hair, but she can't look directly at Ken and Ruby. Instead, she pretends not to watch, but is in fact obviously watching them on the monitor in front of her, her own reflection (it is hard not to notice) mildly covering Ken's head. She bites her lower lip, unwittingly causing a small amount of mauve to color her top front teeth, and, although she probably doesn't realize it, the microphone clipped to her well-fitted pink cotton sweater is still on and is registering the thumping of her heartbeat.

The plummet from queen of the dial to royal has-been has clearly been harsh. Faith's invitation to speak at NYU's graduation was recently revoked, and according to today's Page Six, just last night when she tried to make her weekly dinner reservation at Michael's, the maître d' pretended not to recognize her name. Faster than a sex tape makes a B-list celebrity A-list, Faith's connection with Glossgate has made her such an untouchable, such a detriment to those associated with her, that the circling of the wolves, the gossip documenting her downfall, is probably a little welcome because at least it guarantees some sort of attention. Not good attention, granted, but attention nonetheless. But having Ron Ruby right here on her set, discussing this very story, is calling attention to her again in the worst possible way to have attention called. On her home turf, nonetheless. And, salt to the wounds, the producers aren't even letting her do the interview. They aren't even giving her a shot at grabbing some tattered thread from the reins, which, according to Faith, is absolutely insane. That's what she told Tatcher. Before the show, she told him she could handle Ron Ruby if they let her. She'd interviewed him numerous times before. And she knows he isn't here to help her in any way. She knows he is here to defend Annie and to fluff his own feathers. He can put on quite the show, that man. He'll make mincemeat out of Ken if he wants to, she said to Tom. And, she said, he probably wants to.

But now all Faith can do is sit tight, try to keep her breakfast down, and hope against hope that Ron Ruby doesn't bring her down further with his spin. She gently pulls her sweater (and the microphone with it) away from her chest.

"Ken, you should be happy," says Ron Ruby, picking up the *New Day* coffee mug filled with water and slowly taking a sip. "On the other shows, because the interviews were taped, I was very aware that what I said could be bleeped or edited. So I just read the prepared statement that Ms. Kapner wrote. But since we are live, and since she knows you, she asked that instead I let her, or shall I say let her actions, speak for themselves." He pulls a small DVD player out of his inside jacket pocket. "I can play this from here, or if your director cares about sound and video quality, my associate is standing outside of the control room with a clean copy."

Ken, looking like a deer in the proverbial headlights, stares into camera A, waiting for direction from Tom to enter his ear. The floor director, standing right behind the camera, starts to maniacally signal for Ken to stretch it out, wait for an answer.

"Uh...uh, okay," Ken says, mouth slightly agape.

"Everything all right, Ken?" Ron Ruby asks. "Should I press Play?"

"No, no. Hold on." Ken nods his head as he listens to the instructions coming through his clear plastic, nearly invisible earpiece.

"Um. Tell me a little bit about what we are about to hear," Ken says, the redness of his cheeks clashing with the pink of the blush that was earlier applied. "We need to give them time to load the disk."

"Load it or screen it, Ken? If it doesn't start playing by my count of ten, I am either going to hit Play here or just up and walk. Dead air to fill, Ken. Your call."

There are times in the careers of high powered executives when a split-second decision can be a cause for eternal failure or unbridled success. *New Day's* executive producer Tom Tatcher is thinking that this might be one of those times—though with failure already lapping at his door, there isn't really much of a decision to make. "We'll run it, Ken," he says quietly into the microphone that is a direct line to Ken's ear.

"What?" says Ken, not just to Tom, but because he is on live television, to everyone who is watching.

"We'll run it!" Tom yells, causing Ken to flinch from the pounding on his eardrum. He turns back to Ron Ruby. "Okay," he says, "they are saying we are running it. Can you at least give us an introduction?" He takes a deep, deep breath and, along with Tom and everyone else in the control room, crosses his fingers (out of the line of the camera, of course).

* * *

"What the fuck was that!" Max Meyer, CEO of Corpcom, former major shareholder of Vanity, Big Man on Campus, is— well, was—sitting at his kitchen table, but is now standing, almost hovering, having flung his china coffee cup acrʌss the room, aiming for his CORP-ZE (Corpcom's electronics company) plasma television installed over the sink, but instead hitting and shattering it all over the emerald-pearl granite countertop, causing his latest wife (number four) to curse back at him, since the hot coffee splashes all over her white silk pajamas.

"Max!"

"Did you see that, Stacy? Did you see that? She's going to ruin us."

"It's Stacia. Stacy was your last wife."

"Stacia. Whatever. Did you see that? Jesus Christ. What kind of network do they think I'm running?"

"Calm down, Max. Your heart..."

"And how the hell did that Kapner bitch get ahold of that video from jail? That is ZBC property. This stinks of...oh hell, where are my shoes? This is, oh, goddamn it!" Max sits back down. Because, just then, just when it can't possibly get any worse, on the high definition screen appears an image of Faith Heide as she flings the purple platform espadrille she was set to discuss, nearly decapitating Ron Ruby, and announces that she has her own version of the events that have just ensued, because the events that just ensued, were—mildly put—rather embarrassing for her.

The events went like this: Ron Ruby explained to Ken (who was, at that point, so red in the face that the technicians had to adjust the color settings on the output), that the last video that was shot of Douglas Purnell was in fact of the interview that Faith had started—started but not finished. In all of the newscasts, in all of the Glossgate coverage, it had not yet been shown. It hadn't been shown, because only Annie (and soon Ruby) knew where it was. Ron Ruby did not need to explain how he got hold of the tape. He was, after all, the man who had unearthed the ruinous Dick Cheney hot tub videos; Ron Ruby did have his sources and he took great pride in his gumshoe reputation. The truth, however, is that it didn't take much detective work at all. Annie told Ron that she knew all along that the tape was in her roll-on bag, and she knew she had left the bag at Mark's on the night of the so-called break-in—which, in her newly charged and mildly aggressive state, she referred to as a walk-in. And now, now that Galina had gotten her thinking, now that she was awake and alive enough to put it all together, Annie realized that, embarrassing as it was, that tape was her biggest asset of all. And lucky for her, Mark, confused and in shock from the recent events (it isn't everyday when your lover gets dragged off to jail and gets pegged as an enemy of the state, after all), was both oblivious to the contents of the bag and eager to get rid of any Annie evidence. When one of Ruby's associates came by to pick up Annie's things, he gladly handed it over.

And then there it was, for all the world to see: a video of Faith Heide, standing up mid-interview, brushing off her tight, lavender-colored knee-length skirt, walking off camera, and then heard (as the video remains focused on her vacated chair) announcing her intentions to go to Neiman Marcus. Moments later her producer, one Annabelle Kapner, is heard telling two of the three camera-men to stop rolling, but for the cameraman focused on the subject to keep going and for the soundman to clip an extra lavaliere microphone on her in order to record her questions for context during the transcription, even though they won't be broadcast. She is heard whispering (presumably into a cameraman's ear) that there is something seedy going on and she wants to get to the bottom of it. "This is a much bigger story than it looks like," she says sotto voce. Then Annabelle is seen for a nanosecond walking in front of the camera, a petite figure, almost girl-like but for her professional looking black pantsuit, on her way to the seat opposite the sweaty, bulbous man calling himself Douglas Purnell.

The world then saw (well, heard) how Annabelle does a very poor impression of a storied investigative interviewer (making a disparaging remark about the talent, asking as best as she could about the testing of the lip gloss), and how Purnell storms off, falls over and then scrambles out of the room. Annabelle's back (actually her butt) appears briefly in front of the lens as she bends forward to pick something up. Then the tape stops. It shows static fuzz for a split second, and on comes a still shot of what Annabelle, what Ron Ruby, hoped would solidify the nation's sympathy. It wasn't proof that Annabelle was only doing her job, but it sure came close.

"Let me read this to you," said Ron Ruby, as he recited the words written on the e-mail shown on the screen, an e-mail forwarded to Annie from one Carl Van Dunt, senior supervising producer, but originating, it is clearly seen, from none other than Max Meyer himself. It is a story pitch that said that a producer, it doesn't say which one, should be assigned to do an *American Ideals* segment about a nonprofit called Cosmetic Relief. "And I would like to point out," said Ron Ruby, feeling very good at this moment, "that the e-mail was dated just two weeks before Corpcom, under the direction of Max Meyer, bought all those Vanity shares."

This particular conflict of interest might not have been new news, but the timing was sure to generate some interest.

Ken Klark looked at Ron Ruby, unsure of what to say. Across the set, however, someone else had a lot to say. A purple espadrille came zipping past Ron Ruby's head, just in time for Ruby's show-and-tell video to stop rolling and the cameras to catch the shoe midflight.

"That's not true!" Faith had left the confines of the anchor desk and materialized between Ken Klark and Ron Ruby, hysterical...and live. "None of this is true! And she gave me the signal! I would have continued the interview! I am a professional! She said she got what she needed..." At which point Tom Tatcher, back in the control room, practically screamed that it was time to go to commercial. Go to commercial *now*.

17

You can crush a man with journalism.

—William Randolph Hearst

"Get my agent on the phone! Now!" Faith Heide is standing, her feet apart, her hands on either side of the newspaper spread open across her desk, her arms supporting the one hundred and fifteen pounds of body weight that her slender knees are at risk of dropping.

"Tiffany!" She looks up, suddenly remembering that due to the show's recent cutbacks and her own plummet from grace, her assistant no longer exists. At least they didn't can the makeup artists. "Goddamn it," she says, and, after having to look it up in her Palm Pilot, punches the numbers in herself. It's been a really bad day. Maybe the worst.

Max Meyer, with Tom Tatcher and Carl Van Dunt standing right behind him, had appeared at the threshold of her office, looking more like cowboys circling for a fight in a Western than network executives asking for a meeting. Faith had just stepped off set and was sitting on her sofa, taking off the Manolo heels that she was about to replace with her much more comfortable Chanel slippers.

"Hi, guys," she said, more as a question than anything else. It wasn't a complete surprise to see them all there, exactly. You don't try to hijack a television program with a threatening purple shoe and expect silence. But the last time all three of the big suits had approached her en masse was to congratulate her the day after *New Day* grabbed the highest rating in morning show history. That was a while ago. This time she knew they weren't here to sing her praises. They were here, as Max so gingerly told her, to come up with a solution. He said "solution" as if it were something as horrible as The Final Solution. They needed to distance themselves as much as possible from this Kapner affair for a while, he said. He said it was too late to try to compete with the coverage on the other nets. The ratings damage was done and now they needed to clean up the mess. And, well, Faith was part of the mess.

And so, after a short conversation, a couple of Kleenex and a violent throwing of stiletto heels across the expanse of the room, one just barely clipping Max Meyer's head, Faith told the three of them, three of the most powerful men in the company, to get the hell out of her face.

That was about thirty seconds ago.

Now the phone rings at the other end of the dial and Faith hits the speakerphone key. She then paces, barefoot, around her desk until the ringing stops and someone picks up.

"Sam Fox and company," says a breathless, high-pitched, youthful voice on the other end of the line.

"Maurice? Where is he? Put him on *now*." Faith is leaning forward into the speaker, so close her lipstick is almost rubbing off on it.

"Who's calling?"

"Fuck you. You know who this is, Maurice. Put him on *now,* or I'm going to come over there myself. Sam hasn't returned my calls in three days, and if he doesn't answer right *now* I am going to catch the next plane to Los Angeles and personally come over and rip off his scrotum, but not before I rip off yours, if you even have one. Put. Him. On. The. Phone."

There is a clicking and a clacking and then soft Muzak starts to squeak out from the amplified speaker, calming Faith just enough to allow her to sit down and take a breath. She counts down from ten. At five, the Muzak stops.

"Good morning, Faith," Sam Fox says sonorously, as if he was saying good morning to his own daughter, as if there was absolutely nothing negative at play. Nothing to be concerned about at all.

"It's not morning here, Sam. It's noon. It is noon and I have just been told by my executive producer, the supervising producer *and* our CEO that I am not to appear on the air for the foreseeable future. An extended paid leave, Sam. Max told me like it was some kind of gift from him and Carl and Tom. It was almost surprising they didn't include a card. Or did they mean to, Sam? Did they first send it to you to sign, you son of a bitch." Faith is talking through her laminated teeth now, consciously pacing her words so as not to start screaming. "You are my agent. You are getting ten percent of my salary—that's not chump change—and you should be fighting for me. This is a breach of my contract, and if you don't—"

"Faith, Faith, darling," Sam Fox says, his deep voice mustering all the weight of his three-plus decades in the industry to take the reigns from his biggest client. "You are jumping to conclusions, sweetheart. Don't you think I know what is best for you? To create a little space from you and the program? Especially after what happened on set today. It's really not such a bad idea."

"Don't you sweetheart me, Sam. What are you getting at?" Faith takes a deep breath in through the nose, then lets it out at a count of five—a relaxation technique she learned at Yoga Luxe. The stress level has gotten so high she's been taking three classes a day now.

"It is much better than the alternative, Faith. Remember when Paul Ardent got canned from VNN in '98? When he admitted no wrongdoing because he was only reading a script and didn't know anything about the antimilitary story he had misreported? Not so dissimilar to your situation, but yours is worse. Not only did you not know anything about the story you were supposedly reporting—one that you stood to profit from, I should add—you stood up midinterview and announced that you were going shopping. That doesn't look good for your credibility, Faith."

"Well, I..."

"Now, hear me out here. You have a long way to fall, and it could really hurt. Remember just last year, when Hound News fired O'Snidely once they discovered he was donating thousands of dollars to radical political candidates? I think taking a break, let's call it a vacation, is a much better scenario than what happened to either of them, ultimately winding up on some no-name Internet outlets and then fading off into the dustbins of tape archives. I recently heard that Ardent got a job working for a K Street lobbying firm, doing PR for the sewage disposal industry. If I thought this was a bad move for you, I would be on the next plane—"

"Oh, screw you, Sam. I might not have done much of the reporting on this Cosmetic bullshit, but you know perfectly well I am no two-bit has-been like Ardent or O'Snidely. I'm Faith Heide. And you... You are bullshit if you aren't on the next plane. You better be on the next plane or I swear, you—"

"Faith. Calm down. I'll come out on Monday. That's just three days away. In the meantime, think about this. It would be much better for you to focus on how we are going to resuscitate your image than on wanting to appear daily, in public, on a dying show, continually being associated with this Glossgate affair. We need to break your association now. Take a breather, regroup. Maybe you should go to Belize. Isn't there a spa there that—"

"How *we* are going to resuscitate my career? We? What have I been paying you millions for? Millions of dollars, Sam? Without me, Mr. Beverly Hills, you'd be living in a run-down condo in Florida, you decrepit mother f-*^&@$*%!You #@&*^!!!" Faith shouts out words so hideous even she didn't know she had them in her vocabulary, so hideous and so loud that security comes banging on her door. "Get the hell out!!" she yells at them, and then turns back to the phone and tells Sam Fox in no uncertain terms that if he doesn't figure out a way to rehabilitate her career by the time he lands at LaGuardia Airport on Monday, she is going to sue him, his agency and everyone who ever met him for every penny they've got. She slams down the phone just in time for security to escort her out of the building, and, fortunately or unfortunately, depending on one's perspective, into the lenses of the waiting paparazzi, giving them the perfect angle for the shot that would, in a matter of hours, grace scores of publications and hundreds of Web sites.

Sam Fox gently hangs up the receiver and looks across the expanse of his vast office, the crisp light pouring in from the glass walls separating him from the riffraff in the cubicles on the other side a dramatic contrast to the dark cloud hovering over his head. Until, that is, the proverbial lightbulb goes off on top of it. He had seen the show this morning. It was crazy that it took him this long to think of this.

"Maurice," he says into his intercom, "get me the fax number for Ron Ruby's office. Now!"

18

When women go wrong, men go right after them.

—Mae West

A cell phone rings. It rings again, those grating beeps in the tune of the *William Tell Overture*. Mark had been too busy, and now, with nothing to do, he is too depressed to be bothered to change the default ring tone. Da Da…he looks at the caller ID but does not recognize the number. He doesn't answer. There is a welcome moment of silence, but then William Tell's arrow strikes again. And again. Da Da Dah Da Da Dah Da Da Da Dah. In a resigned, nothing-can-shock-me-now kind of motion, Mark reaches across his coffee table, past the empty pizza boxes and Chinese food containers, and, with a rather pronounced sigh, reluctantly hits the mute button on the television remote and picks up his phone.

It had been a heady morning. Seeing Annie on TV completely solidified his feelings of caddishness, but didn't help at all to free him from his current paralytic grip. The days since Annie's arrest have been among the worst of his life. When the news reports last week suggested to the world that he was on a vacation, Mark had a good hearty laugh, the only laugh he had had in what felt like a very long time. A vacation from all of this would have been a damn sweet thing. But there are no chaise longues or piña coladas in sight, just a few empty beer bottles and a faux-worn leather armchair he bought a couple of months back at Restoration Hardware. In actual fact, Mark Thurber, once glam man about the District, once the well-groomed face the administration wanted to put forward most, is as good as under house arrest. Under strict orders from anyone who is anyone, but the vice president in particular, not to open his blinds, not to pick up his mail, not to answer his home phone, not to make a move to open his door. The Secret Service is handling the business of life for him. For now, Mark Thurber, potential love of Annabelle Kapner's life, potential witness for the prosecution, potential informant, potential he doesn't even know what the hell what, needs to stay low while both he and the White House figure out how to play the card with his face on it.

As well established by the tabloid press, Mark Thurber was as close to Hollywood famous as anyone this side of the Beltway had ever seen. But this being Washington, even celebrity only got you so far without patronage. And, lately, all of those patrons, all of those VIPs and muckedy-mucks, all of those Georgetown ladies and lobbying ex-senators, all of those people who had tapped Mark to be the Party's next big thing, the great hope for the image they were so desperately trying to reconstruct, were more than a little bit flummoxed. When word spread that the White House had sent Mark on a vacation to an undisclosed location, the sighs of relief, the ringing sounds of time being bought could be heard from Old Town to Baltimore. But when word spread again (this time to much, much more limited circles, more ovals than circles, really) that upon his attempted departure, a sweet little beagle named (not too originally) Snoopy, had sniffed out something in the depths of a pocket in the depths of a jacket in the depths of Mark's carry-on bag, it was a whole new series of sounds that were heard—the whispering sounds of stories about to be spun.

Oh, little Snoopy had had a field day, having, after all of these years of errantly scented false alarms, finally shoved his snout into the heart of the matter and pointed it straight at an innocuous looking tube of lip gloss—the shade of it bubblegum pink. He wagged his tail and yelped for pats, because he knew what was in there. Snoopy knew, and the Secret Service knew, that what he found was certainly not something the vice president would want the world to know about.

It all happened about two weeks ago, and it happened very fast, as these things tend to. Annabelle was arrested, the press went nuts, the link between her and Mark was made public, Mark tried to keep his head low and his profile lower, Snoopy had some fun, and then Mark was promptly called back to the Eisenhower Executive Office Building to meet with the second in command. It was a bit like being called into the principal's office, but not exactly. This time, instead of sitting behind a desk made of plywood and laminate, the person with the power to send him to detention was leaning his rigid, aging frame against an ornately crafted hardwood desk that was first used by Theodore Roosevelt. On top of it, a yellowed manila folder sat squarely in the middle, the red "classified" ink slightly faded.

"I am sure, Thurber, that you had no idea what you were getting mixed up with," said the man who was one heartbeat away from, well, oh so much. "And I assume you are no cross-dresser, Thurber."

Mark meekly said thank you, because he thought he knew what the VP was getting at. He knew, in fact, more than Vice President Hacker knew he knew. More, in fact, than anyone knew he knew. He knew about the toxic substance Annie was concerned about, about the girls losing their lips, about the e-mails in Annie's in-box. And thanks to some insider information, he had a pretty good idea why Hacker was so rattled.

Hacker continued. "I am going to give you the benefit of the doubt and assume the lip gloss the dog found was your little girl-friend's." He held up a small Ziploc bag containing a tube shaded, not surprisingly, bubblegum pink. "As I am sure you know, this wasn't left here by Herbert Hoover."

Mark wasn't certain if he should laugh or not, so he let out an ambivalent sound that was neither giggle nor grunt.

"This is no laughing matter, Thurber. There is a lot at stake here."

Hacker put the bag down on top of the classified folder and slowly walked around the desk, tapping his long, ancient fingers across the top as if he were trying to create an ominous sound-track. "This doesn't look good, Thurber," he said, holding up the folder. "Doesn't look good."

"Um, sir?" Mark said, mustering all the courage he could find to see if he could get the veep to fess up to anything at all. "May I ask you what exactly is in that lip gloss that the administration is so concerned about?"

Apparently, it wasn't a question Hacker was in the mood to answer. With the weight of a desk that had served the likes of Dwight Eisenhower and, yes, Herbert Hoover in front of him, he told Mark in no uncertain terms that if he had any hope of continuing his brilliant career, much less of participating in the Hacker administration should he, the VP, win the upcoming election, Mark had better not ever mention the lip gloss again, and that he should keep on keeping his head low, his profile lower, and his distance from the public eye in general, and one Annabelle Kapner specifically, as large as it could be.

Since that meeting, Mark has accrued a shaggy growth of facial hair and bloodshot eyes, which for some might serve as a manner of disguise; for Mark, it would take more than scruff to go out incognito. Even under normal circumstances, with or without the almost-beard and mustache, Mark Thurber would have had trouble going around unrecognized. But under normal circumstances (oh, how a couple of short weeks can feel like a lifetime), it really didn't matter. Sure, it had been annoying at times, trying to complete the thirty-five minutes on the elliptical in peace, or having his up dog zen fall prey to unwarranted titillation when the women surrounding him in yoga class made certain to push their up dog breasts so that they were heaving out of their leotards just so. But that was forever ago. Since then, he has been sitting here watching the coverage, reading the papers, as his once taut glutes flatten, his gut thickens and his ego slowly seeps out of him.

This morning was the worst. Watching Annie on TV, he felt like such a useless cad. He knew how shaken she had been by those strange calls, how creeped out she was by Purnell, how she had gotten herself in over her head. And he knew that while one Douglas Purnell might have existed, it wasn't even his real name. Mark knew, or at least he had a good idea, what was in that classified document Annie had tried to fetch, even if she didn't, even if he hadn't had the chance to tell her. He was sure that was the same folder that was sitting on Hacker's desk, and Mark was sure that it being there wasn't just a strange coincidence. There was definitely something shady going on, but it wasn't anything Annie had anything to do with. His assistant had pulled him some more information (which wasn't so hard, considering who she was sleeping with) and now Mark knew that if anyone could attest to Annie's ignorance, it was him. He also knew, he had known since right before her arrest, what she was up against, more than Annie could possibly know herself.

Which is why he can't get in touch with her. It's not that he doesn't want to. It's not that he doesn't care or doesn't want to see her free. It's that, because he can't contact her without the world knowing, without the VP knowing, without some potentially very dangerous characters knowing, he is petrified. Until he can figure out a safe way to do it, he doesn't know what to do. He can't even count the times he has picked up a pen or the phone to contact her and then put it down, hand frozen and throat dry. He even risked asking that New Day booker, Caitlin, to relay a message when she called him on his private line, but he knew it wasn't enough, that he couldn't trust her to tell Annie what he really wanted to say.

Still, to call it a loss of words would be an exaggeration. This is the man who has put words on presidential lips, who has spun some of the world's greatest spins, written a bestselling book. He has plenty of words, but he's terrified of making the wrong move or saying the wrong thing. Unsure of how to move forward without both jeopardizing his career (which is clearly already in jeopardy) and bringing more attention to her (if that were possible), he sits paralyzed. And the longer he waits, the worse he feels. It is torment. Purgatory. Because Mark is starting to feel that for all his swagger, for all his charm, for all his brain power, he is in actual fact a total wimp.

Sure, he can spin words of silk and froth up factless confections of useless information, and he sure makes the administration look good on camera, but now that shove has been approached by push, he isn't sure what he is actually made of, if anything at all.

Dah Da Da Da Da sings William Tell.

"Hello?" Mark says, preparing to choose his words very carefully as he places the small flip phone to his ear. He needs to sound like he is at the beach, or perhaps taking in the sights of the River Seine.

"Mark? This is Karen. Annie's friend?"

He looks around, as if anyone who might be listening would actually be visible.

"Uhhh." This is odd. First off, no one except close friends and family (and one morning show booker) has this cell number. "Have we met?"

Mark knows about Karen. Annie had mentioned her. Annie called him, he now recalls, when she had gone to visit Karen at her office at the NIH. Karen must have kept the number in the memory of her phone. And, he thinks, if Karen so much as mentions to anyone that he might have had knowledge of *any* of this before the story ever broke, before Annie decided to be Sherlock Holmes, his career might be in bigger trouble than it already is. There is no point in pretending he is in Paris.

"We probably shouldn't talk on the phone," Karen says. "But I didn't know how else to reach you."

"And?"

"And Annie told me you live in Woodley Park? I'm nearby. Can you meet me at the zoo?"

Mark is silent for a moment and then explains to Karen that he isn't supposed to be out and about right now.

"Where do you live? I could come..."

But Mark knows that won't work. He can't let Annie's best friend see what a completely pathetic wasteland he has become. And he can't have a young woman be seen entering his home.

"Small mammals," he says.

"Small mammals?"

"Meet me there. It's dark." It's dark, and as Mark well knows from previous secretive meetings he has had (i.e., dates), the only people who tend to go inside tend to be mothers pushing strollers, too preoccupied with lulling their toddlers to nap to notice much else. Tourists and the unemployed tend to visit the pandas.

"How about the reptile house," says Karen. "Even less people go there."

"Reptiles?"

"Meet me by the Fardish stiletto vipers."

And so it is that Mark Thurber finally takes a shower and gives himself a shave, puts on a hat, a large jacket and sunglasses, slips a one hundred dollar bill into the hand of his so-called security guard, walks out the back of his house, down the alley, over to Connecticut Avenue, and into the National Zoo.

19

Wherever you go, there you are, and today it feels like I'm everywhere. It's a bit overwhelming. I walk down the corridor or through the cafeteria and hear my name mentioned over and over, so many times it sounds like an echo, a ricochet off the cell block bars: the raspy discussion emanating from the old radios a few inmates have managed to obtain, the guards reporting that clips from the morning shows are making viral rounds across the Internet, other inmates returning from the phone booth and reporting that all their relatives, their daughters, their mothers, their sons, all they want to talk about is the inmate's famous friend. Was she set up? Is she innocent? Is she an opportunist in over her head? Love me or hate me, I am the star of the water cooler. If that old wives' tale about ears itching were true, I would be tremendously uncomfortable right now.

Galina bounces into my cell and drums against the metal locker that holds what few possessions I have with me—some prison-issued outfits and underwear, some pens and paper, some tampons. It's not the most glamorous closet, to be sure.

"Cell-e-bration...come on!" she sings in a bad imitation of Kool and the Gang as she grabs my wrist and pulls me off the cot, spinning me around in a quick disco hustle. I fight off a smile and sit back down, bringing my knees to my chest and shrugging my shoulders forward as if defeated.

"Okay," says Galina, sitting down at the opposite end of the cot, "I know not what your problem is, but you cannot be this way. Not now."

I raise a single eyebrow. "Why not? It's my life, my nervous energy."

"Smell of fear, my *zaichick*. Smell of fear. Of course you worry about your spectacle today's morning. You played your one card and now it must play out. And it seem to be doing that, you know. So, karmically speaking, think about it. Sitting scared will do you no good."

"Karmically speaking?"

"You know, power of positive thinking, this sort of thing."

Sometimes I really can't figure Galina out. She was addicted to television shopping networks, buying up extendable dusters, collapsible fire escapes and tons of cheap costume jewelry, and was caught stealing thousands of dollars from some Wall Street firms to pay for the addiction, but she is also one of the smartest, wisest women I have ever come across. And for all the crap that life has tossed her way, she is one of the most refreshing and upbeat (without being annoying) people I know. Her mind is like a cruise ship hostess meets, I don't know, someone really smart and sharp—someone who is clearly not me right now.

"So now you have plans to become a motivational speaker?" I say.

"Why I put up with you?" she says, shaking her head.

And probably out of fear of alienating my one true friend, I smile slightly.

"There you go! Now let us celebrate in today's morning's performance."

I roll my eyes, but verbally give in. "Fine. What was that song again?"

Galina starts to sing and I parrot (with Russian accent and all), "It's time to celebrate…come on, come on, let's have a real good time." And off we waltz into the hallway.

20

If you enter the National Zoo through the back gate (which, in the interest of not being seen, Mark does), the quickest path to the snakes is through the lions' den, a fact that some might find interesting on some animal kingdom-esque metaphorical level. But for Mark, it just makes the trip that much more unsettling. It isn't that the lions are scary. Far from it. Like most of the large animals at the National Zoo, they look as if they've been feeding off fetid slops, not the fresh kill they crave. And they are living in spaces way too small even for their malnourished bodies. *Kind of like a jail cell,* Mark thinks to himself as he watches a lioness skulk over to a shady corner of her undersize lair.

The reptile house itself, however, isn't nearly as dark and creepy as the name implies. Yes, there are scores of slithering, crawling, creeping things, but the building is very well lit and appears to be extremely sanitary. Unlike the elephants and the apes, the reptiles don't attract the same steady stream of traffic, so it is probably a bit easier to maintain.

Mark walks past some small lizardlike creatures, some turtles, some frogs. He stops in front of every species of snake on display, reading the placards describing their personal preferences. This one likes cool climates, that one prefers the desert heat. And it is there, in the desert range, that he finds what he is looking for. Long, thin and black, two Fardish stiletto vipers are coiled around each other under a dusty rock. They are almost still, but there is enough movement—a slow, undulating wave rippling through their bodies—that you know they are alive.

"The Fardish stiletto viper is one of the most poisonous snakes on earth," reads the sign posted to the right of the large glass cage. "A single bite can kill a human being within thirty seconds."

"Jesus," Mark says out loud, and then continues reading about how, though extremely dangerous to collect, the venom from the Fardish stiletto viper is believed by many indigenous peoples to have magical properties if used in extremely small doses.

"Mark?" Someone taps him on his shoulder and he starts. "Are you Mark?"

A young woman, probably in her late twenties or early thirties, is standing very close behind him. She is tall enough, but her thin-limbed, slight build, her uninspired straight, wispy, bobbed light brown hair—all of it adds up to one fairly unnoticeable person.

She isn't what Mark expected. Not as Annie's best friend.

"Karen?" he says tentatively.

But Karen doesn't bother to confirm or deny. Instead, she just launches into the matter at hand.

"This is what I wanted you to see," she says, gesturing at the long, languid creatures in front of them.

"These snakes?"

"Yes, these snakes. The *Fardish* snakes? From Fardistan?"

A scientist at the NIH with a Ph.D. in biochemistry, Karen is obviously extremely bright, but being from southern California she does have an unfortunate tendency to speak a little Valley, often sounding as if she is asking a question when she is really just trying to make a statement. The effect can be detrimental at times, and her poor ability at public speaking is one of the many reasons she chose a career path that would keep her holed up in quiet laboratories with most of her communications issued in the form of long papers published in heady academic journals, instead of in some person-to-person in-your-face kind of way.

Her friendship with Annabelle doesn't make sense to most casual observers. It didn't initially make sense to Annie and Karen themselves, for that matter. Thrown together by the housing lottery the summer prior to their freshman year of college, Annabelle took it upon herself to call Karen for an introduction before the semester began. The conversation started fine, but when Karen suggested to Annie that perhaps they should try to coordinate their bedspreads and window treatments for their dorm room, Annabelle immediately hung up and called the housing office to see if she could find a different roommate. She said she had visions that her college room should be a bohemian nest, filled with batik wall hangings and scarves hanging from the lamps, not a Holly Hobby knockoff with Kmart issue bed dressings and matchy-matchy decor. But the housing office informed her that, sorry, there were no other beds available. She and Karen were stuck together.

Oddly, it worked.

For all of Annie's anxious banter and energetic chattiness, for all of Karen's introverted, studious calm, they balanced each other and helped one another find the best in themselves. Karen could talk Annie out of a self-deprecating neurotic spiral; Annie could get Karen out of the library to actually have some fun in the world.

After college, after graduate school, after all the degrees and the career advancements, all the failed relationships with men and disappointing friendships with other women, they still balanced each other. They were still the best of friends. And now Karen, with all the knowledge she'd acquired, with everything she now knows, she has no choice but to do what any best friend would, given the chance.

"I wouldn't have called," she says to Mark, "but you are the only one who might be able to help me?"

Mark looks at her with a mix of skepticism and hope. As much as he has been wanting to help these days, he's been at a complete loss as to what the hell he could possibly do. But it seems strange that this Valley-accented young woman could be part of the answer.

"I discovered something about the lip gloss?" Karen says. "And I think it might help explain what happened to Annie? I mean, why all of these ridiculous charges?"

"I know about the toxicity levels, Karen. Annie already told me about that."

Karen shakes her head.

Two teenage boys walk by. She waits for them to pass.

"No, it's more than that," she says, once the boys turn the corner heading to the next exhibit. "The toxins I found? I wasn't sure where they came from? I mean, I thought they had something to do with snake venom, but I wasn't exactly sure what, or which species of stiletto viper. But I did more testing and research, and I am pretty sure it comes from these guys? From Fardistan?" She lightly taps the glass in front of them. "And I am pretty sure that that same substance, in different quantities, acts like sodium pentothal."

"Sodium pentothal?"

"Truth serum?"

"And?" says Mark. "So what?"

"And," says Karen impatiently, and hence more definitively, "it acts like sodium pentothal except that this substance could kill you, if it doesn't make your lips explode first. I found some documentation, a paper written by an anthropologist years ago about how some of the smaller tribes who used to live in that area of the world used this substance, both ceremonially and, well, in their—" she makes little quotes sign with her fingers "—courts. It has to be applied on the lips, because, at least according to the paper I found, ingesting it directly could cause sudden death. But putting it on the lips has its own perils."

"Okay? So, that's very interesting, but what am I supposed to do with this information?"

"Mark," says Karen, exasperated, "for somebody supposedly so smart, you are pretty dense."

Mark raises a questioning eyebrow.

Karen sighs. "Look, this whole thing has nothing to do with the war on terror. It's a cover-up. It has to be. This venom is a substance that could come in handy in interrogations, right?" she says. "Don't you think it's weird that this is all revolving around Fardistan, an area that was once deeply infiltrated by the CIA? And didn't that boss of yours, Vice President Hacker, presidential candidate Hacker, head up the CIA around the time that we were infiltrating? I mean, don't you think there is a possibility of some connection here, something that maybe a man running to be president of the United States would prefer people not know?"

Mark turns to Karen and looks her squarely in her eyes.

"I know," he says softly. "I know about Hacker and the Fardish connection. I mean, I have some idea about it. I've done some digging, too. I can't prove it, but I think this might have started because Hacker was having Purnell watched. Purnell was up to no good and most likely Hacker knew he had to protect himself from any association."

"For God's sake, then why aren't you talking about it? Why isn't anybody?"

"Karen," says Mark in a tone more haughty than normal, a tone that infers he not only went to the best schools, but worked in the best places, "do you have any idea what you are suggesting?"

And then Karen, firming up both her posture and her voice, says to Mark with absolutely no equivocation that yes, she has an idea about what she is suggesting. She is suggesting that maybe Annabelle has been made a scapegoat for something, and yes, she is suggesting that maybe something extremely weird is going on, and she thinks that if he, Mark, cared at all about Annabelle, and if he had any spine or soul, he might at the very least try to find out a little bit more what that connection is, if there is one, what it might have to do with the lip gloss story Annie was working on, and maybe try to help.

He sighs audibly, as if this is a hopeless conversation to even try to begin. "I know," he says. "I tried to warn Annie that she was getting in too deep."

"What?" Karen raises her voice. Luckily, there is no one else around to notice. "What did you know? You knew there was something going on and you didn't tell her?"

"I didn't know much," says Mark, taken aback by the sudden strength of Karen's voice. "But right before Annie called me from Purnell's office, I started to think that maybe…"

"She called you from there?"

"Yes, and I told her to get out."

"What did you know?"

"As I said, not much. But my assistant had just told me that Purnell might have actually been former CIA, probably with a different name, and I figured that the Fardish connection—"

"Your assistant?"

"Yes, let me finish."

"So someone else is aware that something extremely fishy is going on?"

"Would you let me finish? Anyway, she didn't know why I was asking for the information."

"Don't you think she might have put it together by now?"

Mark doesn't respond to that, because he knows it is true, but he also knows that his assistant knows that jeopardizing him could be the end of her own career. He does know things about her and Hacker's favorite daughter, after all.

"Regardless," says Karen, "don't you think that maybe you should try to do something about this? Don't you think you owe Annie at least that much?"

"You have no idea how hard this is for me, do you? You have no idea how hard I worked to get to where I am and how quickly I could lose it."

"Oh my God," says Karen, shaking her head in disgust.

"Oh damn it." Mark makes a pained grimace and covers his eyes with his hands. "That came out all wrong. I am not such an ass. I really do care. Really. I mean, look, I am here, right? I just, I mean, it's just that…"

Karen, hand on hip, waits for a better explanation, but one doesn't appear to be forthcoming.

"I have no idea what Annie sees in you," she says impatiently.

"Sees in me? Like, present tense? Have you spoken to her?"

"Good grief, Mark. Of course not. God. There was no way I could call without someone listening in. And if I visited her, it would be even worse. If anyone finds out about these tests I'm doing I would not only lose my job, I'd jeopardize the possibility of helping her at all." Karen is whispering again, but from her tone, there is no question that she is totally appalled. "You are so not what I expected," she says. "I mean, how the hell did you get as far as you have in your career? I know most of politics is about who, not what, you know, but don't you have any brain cells in your head? And more than that, do you have any substance at all in your heart? I mean, what the hell is the point of being in a job that is supposed to be about helping people, helping the country and the world, if in the end all you care about is yourself?"

At which point, the face that the administration liked to put forward, the handsome man with movie-star hair and bedroom eyes, looks away from her and back to the snakes. "I did once," he says, "but it's been a while since I really had to use them."

"Well, now's your chance," Karen says, giving Mark her card with all of her contact information. "Let me know when those synapses start working again and your blood warms up."

Which is pretty much why, a few hours later, without being cleared to do so, Mark returns to the executive office building, places his palms on the desk that once belonged to Roosevelt, Eisenhower and Hoover, and tells the vice president of the United States that he demands he be brought back into the fold and put to work. He has no reason to hide his face or feel shame about his personal relationships, and he deserves to have full access and understanding about what all the concern is about in the first place. Without that he will walk out the door.

Which is what happens.

And everyone who has any working brain cells at all knows that the real power in Washington comes after someone leaves office; that's when people will really leverage their position and work the connections they made along the way.

Mark walks down Pennsylvania Avenue, makes a left turn onto K Street, goes into a printing shop and has his new business cards made up.

Mark Thurber
Political Consultant
(202) 555-2358

Then he starts calling in some favors.

21

Anonymous sources are to journalism what silicon enhancements are to the feminine figure; they look impressive to the gullible, but something doesn't feel right.

—Larry King

"Annie!"

Ron Ruby's large frame is silhouetted, backlit by the row of luminescent vending machines in the front of the reception room. I haven't even had a moment to gather my thoughts, so the best I can do is to wiggle my fingers as a modified wave. Just a few minutes ago, a guard pulled me out of the lunch line to tell me that my lawyer was here, which was odd because I wasn't expecting him until tomorrow. I am hungry, and skinny as I am these days, I really should eat. But when your lawyer comes to jail, you put down whatever you are doing, even if the kitchen is finally serving ice cream for dessert. That said, I pray Ron can read my mind and will stop to get me a candy bar. He doesn't. He just marches forward, greeting me like a long-lost relation.

"Annie, Annie, Annie," he says, like Cary Grant might have said, "Judy, Judy, Judy" had he actually done so, although he never actually did. But it is that sort of vibe: upbeat, giddy and perhaps a little patronizing.

I raise my hands head height, palms facing the ancient, dusty ceiling fans as if to say, "What gives?" though truth be told I have an inkling. It's time to circle the wagons and do another jig. Which is exactly what Ron does when he approaches me. Ron is probably about fifty-five, and though he is large, he is clearly fit, since he easily lifts me high up off the ground and spins me around and around a few times in a fatherly sort of way. It isn't very professional, and I am sure it is very out of character for a prominent lawyer like Ron Ruby, but it feels okay. I might be having a hard time internalizing yesterday morning's success, but I am happy other people are able to externalize it for me.

One of the guards comes over to break us apart. "No touching," she says apologetically, and shuffles away.

Ron lowers me to the ground. "I give it a week," he says in my ear, once both he and the room have stopped spinning. The smell of his spearmint gum is as startling as smelling salts. I pull back.

"A week for what?"

"For something big to give, Annie. You're the talk of the town."

"Apparently. But what are people actually saying?" Word has been filtering in from the outside, suggesting that the impression our stunt made was fairly positive. People are starting to pity me (in a good way), but I am short on details.

"They are saying you are the next big thing. You are the current big thing. You are not only the biggest story around, you are also, finally, gaining a fan base. Our little performance yesterday has gotten everyone all excited—the muckrakers, the public, and most importantly, the agents."

"The agents?" I say as we settle down at a wobbly square table in the corner.

"Take your pick." Ron pulls a small stack of papers from his inside jacket pocket. I can see the fine silk lining—a deep burgundy that just screams success. It is a gesture Ron has obviously perfected over the years, revealing the luxurious fabric to perhaps subconsciously assure a client (or anyone else) that he knows what he's doing.

"They are all here," he says. "William Morris. ICM. Matt Orbitz. Larry Deller. Sam Fox. All of them faxed letters to me right after the show. Have a look." He spins the papers to face me. "We even have invitations from speakers' bureaus, for you to do the rounds as soon as you get out."

I flip through laudatory page after laudatory page.

"This is insane," I say. These people are writing to me as if I just won an Oscar, talking (here's humor for you) about my brilliant performance, my charismatic persona, my camera-loving face. Where were they all those Saturday nights I sat moping because I couldn't get a date, feeling flabby, boring and poorly complexioned? I haven't changed, but my Q rating sure has. I know that the truth is if you judged me by that tape alone, you wouldn't think I was anything at all, except maybe a little foolish and (as was the intent) possibly innocent.

I don't get it at all, and I say as much.

"Come on, Annie. Don't be naive. A story like yours hasn't crossed their paths since, I don't know, Monica."

"Monica?"

"Whoever. It doesn't matter. What matters is that right now you, your story, are hot and juicy. You make a lot of our sacred cows look like they would make low-grade hamburger meat." I've been noticing that Ron has a tendency to get blustery when he speaks. The more animated he becomes, the more bravado he shows. Right now, he is very animated. "Who doesn't like to see the big cones fall from the trees? That's what makes tabloids swirl and movies bust blocks."

"I didn't realize that was our objective, Ron," I say in as snide a tone as possible. Not that I don't like this adulation, but a movie deal won't buy me anything worthwhile if I still get a prison sentence.

"It wasn't? You had me fooled, young lady. Because let me tell you, Oliver Stone couldn't have scripted it better himself."

"Oh, come on," I say. "That's totally ridiculous."

"Jesus, Annie," says Ron, slamming his large palm against the table. "How don't you get this?" He goes off on a rant about how I have shown the most popular television journalist of our time for what she really is: nothing more than a prospective member of Shopper's Anonymous. How I exposed the slippery ethics of conglomerate-owned news networks. How, by his absence and silence, the nation's heartthrob (an exaggeration, I point out, he was popular and all, but come on) has been shown to be a failure as a leading man.

"Mark Thurber has nothing to do with this."

"As you wish, Annabelle. But either way, it's like I told you, just like I told you. Hollywood would come knocking. The balls are all in your court."

"Court?" I say. "I am still in jail, remember? We haven't even gotten to court."

"Patience. Think forward. This will be over soon enough. I am so confident in fact, that I am ready to have you call a Realtor out there. Santa Monica? Hollywood Hills? Where would you prefer?"

"Are you trying to be funny?"

"A little bit. But don't worry, Annie. You are going to be out of here soon."

"Would you mind telling me exactly how? I mean, so I'm now famous the world over, but I am still presumed to be guilty of some pretty nasty things."

"Presumed innocent, Annie. Presumed *innocent*."

"Tell that to the press."

"I don't have to," he says, at which point he pulls out another piece of paper. "I couldn't wait to see the look on your face when you read this." He places on the table the white sheet, clearly a fax of a severely minimized newspaper page, an advanced copy of the front page of tomorrow's *New York Herald*. The print is so tiny it's hard to read most of it, but the headlines are clear.

The Purnell Papers:
Secret Source Claims Vice Presidential Connection To Man At Center Of Cosmetic Relief Scandal

Fugitive Douglas Purnell reported to be former undercover CIA operative, once under direct command of Vice President Hacker.

I pick it up and try to make out the rest of the tiny text.

A confidential White House source alleges that during his tenure at the helm of the Central Intelligence Agency, Vice President Hacker worked directly with a man named Douglas Lenrup. Confidential sources at the CIA believe Lenrup to be the same man currently assuming the identity of Douglas Purnell, the fugitive head of the embroiled nonprofit Cosmetic Relief.

I put it down, in shock. "Holy cow. Hacker might be directly involved? The vice president of the United States could be linked to a man who runs an organization that's being accused of funneling money to terrorists? You buried the lede, Ron."

He looked rather proud of himself. "I took the first flight I could so I could show it to you in person."

"But how…" I have no idea how this article got reported, much less how it landed in Ron's lap prior to publication.

"It's a gift horse. Don't try to brush its teeth. Just figure our little performance raised some questions, as we hoped it would, and the *Herald* decided to ask them."

I quickly skim through what I can make out of the article, looking at its proverbial mouth, looking for Mark's name, which is nowhere to be found. Is this reporter protecting him? I wonder. Maybe (I hope, I pray) maybe Mark is somehow behind the leaks. Maybe he isn't ignoring me at all.

"So, it looks like something big already gave," I say.

"It does, doesn't it? But read on. It's good." He points to a paragraph toward the middle of the story. I hold it close and squint to read the text.

Ms. Kapner's lawyer, Ron Ruby, appeared on the three most popular national morning news programs on Monday, the highlight of which was a live appearance on *New Day USA,* the program Ms. Kapner previously worked for. As has been widely reported, Mr. Ruby forced the program to air a videotaped conversation between Ms. Kapner and the man claiming to be Douglas Purnell.

In an interview at his Madison Avenue office yesterday afternoon, Mr. Ruby repeatedly denied that Ms. Kapner had any knowledge of Mr. Purnell's illegal activity, and said that the intention to play the video was to show that the relationship between Ms. Kapner and Mr. Purnell was nothing beyond that of reporter and subject. "I don't need a court of law to prove her innocence. Right now what we care about is the court of public opinion," he said.

By the end of the day, the clip from the show was the most streamed video on the Internet.

As of this writing, Ms. Kapner is still being held in detention, waiting for her trial date to be set. The verdict, however, is mixed. As one woman at an Internet café in Manhattan succinctly put it, "Either she is a really great actress or she's just really stupid."

"Good?" I say despondently. "How is this 'presumed innocent'?" My heart, momentarily elated, has now sunk deep into the pit of my stomach.

"Annie, come on. Think about it. Have a little faith. The more they chase the real story, the more they will find out that you had nothing to do with it."

"The real story? You have too much faith in the media. It's just going to keep coming back to me and the fact that I am a total idiot."

"You'll be a free idiot, Annie. And—" he pats the stack of letters "—a very famous one with a seven-figure deal."

22

The illusion which exalts us is dearer to us than ten thousand truths.

—Alexander Pushkin

"I pledge," says Galina, putting down the latest copy of the *Herald*, "if I could buy stocks right now, I will buy up shares of your Kapner, Incorporated."

"You've already been arrested for insider trading once, Galina, don't you think you learned your lesson?" I say without looking up from my oatmeal.

"It was the embezzlement, Annie. Do not imagine you know this language of business crime," she says, nonchalantly taking my brown plastic coffee cup off the tray in front of me, pleased with herself for finally being able to correct my English instead of the other way around. She takes a sip.

"Hey!"

"You have not touched in five minutes."

"I was taking it slow," I say, but honestly, I don't really care that much. I wave dismissively, gesturing with a shrug for Galina to drink it down, which she does. I don't need a lot of caffeine these days, especially not from the watery sludge they serve here. My energy level is fueled by adrenaline, by the almost relentless pace of the coverage, by the relentless frustration of my Kafkaesque situation—the situation in which I am still in jail even though whatever case they ever had against me is getting shabbier by the second. That said, the last few days have gotten to be fairly exhausting.

Imagine, if you will, an old movie in which a news story breaks. The headlines splash across the screen, one after the next, to a soundtrack of a typewriter about to blow. Days are compressed into seconds as the words tumble onto the newsprint. Tap tap tatatap. Tap tap tap. The articles came out fast and furious, each one headier than the last:

Tap tap tap...

The *New York Herald*

White House Condemns Leaks Of Classified Information; Denies VP Affiliation With Lenrup

Hacker: "Whoever Is Leaking These Falsehoods Is Steeped in Partisan Politics of the Dirtiest Kind."

Tap tap tap...

The *New York Herald*

Documents Confirm Lenrup Reported To Hacker

Newspaper Obtains Classified Intelligence Documentation Showing Lenrup Directed a Secret CIA Program during Hacker's Reign at Agency.

Tap tap tap…

The *New York Herald*
Kapner Connection Questioned
Evidence Lacking. Government Presses
for Another Delay.

Tap tap tap…

The *New York Star*
Producer To Pariah To Princess
Clothing Designers Compete to Win the Right to Design
Annabelle Kapner's Get-Out-of-Jail-Free Outfit for Her
Eventual Release.

Tap tap tap

Faith Heide Visits Annabelle Kapner In Jail

Okay, the last one isn't a real headline, but it is pretty stunning news to me when one of the guards wakes me up from a mid-afternoon nap to tell me I have a special visitor. I ask who it is and she says, "That girl you got fired," which of course isn't what happened, but I guess is one of the perceptions people have formed. I don't try to argue the point.

I've read in the press about the rumors that Faith Heide has suffered a nervous breakdown. I've also read that she is plotting her comeback. And I read that she ran away with a Moroccan prince and is pregnant with twins, ready to give up the whole TV news thing, anyway. The truth probably rests somewhere between the first two and has nothing to do with the third, but ultimately, short of the fun of the gossip, I couldn't care less. Faith's fate and my fate may have intertwined a couple of months ago, but as far as I am concerned, I didn't respect her before and I don't respect her after and if no one ever mentions her to me again, I won't be giving her a moment's thought. She is, in my mind, a casualty left behind in my little war, and when you are at war you can't look back.

I look forward and see her in front of me, sitting at the same wobbly corner table I've been sitting at with my lawyer (it's like the way celebrities get special tables at restaurants—I now have one in the jail's reception room), and I feel bad for her—the last person in the world I would have ever thought I'd feel bad for. I don't think it would be an exaggeration to say that, as horrid as I look these days (what with the weight loss, the unruly eyebrows, the lack of frizz-taming hair products, the darkening mustache that Galina swears she can't see, even though I know she's just saying that), Faith looks worse. Seeing her like this, with almost no makeup, hair pulled up in a tight ponytail, blond roots creeping into her dyed-brown hair a number of inches, is like seeing a cat without fur. It is pathetic. The person who was once voted the most glamorous woman on television now looks more like a bedraggled housewife whose children (not that Faith has any) have just recovered from a weeklong bout of a rotavirus that she had contracted, too.

She still smells good, though.

"Chanel?" I say as we settle into our chairs. "It's so nice to smell something that isn't ammonia or badly baked beans."

She smiles. And with her flashy beam, those big white teeth, suddenly she is Faith Heide again. Superstar. Some individuals really do have natural star wattage, no matter how badly people try to beat it out of them. I can feel scores of eyes upon us, everyone's hand cupping the side of her mouth, whispering, "Do you see who that is?" It is a sensation I have noticed surrounding me constantly since this all began: the subtle whispers in surround sound, the quickly averted eyes. I am still not at all used to it, but Faith is familiar with fame. She must find comfort in the recognition, whatever they are saying. As the word spreads like a game of telephone through the room, her shoulders lower a little and her posture improves.

We pretend to ignore them and instead act as if we are meeting at an intimate Columbus Avenue café.

"Things are looking up for you, aren't they?" Faith says after we complete a few minutes of awkward small talk. I mean, really. What could we possibly talk about? What she managed to buy at Neiman's that day? Favorite shades of lip gloss? How I had unwittingly but nonetheless single-handedly ruined her career? Boys? I don't think so. And I'm certainly not about to ask her what she's been doing with all her free time these past couple of weeks.

"Yeah," I say. "I suppose so." Of course they are looking up, but *looking up* by its very definition implies that you aren't there yet, wherever there is. Yes, it seems my missteps have set into motion a journalistic investigative frenzy the likes of which we haven't seen since Watergate. Or at least since the last scandal that was tagged a *gate*. It is certainly the largest investigation I have ever been involved in, even if I am not exactly a stand-in for Bob Woodward right now. It's crazy. Purnell is actually a guy named Lenrup, formerly CIA, now run amuck. And, yes, it seems this Lenrup might be privy to some facts that the vice president would prefer to keep secret, and no one seems guiltier than someone keeping secrets. And, yes, the latest Gallup poll suggested that 65 percent of the American public now think I am a victim of circumstance—just a silly morning show producer in the wrong place at the wrong time. But it is so not over yet. Twenty-five percent still think I am possibly involved in the whole affair. Ten percent think I might as well be an Al-Qaeda operative, I am that despicable. Five percent have no idea who I am. (Still, with a 95 percent name recognition, more people know who I am than they know the name of the vice president. Or Faith Heide, for that matter. Anyway, even if you don't pay attention to the polls, or if you claim you don't, however you slice it I am still in jail, awaiting a trial that hasn't even been set yet. Clearly, some big freaking cheese (the vice president, perhaps) has the ear of the judge. Ron's theory for the foot dragging is that as long as I am not free or on the stand, I can't publicly discuss what is in those documents I found. And since I actually have no idea what was in that folder, seeing as I didn't even have enough time to open it (and seeing that when Ruby tried to subpoena it, it seemed to have just floated off into thin air with a poof), I am the only one who can be absolutely certain of my ignorance.

"So," says Faith, trying to make conversation. "What is the first thing you want to do when you get out?"

It is the wrong thing to ask. She is most definitely not the person I want to talk to about wanting to talk to Mark, much less about wanting to investigate what the hell lip gloss had to do with all of this, anyway. Besides, the last time someone asked me that question, my actions caused Faith to chuck a purple espadrille across a television studio. She can't know that that seemingly innocuous question set those events into action, of course, but it still irks me. I am not quite ready to fully embrace Galina's power of positive thinking, fully forming fantasies of my life on the outside, no matter how promising the possibility of having that life is starting to seem. I'd rather not jinx it.

I lean forward in what I hope seems a menacing manner. I almost gag on the perfume.

"Faith, come on," I say, once I stop coughing. "You aren't here to be my friend. What did you come for? The closest mall is the Fashion Center at Pentagon City, and it's really not your style."

She flutters her lashes. Apparently I don't intimidate.

"I am here, you little bitch, because you ruined my career. And fortunately or unfortunately, you are in a position to make it again. And you are going to." Faith's suppressed pseudo-Southern accent has now kicked in, and it seems as if a different person inhabits her mouth.

"Are you threatening me?" I actually laugh.

"I am not threatening you, sweetheart. I don't like you, but I think you might want to hear me out."

"What is it with you people? I am in jail. *J-A-I-L*. You know, with bars and limited phone privileges. Even if I wanted to (finger quotes above my head) make your career, there isn't that much I can do about it right now."

She takes a deep breath and lets it out slowly. "Do you do yoga?" she says.

"Not lately."

"You might want to start."

I shoot her a stern get-to-the-goddamn-point sort of look, or at least one that I hope suggests such a sentiment.

"Now, Annie," she says, tones of Scarlet O'Hara still in evidence. "We both have something the other one wants. And we are in a place to help each other out."

"What could you possibly have that I want?"

"I'm not in jail, now am I?"

She has a point there.

"And so what do I have?"

"You, darling, have fame."

I still don't get it.

She sighs. "Remember that story a few months back? The kid who had an asthma attack and was saved by the man robbing the house?" She has now reverted back to the universal accentless accent of a television personality.

I do remember it. It was a crazy story, as many of the stories that we aired were.

A young boy, about eight, was in his living room playing video games while his mother drove off to the supermarket to pick up some cheese. He was getting very excited as he killed off the alien invaders and saved the earth from certain doom, so excited, in fact, that he started to have an asthma attack. It just so happened that at that very moment a man had watched the car drive away, and assuming the house was empty, took a screwdriver to the doorknob and let himself in. And then he heard the wheezing and the gasping just off the kitchen. He peeked over and, being the father of an asthmatic child himself, found his instincts kicking in.

A little CPR, a little 911—the boy was fine and the man was a hero…and under arrest. The very next day, they were all on the show, the boy, the mother, the hero-robber. Our minute-by-minute ratings points were through the roof. Tom even talked about it in the staff meeting, salivating at the thought of us getting more stories just like this one.

"What about it?" I say.

"Do you remember how we were able to get him, the robber?"

I shake my head.

"Think about it. The story was hot. Everyone wanted it. *Sunrise* was dangling Nintendos and makeovers in their faces, but they came to us with the exclusive."

"They probably wanted to be on the number one show, like most people."

"The guy was supposed to be in jail, honey. But he was on our show." The Southern accent returns. It's almost like I am dealing with a person suffering from dissociative identity disorder.

"So he made bail, I guess. It was a small town. I guess things get processed fast."

"A man of no means and no one to give him any got out on a thousand dollar bond. Now, how do you think that happened?"

It takes me a moment. And then my jaw goes slack.

"We paid his bail?" I say, shaking my head vigorously. "No way." This is completely shocking, this thought. It's sacrilege. It would have been a complete violation of our news standards. Haircuts were one thing, but funding someone's release from jail in order to get him on the show is beyond the pale. I don't care how tight the ratings race, there is no way Tom Tatcher would have allowed this to happen.

"We didn't pay a thing." Faith cocks her head to one side and kind of winks at me. "But maybe one of our friends did."

"Our friends?"

"Do I have to spell it out for you?"

My face must say yes all over it because without much ado, Faith tells me, making me swear on a hypothetical Bible, my mother and my favorite pair of shoes that I won't tell anyone, ever (and obviously I lie that I won't), that her agent was concerned about the slip in the ratings (though she says "agent" the way people say "a friend of mine" when they really mean themselves) and how it might impact her Q rating and speaking fees. Very concerned. Network research had recently come out with a confidential survey showing viewers were feeling that Faith wasn't paying enough attention to regular folk, that she was spending too much time with the glitz and the glam, the movie star interviews, the movers, the shakers. Viewers are mercurial that way. They want to see the celebrities and the politicians, but they also want to see themselves. And if there was a "themselves" story, this was it. Middle-class, overextended mom; sweet, asthmatic boy (what regular kid doesn't have asthma these days); and peril. Faith normally didn't have a thing to do with the booking decisions. She just showed up, read the background material and asked the questions accordingly. But this story, this was one her agent heard about over the radio and immediately called to say she had to have it. It was the regular-folks water cooler story of the week, and he wanted her name all over it.

"So, you bailed him out?" I am at this point fighting to keep my jaw from going slack again.

"No, I already said I didn't. His cousin did."

"His cousin?"

"Stop furrowing your brows so much, Annie. Botox ain't cheap."

"Seriously, what are you talking about?"

"Let's just say a little birdie helped Cousin Johnny find the funds."

"And the funds helped the fame."

Faith nodded. "Well, well. You aren't as dumb as you think, darling."

"But what does this have to do with me?"

"Okay, maybe I take that back, the dumb thing."

"No, I get that you are talking about my bail. But really, Faith, why would you want to front five million dollars of your own money just to help the person who got you into the hell you are in the first place?"

"Whoever said it was my money?" Faith sits back, fingertips to her collarbone as if horrified at the suggestion. "It can't be my money. I do have standards, you know."

"Bozhe moy!"

Galina jumps off of her cot when I tell her who just came to visit me, shouting what I now understand to mean "Oh my God!" She pulls me from the doorway and into her cell, patting the mattress vigorously, motioning for me to sit down. "Tell me all!"

And so I do. I tell her about the wafting perfume, the declining dye job, the near deafening whispers. I tell her about the robber-hero and the little boy. And I tell her about Faith's big plan for redemption.

"This Faith, she will be posting your bail?"

"No. She is going to have someone else post it. Someone who must owe her massively."

"No ropes attached?"

"Now really, Galina. You're not that dumb. Of course there are ropes—we say strings—attached. Faith thinks I am her ticket to her return."

Galina is silent for a moment. A rarity.

"You're thinking," I say.

"So, you are the other's ticket, I mean, ticket for each other?"

"Possibly."

She shakes her head and says something in Russian.

"Very pretty, but I have no idea what you just said."

"Let me think, so I get it correct." She pulls her small English-Russian dictionary out from under the cot and flips through it, muttering a couple of words like *illusion* and *exalt.* "Okay," she says. "It goes this way—'The illusion which exalts us is...' One moment." She consults the dictionary again. "'The illusion which exalts us is dearer to us than ten thousand truths.'"

"Whatever," I say, and get up to walk out of the room.

The presses continue to roll, releasing headline after headline of breathless updates and gossipy projections. They roll and roll until finally, somewhere in the bowels of the *New York Herald's* publishing plant, someone picks up the red, lit up phone that almost never rings. It is ringing now, a light flashing on the receiver to account for the possibility that the noise could drown out the *brrring brrring.* The man is giddy with anticipation. He wipes his dirty, ink-stained hands on his thighs, smearing black across the pant legs, and answers it. This is it. This is the day his number has come in, the day he gets to yell the words every newsman worth his salt has dreamed of shouting since he (or she) first got newsprint smudged on his (or her) hands.

He puts the receiver back in place, clears his throat, and with the vocal strength of a Swiss yodeler, shouts the words he has wanted to shout for oh so long: "Stop Press!"

And then, within less than an hour, the new, revised edition comes spitting out, paper after paper after paper, shouting in 72 point font:

Annabelle Kapner To Be Released Tomorrow
$5 Million Bail Posted by Hollywood Agent
Court Date Still Pending.

23

The plan was to release me in the wee hours of the morning to grant me a moment's peace. Lord knows it is going to be needed. But as Ron Ruby escorts me out of the jailhouse gates, the klieg lights are so bright it might as well be high noon. Given the situation, that would have been preferable. At least then I would have gotten a decent chance at a decent night's sleep.

"What the?" I say, shielding my bloodshot eyes from the staccato flashing of the bulbs and the intense, blinding white beams.

"Despicable," says Ron with a smile, and I know immediately he was the one who tipped off the press. Once a media whore… Well, he is all I have at the moment, so I stick with him as we work our way through the onslaught between us and the Lincoln Town Car just fifty feet and a thousand miles away.

"Annie! Over here!"

"Annie! How are you feeling?"

"What is your relationship with Sam Fox?"

"Annie! Have you heard from Mark?"

"Annie! Who are you wearing?"

Ron is in front of me now, clearing the path with his left hand while dragging me forward with his right, tunneling through to the media staging area that I know is his ultimate destination, and then whipping me forward like a calf to the slaughter.

Shit.

They are all here. All of them. All of the morning shows, each set up a few feet apart from one another, ready to broadcast live from location. And all of them are hoping, praying that the seat on their set will be graced with one thing: me. I see the anchors, one from each show, holding floral bouquets at me as if they were bayonets. Big white teeth, grinning large. A wall of bookers holding up the rear. I see them all, marching forward, vying for my attention, trying to get me to stay.

It is 5:00 a.m. Two hours to air.

"No fucking way," I say, spinning on my heel, aiming for the awaiting car, landing in the chest of— "Ooooph."

"Annie. We are so happy...so, so, happy...we've been so worried..."

Carl.

Of course Carl is here, standing in front of the rest of them, angling for my attention. He tries to hug me.

"Oh, please," I say, pulling away from Carl, from Ron, from everyone and, finally, making a successful dive into the backseat of the waiting car.

I drop my head back and take a deep breath. The driver asks if we should wait, pointing out that my "friend" is still outside. And I see Ron out there, holding court, shaking hands, patting backs, probably making peace with Ken. All is forgiven as long as he delivers a good story.

"He's fine," I say, and I pull open the small plastic shopping bag containing the few possessions I had to check all those weeks ago. Some keys, some clothes, my cell phone. I plug my phone into the car jack on the armrest and turn it on to call my folks in Connecticut. Before I even have a chance to dial, the phone rings.

"Hello?" I say, hopeful that it might be someone I actually might want to talk to, that maybe it might even be, oh, forget that. "Hello? This is Annie."

"Annabelle! Sam Fox here. Let's talk."

I know I need to talk to him. I owe him that much. I owe him about five million things, really. But right now? Right this minute? I beg him to give me a few hours.

"Fine, fine," he says. "We need to solidify the details of your appearance. I'll call you in an hour. Give you time for R and R. I recommend deep nasal breaths. Great for the mellow."

He hangs up and I throw myself lengthwise across the backseat, hopeful if not for sleep, at least for some peace and quiet before daybreak. It's a long drive back to New York and I want to enjoy it. I nestle my head into the inside of my arm and pull my cardigan sweater tight around my neck. Just as I start to close my eyes, the phone rings again. I am tempted to just turn it off, but I see that the caller ID is blocked and curiosity gets the better of me. I hold it up against my exposed ear.

"Hello? This is Annabelle."

And in an accent both extremely foreign and extremely recognizable, the caller says the one thing I really hadn't expected to hear, not right now.

"Cow," he says. *"Cow."*

But since he's on the line, boy do I have a few questions I want to ask him.

PART THREE

Everyone will be famous for fifteen minutes.

—Andy Warhol

If you come to fame not understanding who you are, it will define who you are.

—Oprah Winfrey

24

"Thirty seconds to air!"

"You ready for this?" Faith asks me while scrubbing her front teeth with her forefinger just to be extra certain no lipstick has rubbed off and stained her veneers.

"Probably as ready as you are," I say, retucking a short strand of hair behind my ear. People say it isn't a good idea to change your hairstyle when going through traumatic or dramatic events, but on the stylist's recommendation I decided to chop most of mine off. If I am going to be a respectable public figure, someone people might actually listen to, I need to look the part. Most public figures don't have long, unmanageable frizzy hair.

"Fifteen!"

Silently, I go through my mental list of what I've learned since I've been home, of the points I want to get across. I check the pink lip glosses I brought with me, making sure they are perfectly lined up.

"Yoga breath," says Faith, inhaling loudly and deeply through her nose.

"Right," I say, and try to mimic her.

"Five, four, three, two…" and with a silent "one," a finger points at us like it were a gun.

"Good morning, everyone! It's a New Day, USA!" Faith says to the camera as if this were just another day on the set, as if she hasn't been absent from that seat for more than two months, as if she would even be sitting in it if it weren't for me. "Welcome to our show. I'm Faith Heide."

From across the room, sitting at the acrylic desk, staring into a different camera, Ken Klark meekly pipes in. "And I am Ken Klark. What a program we have for you this morning. Former Hollywood superstar Tom Crust speaks candidly about his battle with depression. Chef Jeff whips up a chocolate confection that has negative calories. That's right! Less than zero! But first, it's the interview you've all been waiting for…Annabelle Kapner, fresh out of jail. She's here to speak with our very own Faith Heide, who has come back from her vacation to speak with Ms. Kapner. Faith, good morning and welcome back."

"Thank you, Ken," Faith says not to Ken, but to the millions and millions of people who have tuned in from their kitchens, their bedrooms, their living rooms. This interview has been promoted in every imaginable location: city buses, bathroom stalls, airplane terminals—Karen told me she even saw someone holding a banner about it behind the weatherman on *Sunrise America,* the competing broadcast, the other day.

Faith continues, telling the viewers how much she values her work as a journalist, how much she missed reporting the past couple of months, and how much she missed each and every one of them. "It was a lovely vacation, but I am just so glad to be back." She might as well be batting her eyelashes at the lens right now.

"But I am sure," she says, her not really native Southern accent peeking in, "it's not little ol' me y'all want to see."

Then she gets serious and it's back to newspeak.

"For months she has been silent. But this morning, the young woman everyone is talking about, the woman everyone wants to speak to, is here with me...for her first exclusive interview since her release from jail two weeks ago. My colleague, Annabelle Kapner." She turns to me and gives me that winning smile, her lipstick a vibrant shade of red. "Good morning, Annie. Welcome home."

Let me set a couple of things straight:

First off, I am not her colleague. I do not now and never will again work for this show or this network, whether they would have me or not. So screw that.

Secondly, the term "exclusive" in TV land is very loosely defined. I might be on *New Day* first, but just because my appearance is being called an exclusive doesn't necessarily mean you won't see the same story elsewhere. You just won't see me on a different channel within two hours of the same hit time. I gave Faith, for a number of reasons (five million, to be specific), the right to have me on her (once my) show before I appeared anywhere else, and with that in her pocket, Faith could march into Max Meyer's office and demand her seat back.

And now, now that I am sitting here across from her, Tom Tatcher and friends can excitedly flash the word *exclusive* in big bold letters across the screen as much as they want. That doesn't mean I won't soon be appearing on just about every other news program and talk show there is. But rest assured that word will be flashed again and again on each subsequent interview I do, define it how you please. It doesn't really matter, just so long as something, anything can differentiate this interview from all the others, just as long as they have a good hook to promote it. But I will give it to her that she has me first. There is no gray area in that designation.

Lastly, this set and this show are pretty far away from being anything close to "home." I may have worked here for almost half a decade, but in my mind home usually doesn't require applying a half inch thick layer of pancake makeup just so you can show up in the living room. In a real home you usually aren't subjected to a litany of false greetings and awkward glances as you make your way down a fluorescent-lit corridor to the blindingly lit armchair like the one I am sitting in now.

Anyway, Faith should get her facts straight. I've been holed up in my home (my real home, my apartment on the Upper West Side) for less than a week now, not two. It feels like years, though. The things I've found out since I've been home, the people I have talked to, the relationships I've been patching up... I am exhausted. I certainly don't need any falsely warm welcomes from Faith. She knows as well as I do that this is truly the last place I want to be. But she needs me and I owe her, so here I am, and I fully intend to use the opportunity as best as I can.

We arrived early, my entourage and I. The Town Car dropped us off outside the large, bronze plated door that leads directly from the street to the green room. Clearly, my arrival was a big deal. Instead of having a page or a production assistant greet us and offer us coffee, there was Franklin, green room doyen, cup already in hand with the exact amount of cream to my liking, treating me not like the pesky java-stealing producer I once was but rather like the A-list guest that I suppose I now am.

"Oh, Annabelle," he said, looking as if he was so moved by my presence his eyes might soon well up with tears. "We are just so happy to have you back."

"I'm not back, Franklin," I said, acting the part I guess I was supposed to act—the part of the diva, the star, the person everyone wants a piece of. "But thanks for the coffee."

I took it (swiping from his other hand the pastry he was offering) and sat down on the tweed chair, trying to act as if I was enjoying this little shift of fate.

They were all like that—the audio techs clipping on my lavaliere microphone, the producers hovering around for their other segments, the makeup artists tweaking the work that had already been done to my face prior to arrival (my people insisted that we hire a stylist and a makeup artist to accompany me to every appearance—to assure a consistency in my look). Everyone treated me with a too respectful and uncomfortably polite distance—a distance that in fact felt icy and (okay, maybe I am projecting here) a bit hungry. Like they were all on the edge of their seats, waiting for me to do I don't even know what, but something that would be good to gossip about later in the day. These are the same people who for years had seen me in unwashed ponytails, without makeup, laughing and crying and basically carrying on just like everyone else, which I so clearly no longer am. I am not one of them. I am Famous.

Famous with an agenda.

The negotiation to get me here, where I am sitting now, opposite Faith, was torturous. I knew it was inevitable, but I was fighting to put it off as long as possible. I wanted to allow myself some time to gather more facts and thoughts, to prepare what I wanted to say, but Sam and Ron and Lizzie (the celebrity publicist they hired for me) were screaming at me in near panic that I had to give the public something, a nibble, to keep the interest at its peak, not to ruin the opportunity, to keep the fame flowing, to keep the momentum up for my interest, their interest and the interest of the Fidas and Lidas, and, yes, as it turns out, the interest of my *cow* caller.

Once agreed to, the network needed a week to pitch, tease, promote and basically plaster the world with the fact that they would have an enormous "get" (that's TV news parlance for a coveted guest) for Faith Heide's triumphant return: they would have the first interview with Annabelle Kapner since her release from jail. Of course, Sam Fox was able to renegotiate Faith's contract now that she had me, a metaphorically enormous if literally underweight carrot, to wave in Max Meyer's face. It didn't matter that I had nothing much to say. At least I didn't yet. That's why I wanted time, so I could have something, find out a little bit more, and not just theories and hypotheses.

But here I am, sitting on the opposite side of the lens. I've been media trained, camera coached, made up and decked out— preened and glossy and seemingly ready to go, but with nothing substantial to say.

Introducing Annabelle Kapner, the television personality.

"I love your skirt, Annie," says Faith, kicking off what will clearly be a hard-hitting interview.

Every detail was parsed before I got here: what we could talk about without killing each other (not much), what I would wear (casual but stylish: a pale, summery skirt, a matching thin cotton jacket, and some fashionable platform espadrilles thrown in for a touch of trend), how I would do my hair (shorter, layered, elegantly tousled), what lipstick shade I needed. We went with a subtle shade called Misty Mauve, though I've been biting my lips since the moment I got on set and I am pretty sure it is all worn off now.

I smile, throwing thought daggers at Faith, trying desperately for her to see that if she doesn't get to it, if she doesn't get to the points set up in our deal, I will walk. And then I will talk.

"Annie, I am not going to pull any punches here. I have to start off with the question everyone is asking. Have you heard from Mark Thurber?"

You bitch! That is totally off topic and uncalled-for. You are on such thin ice, you manipulative whore.

"You know I am not going to answer that, Faith," I say with a smile, wanting to kick her under the table. Hard. She had better behave herself. Yes, I agreed to do her first. But the list of shows and stations and papers and magazines that want a piece of me is endless. Faith might be trying to make a little news, get a bigger splash, but if she doesn't behave she can forget about having me back. And she wants me back. She needs me back. They all do. Because here I am: an attractive, charming young woman with an extremely high Q rating who is in the center of the biggest scandal of the century (or at least of the past few months). The vice president of the United States, until recently the front-runner in the upcoming election, has been connected to a scandal that involves a seedy organization that may or may not be funneling money to terrorists, but is clearly doing something bad. And, boy oh boy, since I've been out I have learned that there is oh, so much more. What this had to do with cosmetics is still a big question mark to the world at large (though I now have some ideas), but, short of the fact that my blunders brought it all to light, what this all really has to do with me is an even bigger one, at least in my opinion.

And yet, I am all the media seems to talk about. I am like a reality show champion, famous for being famous, but with little substance to be famous for. I was in the wrong place at the wrong time and now my every step, my every move is monitored for dissection and analysis, my very existence a fun, gossipy entrance into an important but otherwise way too complicated story. Who wants to talk to political analysts and presidential historians (yawn!) when they can talk to me?

Faith asks me about the court date, which still hasn't been set, and which Ron Ruby believes never will be. Apparently there are bookies in Vegas taking bets on what the date will be when the case gets dismissed. I mention this fact to her (and to the world) and we have a little giggle.

"You want to put some money on it?" I say with a laugh, like we are old pals. "Or have you already done enough of that?" Oops. I probably shouldn't have said that. Even though the whole Sam Fox payout is probably public knowledge by now, it was most certainly not an agreed upon topic of conversation. Faith, thank God, just changes the subject, though she doesn't look happy.

"So, Annie, now that you are out, at least for the foreseeable future, what are your plans?"

"Well, Faith," I say with an enormous smile, revealing my recently whitened teeth, "my plans right now are to make sure that I am out for good."

"And short of praying that the judge throws the case out, how exactly do you intend to do that?"

"I'm here, aren't I? I intend, Faith, to make sure that everyone knows, that the world knows, that while there is a very important story needing to be told, it actually had very little to do with me."

"But it does now, Annie."

"Which is why I am here."

"Sure. So, tell me then, if you want to talk about this, what was he like, Douglas Lenrup?" Faith asks, as if she had never met Purnell herself. As if she hadn't sat across from him, giggling as she patted his knee.

"Purnell?" I say, playing along, speaking in that dishy, insidery tone so popular among pundits. "That's what I knew him as. Purnell. He was quite a character." I tell Faith about his bizarre tone of voice and his resemblance to Tweedledee, saying things like "don't you remember?" and "as you probably recall." She doesn't take the bait at all, preferring to somehow simultaneously distance herself from the story and act like she is an ace reporter all the same. "Anyway, Faith," I finally say, because it really doesn't serve either of us to press that point, "what I'd really like to talk about, and I think you know, is this." I hold up one of the lip glosses. "I have some ideas that—"

Faith gently pushes my hand back down. "Yes, yes. We will get to that. But tell me, did Mark Thurber ever meet him, this Purnell? How much did Mark know about your reporting of the Cosmetic Relief story before you got into trouble?" she asks.

"Faith," I say, this time through my teeth, my cheeks burning up. "I have nothing to say about Mark Thurber. We agreed this interview would only focus on my time in jail and what I know about Cosmetic Relief."

"Now, Annie—" she crosses her arms schoolmarmlike "—you know perfectly well that it is against ZBC News standards to agree to the terms of any interview."

I shake my head dismissively. What crap. Faith doesn't give a rat's behind about news standards; this interview was so planned it may as well have been scripted (not that Faith is sticking to the script). Her agent may have paid my way out of jail, but we had a deal. And the deal was that I could discuss what I thought to be the real reason behind my arrest.

"Annie, honestly, there are probably ten million people watching us right now—" she waves flirtatiously at the camera, acknowledging them "—and they aren't watching because you are some world-renowned investigator. If I recall correctly—" that accent again "—the last time you tried to investigate something, you wound up behind bars." She actually giggles.

"I think, Faith," I say very slowly and deliberately, "trying to wing this interview without reading off questions someone else wrote down isn't working for you. Anyway, if you were half the news-person (air quotes with fingers above my head) you pretend to be, you would probably be interested in knowing—"

"Annie, really. I don't need a producer to know that all we are *all* interested in is if you were sleeping with Mark Thurber at the time of your arrest, and, for that matter, if you still are. Because someone has been leaking some pretty heady stuff to the press and the only person this information really benefits is you."

Knowing the vice president, a man running for the big office, is possibly a corrupt, twisted, evil prick might benefit the American people is clearly beside the point to her. And so long as she looks good (literally and figuratively), the facts that I want to share (some information a cow caller sent my way)—that little Fardish girls were used as testing bunnies for a lip gloss that our own company was invested in—is obviously irrelevant.

She continues. "So why don't you just fess up and tell us. Tell us the truth about you and Mark. We'll find out sooner or later, anyway. Wouldn't you rather we find out from you?"

I have to hand it to her that this line of questioning has the potential to turn our little chat into the first real, possibly even quasi-substantial interview she has ever done. In truth, she isn't doing a bad job playing the part of a journalist hungry for a story. But this is my story we are talking about here. My story. And you know what? Screw all of this. Galina was right. There is only one person who should be doing the reporting here and that person is me. And there is no way in hell I am going to let Faith blow up the sensational tabloid crap even more just so she can look like some news-making hero. I mean, not any more than she already has.

"You are treading on very thin ice, Faith."

"Oh please, Annie. The only one on thin ice anymore is you. You might be out on bail, but your court date could be set any day now. And then who knows what will happen."

Who is this woman, this suddenly aggressive, suddenly uncompromising interviewer? I would almost respect her (for the first time ever) but for the fact that this is totally pissing me off. Not just Faith, but all of this. Seriously, what the hell am I doing here? It's bullshit. All of it. I know I had to appear on this show as part of the bail deal, but beyond that. I mean, the vice president, the man who is trying to sell himself as the next great hope to be the leader of the free world, might actually have some connection to those poor little Fardish girls and that skanky swine Douglas Purnell. That's what we should be talking about. And now that (thanks to my "therapy" sessions with Galina and the productive emotional growth I experienced in jail) I am no longer subject to the tendency to retain all the venom and the despair I am feeling, I do the opposite.

"You are such a fraud, Faith. If the audience only knew the truth about you, what a piece of opportunistic, manipulative—"

"Excuse me?" She interrupts before I can finish. "Who the hell are you to say, I mean, what the? I have earned everything I have, I worked my butt off to get here. But you. If it weren't for the fact that you slept with Mark Thurber, you would be nothing. A flea. That's what you are. A whoreish little flea who got herself into more trouble than she can handle."

And I can't help myself. It is almost out-of-body. I watch from the corner of my right eye as my fist draws back, and then I see it flying across the width of the coffee table, landing smack on Faith's perky little nose. Hard. Her nose starts bleeding.

Faith, with one hand holding back the blood, reaches over and pulls me by my hair to her side. I scratch and slap and get scratched and slapped, and both of us land somehow on the floor, rolling over and over, her on top, me on top, her on top, me on top.

"Go to commercial *now!*" I can hear Tom Tatcher's voice screaming through the earpiece that got knocked out of Faith's head.

The *New York Spectator*

Meow Mix In The Morning

By Alexander Churn

New York Spectator Media Critic

Oh my, oh my, oh…meow. What can I say? A catfight on morning TV? Could live television get any better than this? Because if it was ratings points that ZBC News's *New Day USA* was after, they got them in spades. But where oh where to begin? This is as juicy as an overripe Georgia peach or, with respect to Ms. Faith Heide, perhaps I should say Ohio peach. Oh, oh, stop it, Alex, you are bad.

Okay, for the two of you who didn't happen to tune in yesterday morning and who don't subscribe to *Star Weekly*, here it is from the beginning: We all know that one notorious morning show producer, Annabelle Kapner, was released from jail about a week ago because Hollywood agent Sam Fox bailed her out. Well, he certainly didn't do that, at a cost of a whooping five million dollars, out of the kindness of his heart. And it can't really be a coincidence that Mr. Fox is the same agent that represents the aforementioned imminent train wreck of a woman named Faith Heide, now could it? Well, *he* doesn't have to answer to any bothersome network's news standards, now does he? Of course not.

But how interesting that, as sources at the top of the network game are telling yours truly, with the promise to deliver Ms. Kapner first (who I am sure would have otherwise avoided her former network's airspace as if it were filled with SARS), the once beleaguered, basically out of work disgraced morning queen was able to re-secure her morning throne.

And meanwhile, while we are watching Faith's nose explode and Annie's new hairdo get destroyed (again, for the two of you who didn't watch, this actually happened), does anyone care that the investigation that this whole matter sparked in the first place has driven the vice president's poll numbers lower than my shoe size? But with all the leaks and implications and nasty suggestions, really, Faith Heide is right. Call us crass and shallow minded, but, like she said on the show, isn't it just so much more fun trying to investigate the love life of our favorite coincidentally famous person than get into the nitty-gritty of some way too complicated political intrigue? Give us sex! Give us drama! Give us girl on girl live TV action!

"Oh, for God's sake," I say, pushing the paper across my kitchen table as if it were a tainted, dirty rag. Which I suppose it is. "Can you hand me the *Herald?* Maybe they will at least attempt to take a high road."

Mark skims through Churn's prose and laughs. "At least it's well-written."

Yes. Mark. As in Mark Thurber. He is sitting here, across from me at my kitchen table. The tabloids have no idea what they are missing.

25

Being a reporter seems a ticket out to the world.

—Jacqueline Kennedy Onassis

"Ahh-choo!"

Generally I don't have any pronounced allergies, but my small living room is so overrun with flowers it looks as if a bomb hit a garden show and the carnage all landed on my couch.

"Incoming!" says Maurice, fighting to carry yet another towering bouquet from the front door of my apartment to a place on the living room floor. Maurice, Sam Fox's manorexic-looking assistant, has been tapped to be my interior decorator. While everyone else is running around, taking meetings, hearing offers, pondering deals, he has taken on the increasingly important task of figuring out where to put all these plants. Without him, there might not be a place to sit down. "Let's see," he says once he finds a free spot in the corner, "this one is from Diane Sawyer. Want me to read it?"

I shrug noncommittally, because these notes are all pretty much the same. An invitation to appear on this program or that one, with promises of fancy dinners or editorial discretion or both. My appearance on *New Day* yesterday morning did nothing to assuage the interest of the popular press. Quite the opposite. Apparently, the more outrageous things get, the hungrier they are to have me. Me, but not the whole story, not the real story. I mean, sure, Oprah wants me on the show to discuss conditions in a women's prison, and that is very noble. And *Dateline* wants me to take them back to the scene of the crime, which isn't such a bad idea but in the pre-interview it became pretty clear that the scene they really wanted to reenact was wherever it was that Mark and I went on our dates.

"Ah-choo!" I sneeze again.

"Is there some sort of charity we could donate all these to?" I say, stooping down to get a closer look at one particularly exotic orchid. "Flowers for funerals or something? A pediatric ward?"

Maurice tells me he'll get on it right away.

"Everything but the lilacs and peonies," says Mark, taking off his dark sunglasses and baseball hat as he enters the room, a tray of Starbucks lattes precariously balanced in the other hand.

"Right," I say, avoiding his eyes and trying not to grin.

Mark Thurber.

He's here in my living room, back from a coffee run.

When I was in jail, this was the stuff of my fantasies that I tried desperately not to harbor. Lately, well, things have changed. I mean, sure, I appreciate his attempts to prove to me that he has more spine than he did all those moons ago when he first disappeared from the face of the earth (and from offering me any support, emotional or otherwise). But I've discovered something, now that I have spent some time standing face-to-face with him (his face, I should mention, looks rather different—a full beard, dyed to match the newly blond head of hair, all affected to make him incognito, which is working, but he also looks a bit too much like a cross between Willie Nelson and Simon Le Bon circa 1987 for my liking).

I don't really want to admit this, but I guess while I was in jail I built him up a little in my fantasies. I mean, for someone's brush-off to affect me so much, he must be pretty great, right? But now that he is here in the flesh, I've discovered that, take away the fancy job title, the smooth talking and the accolades from *People* magazine, and Mark Thurber might not be all that, or at least not all that I thought he was. I suppose I had thought I was above such things. I mean, I would like to think that I am, that I always have been, the kind of person who doesn't just take things at face value, the kind of person who can see past the surfaces, who takes greater stock in what's beneath than what's above. But now I realize that maybe I was wrong. I'm looking at him and, aside from recognizing that he's a very nice guy, I realize I never took the time to take stock. I can't figure out exactly who he is. I think he is trying to figure that out as well.

And now, even though we made it through the all-important second date that night after the Lincoln Memorial, even though we spent more than one night in the same bed, even though we told each other things we wouldn't tell most of our friends, it's not like we can just pretend everything is running a normal course. It's not like it would make any sense for me to just jump into his arms and call him my boyfriend. We have to start the dance all over again.

"Skim latte for you. No sugar, right?" he says, handing me the warm paper cup. I readjust the belt on my pink Vietnamese silk robe (a coming home gift from Galina, who saw it on the Virtual

Shopping Network and had a friend with ostensibly good credit order it for me) and then take the coffee into the kitchen—right now the only room in the apartment, aside from command central in my bedroom, with a proper place to sit down. Mark follows.

Mark has been trying to make things up to me not just since I have returned from jail, but apparently long before I even knew he was. I didn't have any idea—they claim it was too dangerous for me to know—that he and Karen were risking their careers, their reputations, even possibly their lives, to help me clear my name. They have both been running around, digging up helpful information, begging for favors, and, in Karen's case anyway, dissecting snakes. And because of all of this, I mean because of his association with me, Mark was fired from his job, stripped of his security clearance, and has been living on the lam.

Still, he could have called.

When I first got home, I just figured I was on my own. Sure, I had an agent, a lawyer and a mass of "people" set up to help me navigate my new terrain. But real people, real friends, forget it. The way I figured it, I had only one friend in the world and she was still in jail.

The Town Car that had picked me up in Alexandria finally arrived in Manhattan, and I took comfort in the familiar noises—the early morning honks, the sanitation workers stopping traffic on the side street we were trying to drive down. When we finally arrived at my place, the sounds of coming to a slow, measured stop gave me solace. It reminded me of my childhood, of my family arriving at some welcoming destination. Although I could hear the popping of the pebbles in the gravel driveway underneath us or the turn of the wheels lining up against a wet cement curb, I would pretend to still be asleep, forcing my father to gather me in his arms and carry my slack body inside. Of course, there was no one to lift me, much less assist me, when we drove up to my apartment building, even though I was at that point very much wishing against hope that this whole time I had just been dreaming and sound asleep. I had to get up and walk in on my own two feet.

We made record time and managed to beat most of the press, so there was no media circus to greet me, just a smattering of reporters that I easily ignored. The doorman wasn't even there. I carried myself and my one shabby bag over the threshold, up the elevator and back into my own personal time capsule. Everything appeared to be more or less how I had left it all those weeks before: closets open, clothing scattered across my bed. It was a little surprising that apparently no federal agents or investigators had come through to knock my possessions around or maybe even try to plant some evidence, but considering the sloppiness of their work throughout this ordeal, it made some sense. Maybe they knew they had mucked things up too much already and didn't want to risk mucking them up any more. Which I figured was the reason there was even an empty cup of coffee, dark residue ringing the bottom, sitting on the corner of my desk. I probably left the cup there myself all those weeks ago. Piled up next to it? A few tubes of the Cosmetic Relief lip glosses. I didn't remember putting them there, but then again, I didn't always remember to feed the cat in the morning, either. It did occur to me, however, that the glosses probably shouldn't be just sitting out like that. I opened the top desk drawer and swept them in. Then I threw my bag down, shoved the clothing to one side and crawled into bed.

Margarita, my cat, climbed up next to me, and I took some

comfort in the fact that at least she was warm to the touch, seemingly well fed and clearly unfazed by my new status as most talked about girl in America. I made a mental note to thank the doorman for taking care of her.

After sniffing at my hair for a while, Margarita pawed the pillow, curled around my head, and we both fell asleep.

I woke up when I felt someone sit down on the foot of the bed, making the mattress bounce a little.

I wasn't sure if she was a dream or an apparition.

"Karen?"

Karen, my best friend from college, the one friend who I had most expected to visit me in detention, but who hadn't, was sitting there with her Dorothy Hamill hair, looking at me eagerly, as if I would have something to say.

"I didn't want to wake you, Annie. But we—"

"We?" I sat up. "What? What are you doing here? Who's we? Why…?" I looked at my alarm clock. It was one in the afternoon. I had slept almost four hours.

"What the?" I threw my legs over the side of the bed, stood up and walked away to distance myself.

"Annie," Karen said, standing up in turn, attempting to put her hand on my shoulder, but I quickly swiped it off.

"Don't."

She retracted. "Annie," she said again. "I'm trying to help you—"

"Are you?" I said, in a tone bitchier than intended. Then I took a deep breath. "I thought you were avoiding me."

"Avoiding you? No, I, I mean, Annie, I wanted to call, or come by, but I—"

"But you didn't, Karen. And it hurt."

"If I hurt you I am so sorry. But I couldn't. I—"

"Couldn't?" I cut in again. Now I wanted to sound bitchy. "You could have contacted me if you really wanted to. You could have checked in."

"Do you have any idea—" she started to say.

"Any idea? Of what? The danger? I didn't say you should have visited. A stupid greeting card would have been nice. Christ, you could have even sent it in code. I would have figured it out. But no, you didn't even think of contacting me, even though I wasn't more than ten miles from where you live, and now you think you can let yourself into my apartment and welcome me home like nothing ever happened? What is that?"

"Annie, I—"

"No," I said. "I don't think you should..."

I wanted to say more, to yell at her, maybe even hit her, but instead I just started to cry. Tormented, hysterical sobs. Sobs of relief, of frustration, of fear, of I don't even know what. I had held it together so tightly all that time in jail, but I guess I couldn't any longer. Yes, I was home, but I didn't know for how long. Yes, my friend was here, but I didn't know if I should trust her.

Karen, who is taller and larger than me, easily wrapped me in her arms and lowered me back onto the bed as I heaved against her, crying, hiccupping, drenching her T-shirt with unstoppable tears.

"Annie," she said. "I am really sorry. I'm here now."

Then she explained to me, once the sobbing had subsided, why her absence and why her presence.

"Someone needed to take care of the cat," she said, and smiled.

I had to smile back at that point. Apparently she'd been

scooping out Margarita's litter for weeks. How could I hold a grudge after that? Karen told me she'd been sleeping in my bed, throwing out the spoiled milk, taking in my mail.

"Man, you get a lot of junk mail," she said. And then she apologized for the state of the room. "It was even worse when I got here," she said.

"Worse?"

"They were here. I mean, someone was here. Someone went through your stuff."

So I was totally wrong.

"Who?"

"Probably someone working for Hacker."

"They left the lip gloss?"

"No, I brought those. From when I was doing those tests. I figured they were safer with me than in D.C."

"But. Wait. What about D.C.?" I said, meaning what about her life in D.C., her job, her everything.

She said she had accrued a lot of vacation days over the years. "Anyway," she said, "it's a government job? They never fire anyone."

Then her cell phone rang. She took it out of her back pocket and looked at the caller ID.

"Well," she said, smirking, "some people in Washington do find a way to get themselves fired, but it takes a lot of work."

Then she answered the phone.

"Hello…yup. Uh-huh. She's here. Oh, and we need more milk?" She held the phone in my direction. "There's someone who wants to speak to you?"

I knew she wasn't asking a question, that is just how she talks, so I took the phone and said hello.

It was Mark.

"Hi, Annie," he said. It wasn't much, but I couldn't respond. I had no idea what to say.

"Annie?" he said again. "Okay, well, I understand if you don't want to talk to me now. Well, I guess I will, uh, see you in a bit." He paused for a moment to give me another chance to speak, but I didn't so he just added an awkward, "Okay, well, uh, see you later."

I dropped the phone onto the bed as if it was tainted.

"What is going on here? Both of you? Do you think this was just a little vacation?" I shake my head dismissively. "I mean, thanks for looking after the cat, but seriously, am I supposed to just pick up where we left off or something?"

"Let me explain," said Karen.

"I'm all ears." I crossed my arms and leaned back against the headboard, ready to listen.

"Blah blah blah." That's what she said. Something about Mark. Something about Purnell. Something about snakes. Nothing made any sense.

"Huh?" I finally said, "What the hell are you talking about?"

Karen got up and brought each of us a glass of water from the kitchen. Then she explained again. Slowly. Point by point. She told me that after I was arrested, some more test results came back that proved the toxin that was causing the lip gloss problems actually came from a substance developed in Fardistan years ago, before there ever was any such thing as Cosmetic Relief, before women there even knew there was such a thing as lip gloss. She told me about the history of the Fardish stiletto viper venom and about how, while it obviously had something to do with Purnell (or Lenrup, whatever his name was), she thought it might have a connection to Vice President Hacker, that maybe this weird inflammatory lip gloss formula might actually have something to do with an old CIA program to develop a truth serum. Which was maybe why they were casing the Cosmetic Relief office in the first place. Hacker must be afraid of something. There must have been something there that could damage him.

"Karen," I said, "I might have been in jail, but it wasn't a black hole. I've been following the news. I don't know about your conspiracy theory, but I know there is a connection between Purnell and Hacker. But what does this have to do with you and Mark?"

"How do you think it got there—the news?"

My jaw dropped. "So Mark really was the leaker?"

"Some stuff."

"Some stuff?"

"It's bigger than you think."

I was still totally confused.

"But how did you and Mark...?"

"I called him. For help. I mean, I thought he could help."

"And he did?"

"He did. And he was so disgusted with what he found out that he quit his job."

"He did?"

"Well, he tried to. But there was a lot of politicking around it, so I guess, like I said, technically they fired him. We've both been staying here. He's been sleeping on the couch."

This was a lot to process, especially considering that I had been released from jail just a few hours before.

"But there hasn't been any mention of his firing in the papers," I said.

"It hasn't been announced. I am sure they are just trying to figure out how to spin it? I guess the world just thinks Mark is still on some extended vacation? Unfortunately, his absence seems to make people even more curious. That's why he's here. It's the last place anyone would expect him to be right now, with all the attention on you."

I was desperate for an Advil at this point, but I had too many questions to ask to bother getting up to find one.

"But why didn't you come tell me all of this before?" I said. "No one knows who you are. You could have come."

"It was too risky?"

"Are you asking me?"

"No," said Karen, adjusting her tone. "It was too risky."

"To visit?"

"Annie, this is a big deal. There is a lot at stake here for a lot of people."

I could see that.

"And then I got a letter from a friend of yours. Galina?"

"Galina wrote you?"

"She thought you would need some help when you got out. So I came here, we came here, to take care of things."

"Mark is helping you feed Margarita?" I said, still rather confused. Did Karen just tell Mark to pick up milk? What was their relationship about? What the hell was Galina writing Karen for? I took another sip of water and with my free hand motioned for her to continue.

"She thought you might need help with your reporting."

"My reporting? I thought she and I covered that. I did what I could."

"Look, Annie, I'm not really sure what your friend Galina is thinking, or who she is, for that matter, but I am here to help you figure out what you want to do now that you aren't locked up."

"Right now I just want to avoid getting locked up again."

Karen rolled her eyes. "Ha, ha."

Then she got serious.

"Listen, most of the stuff in the press, the stuff about Hacker? You need to know that we didn't have anything to do with that. I mean, Mark did make a few calls, but aside from the possible CIA connection with Purnell, or whatever his name is, there wasn't that much for him to leak. The reporters took it from there. I mean, they haven't really looked at the venom angle yet, but the papers seem to be doing a pretty good job of getting to the bottom of things that even Mark didn't know, especially the *Herald*. So maybe right now we just have to sit tight and focus on how to handle all this press attention on you and trying to get your trial dismissed. Mark has some people who owe him some favors over at Justice, and they—"

"Karen, that's ridiculous." I stood up. In fact, just then, I suppose you could say I woke up.

"He really does, he's—"

"No, not Mark. The press. Do you really think the press is doing a good job with this story?" I said. It felt like a fog was lifting, like a puzzle was putting itself together in my brain. Suddenly, everything, literally everything, started to make some sense. Even the snake venom made sense.

"I mean, if you ask me, if they were really going to explore what connection Hacker has to the lip gloss, not just to Purnell or to Fardistan, don't you think they would have done that by now? I mean, there's hardly been any mention of why the feds were casing Purnell's office in the first place. Just cursory. Like, oh yeah, that happened, and that was that. Think about it, there's got to be more." I was getting very excited at this point, practically jumping up and down. "They might be covering some of the story, but mostly they just gloss over it as an excuse to talk about me. Me and Mark, actually."

"Don't you think you are being a little self-centered?"

"Am I? Didn't you just basically say that you guys have leads to some more information—stuff that I *haven't* read about? The snakes and the serum? I mean, isn't it possible that Hacker could have been directly involved with the snake stuff? Or why were the feds there that night? There has to be a bigger story than some stupid coincidence that Hacker and Purnell knew each other once upon a time, some bigger reason for the feds to have been casing that office, and even you seem to think there is or you wouldn't have gotten this involved, right? But whatever it is, it's not like *that* is making front page news. Are we just supposed to wait for some reporter to trip over it? And what about those girls I saw? What about Fida and Lida and those JPEGs? There hasn't been one mention of that stuff in the papers or on TV, at least not that I've seen."

Karen didn't say anything, but I could tell she was trying to fight a smile from creeping over her face.

"What?"

"Maybe Galina was right."

"What?"

"It's your story, Annie. It should be."

And that was that. For the first time in a really long time I smiled a heartfelt I-really-mean-it smile. Because I knew she was right. And I knew that for the first time in my life I was actually in a position to tell a story the way I thought it should be told, not just produce it in some formulaic way and deliver the expected. Or at least at that moment that's what I thought. Everyone from ABC to Al-Jazeera was begging me to be on their air. I figured I would be able to talk about whatever I wanted to.

Or at least that is what I thought until yesterday, when I arrived at the *New Day* set and sat down across from Faith.

Now, one week and a day later, the day after that fateful interview, I am sitting across from Mark at my kitchen table, flipping through the self-perpetuating dreck churned out by the likes of Alexander Churn, and I know this isn't going to work. There was no way that any of these people, these shows, are going to let me get a word in edgewise to talk about conspiracy theories and exploding lips. Right now, the only thing I can gain from being a passive subject, interviewed across the dial in preformatted programming with preformatted hosts, is more fame. But without any real substance behind it, that fame will be fleeting, not to mention useless.

There are presidential campaigns to derail, strange conspiracies to unravel, young girls to save, and my court date is still pending. Left to the mainstream media, there will be some lip service to the important stuff, but it will be quickly glossed over to focus on the gossip. This is my story and I am the one who is going to report it—with a little help from my friends.

"So, are you ready?" Mark asks after I announce my intention to send all the flowers back, return to sender.

"I think so," I say, and my timing couldn't be better. Because just then, the phone rings.

Mark answers it.

"It's your lawyer," he says, handing it over to me. And then, watching me get the news Ron Ruby needed to report, he sees me turn translucent.

"What? What's wrong?"

I limply hand him back the receiver so he can put it back in the cradle.

"The court date was set," I say. "Three weeks from tomorrow."

"Oh, fuck."

"Yup. So much for the dismissal. So much for clearing my name." I can feel myself shaking, but I am trying to act cool, like this isn't a big deal. Clearly, Mark isn't buying it.

He goes over to the sink and wets a paper towel, which he brings to me and places on my forehead.

"I am so sorry," he says. "I thought my friends at Justice were working on things—"

"Apparently you don't instill much fear in those parts anymore."

Mark doesn't initially respond. Then, gently, he takes my chin in his fingers and moves my head so that he can look directly into my eyes. "No, Annie," he says softly. "I guess I don't. But we can do this. You can do this. We can get this story out."

Maybe it's because I grew up in New York City, but sometimes it is hard to trust someone who is being gratuitously nice to me. And while I am fairly sure Mark's effort is far from gratuitous, I still don't fully get it.

Which is exactly what I say to him.

"I don't get it."

"Get what?"

"This," I say, letting my fear and my irritability get the better of me. "You. I don't get you. What are you doing here, really? Do you really think that you're going to somehow ride on my coattails to some bizarre career redemption? Do you really think you're in a position to help me at this point, anyway? I mean, who do you think you are? Some knight in shining armor? Why don't you just let me go down? It would make a hell of a lot more sense."

I am losing my grip.

Even as I'm saying all of this, even as I start to spiral into this attack on Mark, on his character and his motives and even his appearance, I know that I am totally out of line. I know I don't even remotely believe what I'm saying.

Mark looks at me blankly, not so much with stunned shock but with complete dismay. As if he isn't sure who I am, either. My cheeks are in flames.

"Shit," I say. "I didn't mean that. I mean, I didn't mean that you…" I put my head on the table, afraid of what else I might say, afraid I might see him walk out of the room.

He doesn't.

Instead, I feel the heat of his hand on my shoulder.

"Annie," he says softly. "I know you're scared. Honestly. I'm scared, too. I never thought things would get to this point, that they would be so out of control, but they have, they are. But it's not your fault. It's not mine, either."

I lift my head. I am sure my face is all blotchy and my nose all red, but really, who cares? I am sure a little postnasal drip can't do any more damage than I've probably already done.

"You're too nice," I say, sort of whining.

"No, it's not that. I'm not nice. If I was nice I would have figured out a way to contact you when you were in detention, when you probably really needed a friend."

"No, no," I protest. "Really, it's fine. I mean, I understand."

But it is obvious his silence still bothers both of us a little. Mark takes his hand off my neck and places it on my wrist (which I should mention is now covered with the snot and tears I've just wiped from my face).

"Annie, look," he says. "It's not just that I believe what we're doing is right, what I'm doing is right, which I do. And it's not just that I felt, after finding out what I did, that I couldn't work for the White House anymore, and I needed to help set things straight. That is all pretty bad stuff. But I wouldn't have thrown my career away just like that if I wasn't..." He stops midsentence.

I think I know what he is about to say. And, considering what I just said, I feel kind of awkward about it. I mean, not only am I feeling rather obnoxious and pretty far from romantic, it's not like I am exactly a great prospect for girlfriend material right now.

"Thank you," I say, jumping out of my chair and changing the subject. "Do you want me to heat up your coffee again?" I grab my cup and walk over to the microwave.

"Annie."

I sigh. "Yes. I..." I don't finish. I don't know what else to say.

But Mark, well, words never seem to elude him.

"Okay," he says. "Let's just focus on what's in front of us right now."

I sit back down at the table, grateful. I smile. And then. Shit. Shit. We have only three weeks to somehow prove that the sole reason I was arrested was because Hacker was a paranoid lunatic who was trying to prevent his old protégé Douglas Purnell from tarnishing his name. That in this weird world it really could be possible that a lip gloss marketed to little girls was in fact derived from the same snake venom the CIA was once testing for use as a truth serum.

"Shit." I throw my head onto the table. "I might as well just show up in handcuffs today. I am so fucked."

Mark doesn't even try to respond, because just then the microwave beeps to alert me to my newly reheated coffee.

And then the phone rings again. And yes, as coincidences go, it probably seems like a big one. But it isn't so big if the person causing it has a proven record of having a very good intuitive sense of timing.

Mark looks at me and I nod.

He picks up the phone.

"Hello?" he says.

His eyebrows rise a little. *"Cow?"* he says. "You want to talk to Ms. Kapner?"

As I have mentioned a few times already, it used to take a lot to get me angry. But not anymore. Just hearing that word is enough to set me off entirely. My life (and, yes, Mark's life) is entering an even bigger tailspin than I ever thought possible, and the very person who set this hell in motion, this person who has basically been crank calling for months now, calling and taunting me and then hanging up, is now calling again. I am just about ready to explode.

I grab the phone out of Mark's hand.

"Listen, you schmuck," I say with not a little bit of vinegar, "let's cut the cow calling bullshit and set up a meeting already. Your phone calls and your unsubstantiated dribbles of information are starting to bore me. If you want to harass me because you think I didn't get your story right, then you've got the wrong reporter now. Harass some other hack. If you want to use me as your fucking messenger, than you need to start telling me what the hell you actually want and what the hell you actually know."

There is a pause and a deep, exaggerated sigh before the man starts to speak. "You know what, Annabelle?" he says, this time with no discernable Fardish accent, but rather a slight touch of Ivy League nasality. "I'm glad to hear it. I've been watching you and I've started to think the same thing."

It was an accent that sounded extremely familiar. It sounded like the accent of half the journalists I know, an accent particular to a certain type of the media elite.

"Who the fuck are you? Where the hell—"

"Tell Mark I'll call him later today to set it all up," he says, interrupting me and not answering the question. And then he hangs up. It is a very annoying habit.

26

"You want to do what?" Sam Fox is yelling at me. Screaming. Even over the phone, thousands of miles away, I can picture him. He's standing over his desk, arms tense and spread wide, his head pushed forward so that the words emitted from his mouth are enhanced by a strong gravitational pull to the speakerphone directly below. "Are you fucking nuts? Do you know how much money we stand to lose?"

To be fair, about five million more than he knows.

But beyond that, I do understand that when someone's livelihood is derived from ten percent of someone else's earnings, it is probably not a good thing to hear that that someone else is turning down all of the offers for the purchase of said person's life story, all of the movie deals and book contracts.

"I am not saying never, Sam. Just not right now," I say, trying to bring him over to my line of thinking—that once I am done doing what I want to do, all of that—the movies, the books, the fame— will be even more valuable, morally and monetarily. "Just think of the net worth of Bob Woodward. He's done fine by his work."

"Bob Woodward is a real reporter. All you are, Annabelle, is famous. And, O.J. Simpson aside, fame is going to get you only so far. You are letting it go to your head."

Then, probably realizing that his hysteria isn't having the desired effect, Sam Fox calms down a little and gets all fatherly and advisorly on me.

"Listen, kid," he says. "I'm here to help you. But I've been around long enough to know that you are down to about five minutes of your glorious fifteen. Screw with it and you will lose it. Don't be a fool. Let the real reporters do the reporting. You can't go anywhere, anyway. You should focus on your court date, not on trying to be a reporter. Ron Ruby knows what he is doing. You'll have your chance later."

"I'm not a kid, Sam," I say wearily. "Let me do my part here and you do yours. It will be the easiest sale of your life. At this point, *New Day* has nothing to lose."

"Don't be so naive, Annie…"

But this is not an argument I can lose. Sam doesn't need to know how I, how we, are going to do this, but when we get the information and the proof we need, he needs to know that it has to air on *New Day*. It's the only way to fully clear my name. My credibility was ruined on their air, and really, the only way to regain it is to return to the scene, prove I have absolutely nothing to hide, no agenda but the truth. But to do this, to get it past Max Meyer, we have to work with someone who knows the way the network game is played. Sam Fox knows the game. He also knows that sometimes to get someone to do something for you, you have to play hardball.

"I am getting off the phone now, Sam. When you get the tapes, you can make the call or not, but I am moving forward either way. It's your choice if you want to come along for the ride. But if you do, you can set the asking price, Sam. Get it on the air and you can even keep the change."

I hang up.

"Okay," I say to Karen and Mark, who are sitting on my now flowerless couch, Margarita curled up between them. "I think this will work."

And so it is planned. Karen will be the point person, the only one who will be able to reach us, and even so only indirectly. If Sam, if Max, if Ron Ruby have anything to say to us, they will have to go through her, because Mark and I, well, we're going off to figure out all of the devilish details.

27

The big difference between television journalism and print journalism should be that television is a visual medium. Unfortunately, that fact is often forgotten in the telling of stories, with producers and correspondents alike assuming the audience needs to be spoonfed the obvious at every turn, putting too many words into the story when pictures should really be enough. See video of a baby crawling and we will tell you that a baby is starting to crawl. See a blazing fire, and we will tell you a fire is blazing. But I think the audience is smarter than that. I think that if they were shown, say, the following sequence, they could figure it out:

A shot of me taking some lip gloss tubes out of my desk drawer and putting them in the side pocket of an overstuffed duffel bag.
Cut to a shot of Mark closing the hard plastic suitcase that protects a small video camera.
Cut to a car pulling up to my building in the middle of a dark, rainy night.

Cut to Karen unlocking the car doors and me and Mark piling inside.

Dissolve to the vehicle speeding off down the street.

Cut to car pulling away from the Montreal airport and then dissolve to video of me, hair newly blond, standing next to a man who looks like a Hasidic version of the very non-Jewish Mark Thurber, complete with long dark beard and exaggerated sideburns.

Tight zoom in to show a falsified passport, fake names and numbers.

Dissolve to clichéd image of an airplane flying off into thin air.

Cut to a television set, a well-coiffed man and a well-coiffed woman staring right at you. The woman is speaking.

"Good morning, Ken."

"Good morning to you, Faith," says Ken Klark, his teeth now almost iridescent. "What a show we have today."

Faith nods eagerly just as the video cuts to a single shot of Ken, square on.

Ken lists off the usual list of the day's stories…nothing too surprising. A movie star here, a low-fat recipe there.

Across the country, in homes, in offices, and yes, even in detention centers, an enviable eight point five ratings share of people are tuned in, waiting for Faith to do something deliciously dumb, waiting for a follow-up to the Kapner appearance a few days back.

Today, they will get one.

"Here it is come," Galina says to the other inmates sitting around her, staring intently at the chained-up TV. And then, looking just as surprised as he did when he first heard the news, Ken Klark prepares to announce to the world the juiciest story he has announced in a long time.

"But first," he says once his list of teasers and promos winds down, "a short while ago, ZBC News learned that just two and a half weeks before she is due to appear in court, our former producer Annabelle Kapner, out on bail for a host of charges including espionage, is missing. Authorities believe she may have left the country, skipping out on her five million dollar bond."

Sam Fox, watching the East Coast feed on his wall-size plasma television set at the foot of his large sleigh bed, screams so loudly his feral cry echoes across Hollywood Hills all the way to the beach. Local authorities immediately consider announcing a wild coyote alert.

Galina, on the other hand, just smiles that wide Slavic smile and, most likely, makes a mental note to send a thank-you card to her pal Stungun for the passport help. Never forget who your friends are, especially if you are still behind bars.

Ken Klark continues. "Ms. Kapner's lawyer, Ron Ruby, is here with us this morning to discuss this shocking turn of events." The camera viewfinder widens to reveal Ron Ruby sitting there opposite Ken, sitting, in fact, in the same chair Annie sat in when she clocked Faith a few days ago. "Good morning, Ron. Welcome back," he says, as if Ron were an alcoholic newly returned to the folds of AA.

Ron nods in acknowledgment but doesn't have a chance to mouth any pleasantries because Ken jumps right in with his first question—"What the hell is going on, Ron?"—the informality of which startles the attorney.

"Well, Ken," he says once he has regained his composure, "I can only tell you that this action of Ms. Kapner's was not taken under my advisement. Her court date is just weeks away and we have a lot of work to do. In fact, I had been planning to meet her for lunch later today."

Galina snorts.

"It is tomorrow already where she goes," she says, and the inmates around her (all of whom have been closely following the story) break into chortles of laughter and evocations of awe: "You go, girl!"

28

The very first story I ever produced for network air was about plastic poopy pickup bags. News you can use. A company had developed mitten-shaped plastic bags that you would put over your hand and then use to pick up your doggy's droppings in one simple, neat swoop. It was a cute piece told from the perspective of a dog named Igor. There were plenty of puppy point of view shots across the grass, some funny suggestive angles that showed "everything but" the action in question, numerous snouts and tongues pushed directly up against the camera lens. I'm not complaining. It was fun to do and the response was good and I will never forget the rush I had when I saw it on air, broadcast to millions.

But the thing is, that became my foundation to work from—fun narratives, wagging tales. In fact, I can't recall a single time since graduate school when I had to do any real reporting, when I was in a position to ask really hard questions or find some unfindable facts.

I am in that position now.

But it isn't like I haven't learned anything at all in my years in television; I have learned, for example, that to tell a story properly, to tell it with the most dramatic impact and emotional charge, it is often a good thing not to tell it straight. Just like a good mystery novel or a thriller film, it is often best to leave gaps unresolved and questions unanswered until the bitter end, take the linear out of the equation. Start the story with, say, the fact that the little boy is alive. That point alone hints to the audience that something went terribly wrong, or why would we be reporting such innocuous trivia?

So, let me just say this: a kiss is not a kiss when a gun was just pointed at your head.

Nice tease, right?

Now let me back up. Back to a time when Fardistan, or the country that once was Fardistan, was just a tiny piece of land at the southern edge of the Soviet Empire. A piece that would have been disposable—once Boris Yeltsin got into the habit of climbing on tanks, and the union that had been held together with the glue of terror had finally splintered apart—had it not been for the fact that it sat on top of a lot of oil. Back to the end of the USSR, babe. Take away the iron-fisted authority of the Kremlin and it was a free-for-all. Some wanted the Russians back. Some didn't. Years passed. Things got ugly. Religious fundamentalism took hold. CIA spooks were crawling under every rock. The U.S. tried to develop "Democracy," big D. Things got uglier. Wars broke out; neighbors turned on each other.

Long story short, half the population (mostly the women and children) fled over the mountains to a neighboring and moderately tolerant republic. That is where you will now find vast tent cities, temporary shelters that have been housing families for decades. And that is where I now find myself. More specifically, it is where I now find myself with a very large gun pointed at me.

This sort of thing never happened to me when I was reporting on diet trends and spelling bee championships.

Shit.

I repeat. There is a gun pointed right at me.

Without moving, I try to shoot a questioning look at Mark, hoping maybe he'll have a brilliant idea. After all, he and Karen were basically the ones who got me into this part of this predicament in the first place.

"?"

"?"

Then Mark holds up a finger. Wait a second. He pulls out his now tattered Fardish-English phrase book, holding it up for the gunman to see, gesturing madly for him to give us a moment.

The man at the safer end of the barrel says something indecipherable to his comrade beside him and puts down the gun.

God, oh God, oh God, please let Mark pull this off.

He frantically flips through the pages (while sweat from both the oppressive heat and the intense stress is beading on his forehead), trying to find the right thing to say. But, seriously, what is the chance that a twenty-year-old tourist phrase book would have a sentence like "please don't kill us" right next to fundamentals such as "I am hungry" or "do you speak English?"

Finally, after what seems like hours but is probably only a few seconds, Mark looks up and points to a line in the text, holding it out for the gunman to read.

"*Cow,*" Mark says hopefully, waiting for a response. He does have a way with words.

The gunman laughs and says, *"Cow"* back. Then he takes the book and shows it to his coworker. They turn the pages and have a good laugh, repeating English words like *car* and *hamburger* and *cat*.

He hands the book back to Mark and motions for us to follow him inside.

"What was the phrase you showed them?" I whisper as we enter the cool foyer of what happens to be the only solid structure in town.

Mark opens the book again and shows me the line on the page: "I have money."

This is how we manage to get into the home of the self-declared president of the displaced republic, the man who, it is said, is now prospering from a bumper year for poppy crops, but who once prospered as an informant to none other than America's very own CIA, and, our sources (actually, one obsessive "cow" caller if you want to be specific about it) now tell us, more directly from one Douglas Lenrup, aka Douglas Purnell. His name is Alkalied Alfiedazied, and, we have been learning the hard way, you kind of have to go through him if you want to talk to anyone in this ramshackle place.

The gunman leads us into a cool, dark sitting room that is covered floor-to-ceiling with lush Persian carpets in shades of red and green. Then, signaling for us to wait, he leaves us alone with his friend for a moment.

Which is when Mark decides would be a perfectly acceptable opportunity to try to get romantic on me for the first time since I interrupted the moment in my kitchen.

"I know this is completely insane, Annie," he says, ignoring our chaperone and taking my hand, pulling me closer, "but I am so glad we are here."

Mark, I should mention, doesn't smell all that great right now. I probably don't, either. We've been traveling for three days straight to get to where we are, sleeping on whatever planes, trains and buses we were able to catch. My au courant (and yes, still blond) hairdo looks more like a helmet, and at this point Mark could easily be mistaken for Moses after he just crossed the desert. I am still very much confused about my romantic feelings for him (like if I deserve to have any, for starters, and if I do, can I handle them), and the fact that neither of us has had a chance to brush our teeth hasn't been helping the matter. But having a gun pointed at your head does something to your adrenaline.

I see Mark leaning in toward me and I close my eyes. His lips, dry and slightly chapped from all the travel, gently brush against mine. I pull back a moment and then kind of decide to stop questioning things, thinking maybe a kiss could jump-start my emotional confidence, so I part my own (also dry) lips a tiny bit and I am sure that things would keep progressing in this slow, tentative way, except that—

"Hello!"

—it is very bad timing.

"Mark! Annabelle!" says a tall, bearded and oddly familiar looking man who emerges from the depth of the dark, damp house to greet us. "Please excuse the rude welcome."

His accent is almost indecipherable, but it is recognizable. American, Eastern, a slight touch of that very recognizable Ivy League nasality. As he continues talking, seemingly oblivious to the attempted romantic activity he walked in on, I have a good hunch who he is. On a couple of levels.

"It was just a precaution," he says, and then, looking right at me (with a little glint in his eye) he tells me he knew from the beginning that I had it in me, that while he never really thought everything would unravel as much as it has, it was all going to work out in the end. Sorry about the whole jail thing."

"Are you——?" I start to say.

"Alfiedazied? No. I am his press secretary. Did I forget to tell you that? Oh, well." He stretches out a large, callused hand and vigorously shakes my limp one. "John Sage. I never really thought it would all come to this, but I am pleased to see you here."

"You're an American?" I knew he wasn't Alfiedazied, but I didn't expect that the caller was one of us. And now that I am looking at him, I realize he is more familiar than I thought. He looks like someone I once knew.

"I was born there. Been here on and off since the war."

"What did you——?"

"I covered it for one of the networks."

"Wait a second. Mitchell? Are you John Mitchell?" I know him. I am sure of it. He's the producer who taught me how to pad my expense reports, the one who once expensed a cow.

He smiles, baring those very poorly cared for crooked teeth I remember so well. "John Mitchell Sage, if you really want to get down to it," he says. "I never use Sage back home. Too fruity. But Mitchell is hard for the Fards to pronounce, the "tch" part. Nice to see you again, Annie." He winks at me.

Mark looks from Mitchell to me and back again. "You know this guy?"

"I used to work for him, sort of," I say, still baffled by this revelation. "I mean, he was a producer at *Newsline* when I interned there."

I turn back to Mitchell. "I still don't get it. So you're Mr. Sage? From Media-Aid? You're the cow call…?"

"Annie, you seemed to be catching on, really. Don't slip up now."

John Mitchell always did have a way of interrupting me. He gestures for us to follow him into the house, and I scurry behind with a thousand things to ask.

"But I…?"

"Don't worry, don't worry." He waves his hand, suggesting there will be time for questions later. "I am sorry we don't have lunch quite ready," he says, changing the subject before I can start it. "We didn't expect you so soon."

"We would have phoned first," I say, now that I am sure it is him; that this large hairy man, my former mentor of sorts, is the caller. "But we didn't have your number."

He laughs a hearty Santalike laugh.

"Make yourselves comfortable. I am going to go talk to the chef," Mitchell says once we arrive in what looks like an American living room except for all of the rugs scattered about the walls and floor. There is a plush velour sofa, two overstuffed armchairs and a large coffee table. There is even a large-screen, satellite TV (currently tuned to CNN). "As a great reporter once told me," he says as he is walking out the door, "you can't do journalism on an empty stomach."

Mark and I glance at each other, both amused and confused and, truth be told, a little excited. We sit down on a carpet-covered couch and Mark picks up the remote that is sitting next to the hookah to the side of it.

"Oh," Mitchell shouts from the hallway, "ZBC is on channel 54. Your program is on in an hour."

* * *

"Faith! You're on!"

Tom Tatcher is in the control room, shouting into the thin microphone that is supposed to be a direct line to Faith Heide's ear. Faith, however, is staring intently at the newspaper copy in front of her, yet another dismissive slap in her face, yet another insult to bear.

"Faith! You're live!"

Finally, she looks up. Uh-oh. She gently touches her hair and smiles at the camera. "Good morning," she says. "We are back...."

Carl Van Dunt, senior supervising producer, just shakes his head and grimaces as he watches from behind Tom Tatcher. At this point, it is hard to do pretty much anything other than laugh or cry.

"Camera *two*, Faith!" the director is shouting, implying that she is looking at the wrong lens with the wrong teleprompter, about to launch into the wrong segment.

"Oh, uh..." Finally, she looks at the correct camera and reads from the proper prompter. "With us this morning to discuss his latest role..." But her mind is obviously elsewhere. Most likely, like everyone else's at the show, it is on the latest dispatch from one Mr. Alexander Churn.

The *New York Spectator*
Up, Up, And Away!
New Day Ratings ROSE to the Top—But from the Top
There Was Only One Way to Go
By Alexander Churn
New York Spectator Media Critic

I love my job. I really do. As the media critic for an insider rag, I am being paid to sit back, watch mind-numbingly bad

TV, and analyze why oh why the rest of the country is doing the same. Normally, I can do it in my sleep. But today my woes are large. After plumbing the depths of Freud, Jung, Nietzsche and the Dante Code, I can't for the life of me figure out why anyone in their right mind is still watching *New Day USA,* although it seems, looking at last week's numbers, some people, although increasingly less and less, still are. The much hyped appearance of once prodigal producer Annabelle Kapner made a big splash the other week, as did the delicious catfight between her and my favorite heap of unethical instability, Faith Has Been, er, I mean Faith Heide.

But now that it seems Ms. Kapner has skipped town (and bail) along with that abetting hottie Mark Thurber, taking with them the possibility of any imminent reappearance on the program, the show that once ruled the morning has been unable to maintain its position at the helm. How could it? With Annabelle Kapner unlikely to reappear for another catfight on the couch, it makes sense that the viewers are starting to turn the dial to the networks that have no conflicts with this story and at least have watchable talent.

Seriously, without Annabelle Kapner in her pocket, what the heck is Faith Has Been, I mean Faith Heide, still doing on set? Doesn't Corpcom CEO Max Meyer see what a ratings drain she is oh so quickly becoming? Or did that unscrupulous agent Sam Fox actually get her such an ironclad contract this time around that it would take nothing short of an act of God to remove her from that anchor chair?

So, *New Day* and Corpcom execs, if you are reading this co-

lumn (and you probably are, because everyone in the in-
dustry does), here's my three cents worth of advice:
Cover your asses. It's called Mea Culpa, babies, and it has
your names all over it. Stop cowering behind your monitors
and slumping in your seats at Michael's. Just tell it like it is.
Tell us, once and for all, how you got into this mess to begin
with. Lay it on the line. "Here's why we pushed the Cosmetic
Relief story, here's what we knew, here's what we didn't."
Tell us why you assigned the damn cesspool of a story to Ms.
Kapner in the first place. Tell us what Faith really did as far
her reporting went. Tell us why Corpcom invested and why
it pulled out. Yes, it will all smell like you know what. But
seriously, fellows (and Faith), it's the only way we are going
to respect you in the morning.

"Oh, please," says Max Meyer, trying to act very nonchalant as
he puts down the paper and takes another bite of the thirty dollar
burger he is eating.

"Churn might have a point, Max," says Carl Van Dunt, who has
now joined Meyer at Michael's Restaurant for a so-called power
lunch. Carl might not do a lot of work, but he clearly knows how,
and with whom, to break bread.

"A point? The only point this know-it-all queen has is the one
in his pants. It must be a large one. I mean, who does he think he
is, saying that—"

"Max, calm down." Carl signals to the waiter approaching to
take his order that he should wait a minute. "Now, come on. There
is no denying that our ratings are a problem. A huge problem. All
I am suggesting is that maybe we consider some of what he's

saying while we try to figure out how to dig ourselves out of this hole."

Max takes another bite of his burger, gently pats his lips with the linen napkin and stands up.

"Carl," he says, "we pay you a lot of money. Maybe it is time you actually proved your worth. So why don't you figure out a way to fix this problem yourself instead of just parroting the false wisdom of some pseudo reporter who just happens to be able to turn a phrase?"

Carl, not usually at a loss for words, doesn't say anything back.

29

There was an old correspondent I knew, a woman who had been in the field since my mother was in diapers. They put this reporter out to pasture when her jowls started to quiver, naming her "special correspondent" and giving her an even bigger salary and a lifetime appointment, but never ever letting her back on the air. It was a shame, really; of all the television journalists out there, she was the one who could work the medium the best. Because, done right, it is a lot more complicated than turning on the camera and taking out a pen and a piece of paper. You have to know how to use the pictures your shooter got for you, how to write them up and get them to speak for themselves. These days, you see a lot of what we call "wallpaper"—shots plastered over the screen to bridge the gap between the sound bites and the stand-ups, but that in and of themselves don't add much to the story. But I know that right now, more than ever, every single shot I lay down, every edit I make has to speak volumes. In two minutes or less, it has to grab the audience, make them see and understand the whole truth and urgency of the matter. And I have only two weeks to do it.

"How about this?" says Mark, hovering over me as I struggle to figure out how to make an L-cut on our MacBook's editing program. He leans forward and hits the shift key, cuing the video back a few frames.

"Let's try it," I say, and hit Play.

The image shows three little girls with bandages over their mouths. They were the bunnies for the lip gloss testing; they were the ones whose lips bore the scars so that little American girls wouldn't have to. Underneath the video, a man begins to speak.

"They are the victims of an old CIA project that spun out of control," he says. And then his face, John Mitchell's face, shows up on the screen. "And some of the most powerful people in America have profited from this pain."

"Mark," I say. "I think you have a talent for this stuff."

He smiles. "Pacing. It's like writing a speech. It's all about pacing. Such as here…" He shuttles forward to another part of the tape. "I think this is where we need to put the part about Hacker's connection to Max Meyer. Right after the part about Meyer's old chemical company trying to find some commercial use for the venom, the whole thing about the truth serum?"

"What about this bite?" I say, taking the mouse and clicking on a small picture of an old, weathered man. Once I hit it, he starts talking, telling us in thickly accented English how the venom was applied and how, once applied, it had two main side effects: in large doses it worked as a truth serum; in smaller doses, it was generally safe but could make lips swell up for hours at a time. The wrong amount, though, could be dangerous.

"Don't you think that should go a little later?" says Mark.

I think about it a moment and, you know what? He's right. "But don't forget that photo we found in Alfiedazied's files. Maybe that could work," I say. "Over here."

I click on a small icon to pull up an old weathered photograph, now digitized. The resolution is so good you can see every detail. It must be about forty or fifty years old.

"Perfect," says Mark. "Let's lay it in."

The show ends at nine and the first big meeting of the day is at ten, which gives Tom Tatcher an hour to zip through the tapes of all the morning's broadcasts, time to study the competition to see what he should try to steal, what weaknesses he can attack. Most of the staff, the staffers who don't have segments airing that particular day, won't arrive until one minute to, so it's quiet. This is usually Tom's favorite time of day. No one calling, no one knocking. Just him, some monitors and a remote. But lately, there is nothing favorite about it. He just closes his door and puts his head down on his enormous (but possibly temporary) desk.

All of the other morning programs have been covering the Kapner disappearance like gangbusters, but not *New Day*. Right after Annie fell off the face of the earth and Alexander Churn and friends went on yet another rampage about it, Max Meyer declared that they would distance themselves from the horror show once and for all. There was nothing else they could do, he said. The world would eventually get enraptured by another story and the focus would shift. Faith would get her groove back and everything would be fine. Audiences are fickle. Give it time.

But time is not on Tom Tatcher's side. At this rate, there is no way that the ratings are going to improve on his watch. It is way too late and it simply isn't working. Just look at the last week of shows. Not talking about Annie was like not talking about a feral white rhino sitting at your kitchen table. Churn's prophecy of another tailspin is coming true; Tom Tatcher has a failing show with a failing anchor who is tethered to a story that has disappeared.

He fumbles through his top drawer for an aspirin, finds one, takes it and then puts his head back down.

Tom knows (he's been trying to convince Max; he's been trying to convince everyone in the front office) that they've got it wrong. He believes that Alexander Churn might have it right. Tom is trying to convince the front office that since they, *New Day,* have wasted everything on this Kapner cosmetics thing—first to promote it, then to hide from it, then to try to profit from it all over again, the only hope of rebuilding the show's (and his) cred-ibility and reputation rests on proving that they, and yes, Faith, could get back on top of this Glossgate story once and for all, the story that they pushed forward for all the wrong reasons and then let get away. But he knows that to do that would take an act of God.

"Jesus," he says aloud but to himself, "I am as desperate as Faith."

Lucky for Tom, sometimes acts of God (or at least of incredibly fortunate coincidence) really do fall from the sky (or at least out of the Ethernet).

Of course, when his phone rings and he sees on the illuminated caller ID that it is Max Meyer's office on the line, that's probably not what he is thinking. He is probably thinking that since Meyer is calling his private line, not going through the secretary, Tom should start polishing his résumé again, metaphorically speaking. At this level, no one really needs a résumé anymore.

"Fuck," he mutters before hitting the speakerphone button, "this can't be good."

30

When I was a little girl, I had some big aspirations for my life: to dance at Lincoln Center, to argue a case before the Supreme Court, to find the cure for cancer. When I got older and decided to become a journalist, my aspirations took a while to dim. Initially, I planned on winning Emmys, interviewing presidents—big stuff. But as active as my imagination might have been, never in my wildest dreams would I have wound up here, in this tangle of absurd and strange predicaments:

- I have skipped out on five million dollars bail, my court date is in one week and there are probably international bounty hunters out for my head.
- I am sitting next to a guy who until recently was one of the most respected men in Washington, but who has destroyed his career so that he, in turn, could sit next to me.
- We are here, in this remote refugee camp at the foot of the Vlasic Mountains, because he and I believe we will be able to

report a story the likes of which will not only blow the world away, it will clear my name and make a new one for him.

• I am, for the first time in my life, smoking tobacco out of a hookah, passing the pipe to a different man who, frustrated by its increasing limitations, gave up on journalism a long time ago because he believed he would have more value trying to spin stories from the other side—the other side in his case being the impoverished, homeless nation of Fardistan. Not that he is so innocent. John Mitchell openly supports (and often indulges in the fruits of) poppy farming.

Weird, right?

"Hey," Mitchell says, taking a deep draw on one of the pipes attached to the hookah, causing the water to bubble loudly at the base. "When the Americans left, it's not like they gave the Fards any other means of making a living." He leans back into a large pillow and strokes his beard. I look to Mark to argue this point, but he is actually nodding in agreement.

"What about all of those aid programs—the push to get girls into school, the democracy-building initiatives?" I say, because those are truthfully the only things I actually remember reading about. "Didn't we throw millions of dollars this way?"

"Yeah. And people like Douglas Purnell, Lenrup, whatever you want to call him, were the middlemen."

"Man, what a character, huh?" says Mark, taking his turn at the pipe.

"Mmm," I say. Mitchell told us it was a combination of cinnamon and cloves, but while I haven't inhaled much of anything in my life, I'm beginning to have some suspicions. I lean back and slouch down, my head somehow feeling light and heavy at the same time. "Are you sure this is just tobacco and spices?"

"Well," says Mitchell, taking another drag, "there might be some hash left over in the pipe. Just a little. But really, Annie, it's good for you. You're a nervous wreck. Always were."

"You're kidding, right?"

"Nope. But seriously, you could use it. Take another hit." Mitchell holds one of the pipes up to my face.

I cross my arms, refusing to cooperate. "For God's sake, John," I say, "sorry if I seem a little tense. Sorry if the fact that my entire life is on the line right now isn't making me mellow."

Okay, maybe he has a point.

I uncross my arms and grab the pipe back. "Fine," I say, taking a deep, long draw. It makes me cough. Hard. Then I take another hit.

I can see Mark eyeballing Mitchell, as if searching for a way to gauge how to respond to me. He's been seeking a lot of direction from Mitchell since we got here. They are even starting to look alike, with the long scraggily beards, the billowy native shirts, the I-wanna-look-like-a-sheep-herder chic. I guess I understand it. I mean, I had a whole year of graduate school and ten years in the field to learn how to do this, how to put a story together using the images on videotape. But there is something slightly too sycophantic about the way Mark hangs on Mitchell's every word. It's irritating.

"I am feeling rather confident that this will all pan out well for you, Annie," says Mitchell.

"Yeah," says Mark, "I still think this is going to work."

I look at Mark, mildly disgusted. How can he possibly be so positive?

"Are you incapable of thinking for yourself?" I say, not so nicely.

"Annie…" Mark tries to interrupt.

"Seriously, if John says 'jump!' will you—"

"Annie, I think you need to put the pipe down." Mark leans over and tries to take it away from me, but I petulantly pull it back and inhale some more. He sits back and shakes his head. "Fine, Annie," he says. "Smoke away. But I think we both know that it isn't me you are mad at."

"Do we now? So, tell me who it is," I say, blowing out some smoke. "I'm all ears." In truth, it feels really gross, all this smoke surrounding me and filling me up, but I like this bad-girl vibe it is giving me.

"Me, too," says Mitchell, leaning back against the wall, placing his hands behind his head and stretching out and crossing his legs.

Mark ignores Mitchell and takes a deep breath. "Annie," he says in a much gentler tone. "Come on. This isn't you speaking. You do this. You freak out and then you turn on me and…" He stops midsentence.

Fuck. He's right. I am doing it again. I am pathetic. God, I totally don't deserve Mark, not his friendship, not his partnership, and certainly not his romantic inclinations. Just look at me. I've been wearing the same old gray tunic and worn-out khakis for weeks now, I haven't washed my hair in days and, worse, I've become a complete bitch. I look over at Mitchell, appearing all smug and full of himself against the wall, and I realize that I might have gotten better at getting angry, but I haven't figured out how to focus it. I have no reason to be angry with Mark at all.

My cheeks are burning hotter than this stupid pipe I am holding. God, I can be so dumb sometimes.

"Mark," I say. "I am so sorry." I put the pipe down and take his hand. "You're totally right." I giggle nervously. "I'm like a third grade boy who pulls the hair of a girl he likes."

Mark smiles and our eyes lock for a quiet, happy moment.

We laugh. I squeeze his hand and tell him again that I am sorry.

Then he turns to Mitchell. "Would you mind leaving the room for a minute?" he asks.

Mitchell snorts. "Hell no, I'm not going anywhere. I wouldn't miss this for the world."

I can see Mark's teeth grinding a little. He looks directly at me. "This is so not how I wanted this moment to be."

I bite my lower lip.

Mark just looks down at his feet and says, "Never mind."

And seeing him look so sad and frustrated and, well, kind of dejected, really pisses me off. In fact, I am furious. For both of us. I mean, we've been running around this shitty hellhole, interviewing girls with missing lips, talking to half-senile old men about their ancient connections to espionage, testing venomous truth serum, dodging guns (well, once anyway) and sleeping in tents. All because this asshole Mitchell sent me on a "tale spin" that not only wound up landing me in jail, but now has the potential to completely ruin my life as well as Mark's if we can't get this story out and accurate before I have to show up for court, before all the government lawyers do everything they can do to silence any information I might be able to eke out. I have less than one week to finish reporting this story, to find Douglas Purnell and to somehow have Sam Fox convince the network suits that they should air this crap on TV. And now Mitchell's gotten me stoned, and then ruined this chance of a real, sincere kiss?

I knock over the hookah, spilling hot dirty water all over the rug, and stand up.

"What the fuck do you want from me, John?" I say to Mitchell, kicking one of his feet. "You think you are so freaking high and mighty, that you are some truth-sayer. That's great. But why the hell did you need to bring me into this? I never said I was a great reporter. I never promised you jack shit. You are the one who was pushing this whole fucking agenda. Why don't you do your own fucking reporting? This is bullshit."

Holy cow.

But if I am shocked at my own outburst, the two of them are even more so.

I stand there, waiting for a response.

Finally Mitchell says, very slowly and calmly, that he wasn't the one who assigned me the story, but I was the one who got it, so it was my responsibility to tell it right.

"Why don't you just tell it yourself?" I snap.

"Who is going to listen to me, Annie? The only way anyone is going to listen to anything is if it is on TV, and believe me, I knew it would take a hell of a lot of work to get anyone to put this on TV anytime soon."

"What made you think I could get it there?" I am standing over him like a dominatrix—arms crossed over my chest, stance wide.

"There is a reason Carl picked you to do the assignment."

"Carl?" My arms fall to my sides.

"He thought you had it in you not to just drop the story. He said that with a little push you might actually be curious enough to try to pursue it. And he thought that if you did, he might be in a position to get it on the air."

I am still a bit in shock. "Carl?"

"Yes. Carl," he says. "I know him from back when. We really

didn't expect things to unfold as they have. We certainly didn't expect that you would get tangled up with him." He points at Mark, who is looking as bewildered as I feel. "But quite honestly, now that you are famous, this story has the best chance yet of being heard."

I sit back down. I don't need truth serum to know that he's right.

"Give me that," I say, motioning to Mark to pass me a pipe. He does so reluctantly and I take another big drag.

"Let me ask you something, John," I say once I have calmed down some more. "Why do you even care? I know, you are on some great journalistic crusade, but come on."

He reaches under the white poncho-like garb he is wearing and pulls something out of an inside pocket.

"Because," he says, passing a photo over to me, "these are my granddaughters."

The two girls in the picture have large smiles and lively eyes and they look incredibly familiar.

"Fida and Lida?" I say, and he silently nods.

Which is when it really hits me. I am a total ass. I've been given the opportunity of a lifetime to tell the story of my lifetime, with the nicest guy in my lifetime, and I am, as Ron Ruby might say, trying to break a gift horse's teeth.

I look over at Mark. I look over at John.

I don't say anything, but with lips that are unscarred and healthy, I mouth, "Thank you."

31

The marketplace is exerting a far more dangerous influence on what gets on and what doesn't get on television news programming these days than any...fear of political repercussions or consequences.

—Ted Koppel

"Over my dead body will this make air!"

Max Meyer is pacing the length of his Corpcom office, spitting and cursing, with steam practically coming out his ears. The office is fifty-five stories above midtown Manhattan. There are windows on three sides. On the fourth side there is a wall-size plasma television screen, which is usually cued 24/7 to whatever is airing on his network. Right now, however, there is an oversize grainy image from a stilled videotape. An extreme closeup on a set of extremely scarred lips—bloody, cracked, half-missing lips that, across this screen, now measure about fifteen feet. It is pretty hard to look at, but Tom Tatcher and Sam Fox are staring at it square on.

"This is your brilliant plan, Sam? This is why you flew on the red-eye? To try to get me to buy the rights to the very images that could completely destroy me? Are you fucking insane?"

Sam Fox wipes some spit off his cheek, but doesn't respond.

Tom, still comparatively dry, desperately tries to calm Max down a notch.

"Max, think about it a moment. Yes, it will look bad for us if we air this. It will look like we should have known about the testing when Corpcom bought Vanity. But it will look even worse if we don't air it," he says, knowing that isn't argument enough. But he knows what might be.

"Guaranteed," he adds with a meek but hopeful grimace, "it would be a ratings hit."

"For Christ's sake," Max says, throwing the disk's clear plastic cover across the room, hitting the wall and startling both other men in the process. "Don't you fucking get it?" Max is speaking in decibels that would upset a teenager's mother. "It's bad enough that we invested in this goddamn lip gloss to begin with, that we actually profited from it. No one will believe us if we say we thought they were testing on little bunnies, not babies. Which is true. But even if we said that, the animal rights crazies would have a field day. Shit. Do we really need to point out how insidious it was? Who ever heard of some fucking lip gloss being used as an interrogation technique? Jesus."

"That's not exactly—"

"And what the fuck," says Max, ignoring Tom's protestations. "How do we even know what she is saying is true?"

Tom and Sam look at each other, silently daring the other to speak up first. Finally, Tom realizes he has no choice.

"If we don't air it, Max, someone else will. You can be sure of it."

At which point Sam Fox interjects, "No question there."

"Sam, are you trying to ruin us?" Max starts spitting again. "You know perfectly well this isn't morning show material. We can't show this over Cheerios."

"But, Max," Tom Tatcher begins. "We have an obligation as journalists—"

"Air that shit, Tatcher, and you can go beg for a job in market 207. That's right, if you're lucky, you can go freeze your ass off in fucking Juneau."

And while that is a pretty clear signal that the meeting is over, it certainly doesn't seem like an act of God. Not yet, anyway. But as they say in TV land, stay tuned.

32

A journalist is a reporter out of a job.

—Mark Twain

Unlike the convention center in Sweetwater, Texas, these snake pits do not come equipped with protective gear for the visitors to don. There aren't really even pits. It is just a large room, cement on all sides, with hundreds of black, shiny snakes slithering around, across the floor, up the pipes that run along the walls, dangling from the rusty light fixtures above. The only thing keeping us apart from this mad army of Fardish stiletto vipers is a thin glass window in the middle of the heavy entrance door.

"Do we really need this shot?" I say, pointing at the glass. Mark grins at me, because of course we do. It is essential to the story.

"Well, I guess if they bite me, I won't need to worry about the court date. That's something."

We tuck our pant legs into our boots and I open the door. Mark holds the camera up to his eye and hits Record.

* * *

"Holy cow!"

Tom Tatcher looks away from the video of the mound of glossy black snakes and hits the pause button. He turns toward the man standing at the threshold of his office.

"Hey, Carl," he says, and then looks back at the screen. "Take a look at this, would you. And shut the door."

Carl steps in with a satisfied smirk stretching across his face. Tom Tatcher rarely defers to him for advice or opinion. It was pretty clear to everyone that Tatcher barely tolerated Carl's presence at his broadcast, but knew he had to coddle this man who, while once upon a time might have been something, currently was better known for taking up oxygen than for adding anything positive or constructive to the editorial decisions about running the show. And Carl, for his part, never failed to get a dismissive word in edgewise that Tatcher, two decades his junior, was too young to know anything about television news. "He wouldn't know a real news story if it hit him in the face," Carl liked to say to just about anyone who would listen.

So it is an extraordinary event that Tom has called Carl into his office for a confidential consultation, but these are extraordinary times. Besides, at this point neither of them has much to lose. As Tom told Carl on the phone when he summoned him over, he needs a confidant, and he needs someone with enough venerability that Max Meyer might be willing to bend an ear. And Carl, well, no one has to say it but everyone knows that with young guns like Tom around, he's on his way out, anyway. He's been on his way out for a long, long time.

"Whatcha got there?" Carl says, taking a seat on the leather couch near Tom's desk, first tugging up his pant legs so they won't pull when he sits down. But he definitely knows. At this point he should know better than anyone at the network what that is on the screen.

"Honestly, Carl? It's not shot very well, but this is the best piece of video journalism I've seen in a long, long time."

Carl bites his tongue and focuses on the screen as Tom shuttles the disk to the top and once again hits Play.

Two minutes later Tom looks at Carl. "I've got two other reports that are just as good. Just as disturbing," he says.

Carl nods but waits for Tom to continue, which he does.

"But, for obvious reasons, if I air them, I'll lose my job…and probably any hope of ever getting another one."

Carl, looking like an understanding physician pondering a diagnosis, bites his lower lip and says, "hmm."

"What?"

"You think they might show up somewhere else if we don't air them first?"

"Max paid Sam Fox off—five millions dollars for exclusive rights. Anyone else airs them, Corpcom will sue."

"Sam Fox owns the rights? He can do that?"

"Annie's a bit too far away to fight that fight, I guess. And what's she gonna do? Sue *him*? She isn't even going to make her own day in court. She can't set up another one. My gut? Max and Sam are just buying time. Once Annie's case begins, this can all be subpoenaed, and with all the lawyers involved, it will probably never see the light of day."

"What about Sam's bail money?"

"Clearly, Max took care of that."

"Right." Carl thinks about this a moment, and then, in the way the older generation does, he gets excited for a second with his very modern thought. "She could always post the video on the Internet."

This doesn't impress Tom.

"She could," he says wearily. "But if she really wants to credibly state her case and clear her name, she needs network airtime. *New Day* airtime. Besides, if we want to gain back any of our lost credibility ourselves, we have to air it."

"If you want it back, you mean."

"You want it, too, Carl. You know it."

The two men sit silently, both staring at the image stilled at the end of the tape: Annie, standing in front of what appears to be a makeshift beauty parlor, complete with cheesy photographs of excessively laminated fingernails on the wall, and a row of women, faces covered but heads under drying lamps to set their curls.

Tom turns the monitor off.

"Crazy story, huh?" says Carl.

"Do you believe it? I mean, if this is true…"

Carl stands up and walks over to Tom's desk, putting his hands flat on the surface and leaning forward to emphasize his point. "It's true, Tom. I'm sure it is. All of the sources she has are completely reliable."

Tom looks at him. "How do you know that?"

Carl closes his eyes a moment and gently bobs his head, the way someone might when recalling fond memories, savoring thoughts of old times. "God," he says, not really to Tom but to, well, God or something, "remember those days? When we could spend months, even years, investigating a story? When we could spend all the money we needed and travel to the ends of the earth to get to the bottom of it?"

Tom looks at him with a get-to-the-point type of expression, but since Carl's eyes are still closed it probably doesn't register.

"I remember once," Carl continues, "we were reporting on the conflict along the Zapistan-Nardal border. Remember that story? The transfer of the nuclear material to the CIA-funded paramilitary units, how the Nardalize found out and were threatening all sorts of crap against the United States?" He opens his eyes and stares at Tom, who doesn't look as if he is registering anything.

"Anyway," says Carl, now with a slight touch of disdain mixed in with the nostalgia, "back in the day, back in the conflict zones, there were always a few other journalists you knew you could count on, who would share information, even if they worked for a competing network or paper. What mattered was getting the story, getting the true story. I mean, sure, we were competing with each other, but at the end of the day we were fighting the same fight."

Tom is now looking rather bewildered—as if he's wondering what the hell Carl is getting at and is impatient for him to get to the point.

"Look," says Carl, standing up and grabbing the remote control so he can shuttle to a certain shot on the tape, which he does. "See this guy? His name is John Mitchell Sage. I haven't seen him in years, but I would trust him with my life."

"Are you still in touch with him?"

"Let's just say that he's in touch with me." Carl looks over at Tom. "The information is good," he says, with more conviction than he has said anything in years.

And that appears to register.

"We're going to put it on, aren't we?" says Tom, as if he is not the one in charge. As if, because it has in fact happened, the ghost of the old newsman in Carl has emerged and he is speaking the gospel truth.

"That depends, Tom." Carl crosses his arms. He looks over at the wall of plaques and awards and ribbons, at all of Tom's photographs and degrees. He has a wall just like it a few doors down. "Are we journalists or are we businessmen? Should we be loyal to ourselves or to Max Meyer?"

And Tom, probably realizing that there really can only be one correct answer to this question if he has any intention of ever looking at himself in the mirror again, probably making a mental note that he has enough in his checking account to cover his mortgage for the next few months, and that if he sells his car it can stretch out a bit further, sighs a deep, audible sigh.

"Okay," he says. "Let's do it."

33

When a dog bites a man, that is not news. But when a man bites a dog, that is news.

—Charles A. Dana

"Thirty seconds to air!" The stage manager skips over the wires strewn about the floor and, as she does every morning, jumps behind the row of semirobotic cameras.

A frail makeup artist rushes forward with her powder puff, Ken Klark tugs at the bottom of his blazer, Faith Heide checks her teeth for a lipstick smudge. To the rest of the staff, there is nothing unusual about this morning. The bookers are hovering over their guests in the green room, Franklin is offering up cups of joe. The director, with the show rundown ready on the screen in front of him, counts down from the control room, cuing to everyone on set and off that the show is about to begin.

"Three! Two!"

On the unspoken count of "One," the stage manager mimes a

gunshot at Klark, who smiles and leans forward slightly, waiting a beat for the zooming camera lens to settle on him.

"Good morning, everyone! It's a New Day, USA!" he says, reading off the teleprompter. "Today is August 3rd, and this is ZBC News. I'm Ken Klark."

As mornings go, neither Tom Tatcher nor Carl Van Dunt could consider this a good one. They know, and only they know, that what will happen in exactly fourteen minutes and thirty seconds will most likely cost them their jobs. They had put it off for a few days, working out the details of how to slide it in, planning the response, adjusting their personal assets. The news industry has been very good to them, and at the end of the day (or in the beginning, in this case), it is their turn to be good to the industry, cost them what it will.

The camera pans across the screaming crowds gathered in front of the plaza outside the studio, their placards waving, sending love to Mom and birthday greetings to Aunt Betty in Kalamazoo.

If it were to swoop up over the trees of Central Park, all lush and green from the damp summer, turning a sharp right and landing above Park Avenue, and zoom into an open bedroom window, it would find there, with eyeshades doubling as a hair band and thousand-count sheets doubling as a robe, Stacia Meyer, fourth wife of one Max Meyer, CEO of Corpcom. She picks up the remote from her bed stand and turns on the TV. Max walks into the room, fresh from his workout in their adjacent private gym, scratches the white hairs on his chest, gives Stacia a quick pat on her thigh and then heads off to take a shower. The camera might then follow Max into the opulent bathroom, watch him turn on the taps located at the foot of the marble tub.

And then, as if bored or huffy, the lens might spin off in another direction. It might sail back out, fast, fast, across the park, across the river, two hundred miles down Interstate 95, checking in briefly, no more than three seconds, with the inmates who are gathered around the television set in the recreation room of the detention center in Alexandria, Virginia, before it zips out and east, across the ocean, across mountains and lakes and dams, finally slowing down as it approaches a tent city, and then zooming into the one cement structure for miles around, one with satellite dishes breaking up its otherwise straight, harsh lines. If it does that, the camera would find Annabelle. She's sitting with Mark and John Mitchell, and they are trying to get her to drink some tepid tea.

"Come on, Annie," Mark is telling me as he holds a chipped china cup in front of my face. "You'll feel better."

"Try taking it with this," says John, unscrewing a small glass vial and pouring some pills into his palm. "These will help."

I knock his hand away, causing whatever it is he is offering to fly across the room, and then proceed with the crying bout I was in the middle of.

There are only three days left before I am supposed to appear in front of a judge and a jury somewhere in Washington, D.C., and that's just about the amount of time required for me to travel there. So now not only have I jumped bail, I am about to skip out on my court date. Sure, we've reported the hell out of this story. I've interviewed everyone from tribal chiefs to religious leaders to little girls. We've shot in every corner, every crevice of this refugee camp—tents, tunnels, outhouses, you name it. We even found Purnell, living in an oddly well-appointed cave, surrounded by scores of bodyguards. I have all the evidence I need, but no reputable venue in which to argue or air it. We had counted on *New Day* taking the bait, that maybe the ratings boost my pieces could give them would be reason enough to put them on the air, but maybe we counted wrong. All we have heard from Sam Fox, via Karen, is that he is working on things. He says his attempts to get another network to pick up the tapes have gotten no response. I might as well go join Purnell and live in some cave with him. Short of that, my options seem even bleaker.

I don't know what Mark is all freaking cheery and optimistic about, because at this point, his prospects aren't much better. If they don't air it today, we are both pretty much cooked. And given the teasers at the top of the show, it doesn't seem that they will.

As soon as we saw Ken's intro, I stormed out of the room, because, really, why watch? And now we are sitting on my bed, just like I used to do with Galina, and Mitchell and Mark are trying to make me cheer up.

"Don't worry," Mark says for the gazillionth time, putting down the teacup and attempting to rub my shoulders.

"Don't worry? Don't worry? Are you kidding?" I start sobbing again, and Mark, justifiably getting a little fed up with me, stands and announces that he's going to go watch TV in the other room, just in case.

He walks off and John follows, and within a few moments I am hearing the cloying, saccharine *New Day* theme song seeping from under the door.

"Would you turn that shit off?" I shout, but either they can't hear me or have chosen to ignore me. My face goes into my palms, but even from here I can make out Faith chirping away about some stupid cooking segment coming up later in the show.

It is now ten minutes and sixteen seconds past the hour. Four minutes and fourteen seconds to go. Tom and Carl chose that point of the newscast because it is at that moment when, statistically, the most viewers are actually watching, not just listening to, the show. It is, needless to say, very precious airtime.

Tom, trying to remain calm and leaderly, turns to ask Caitlin an innocuous question about her upcoming booking—the guest will be talking about how the rise in interest rates will affect the entertainment industry—even though he knows, as Carl knows, that that guest will be bumped right off the air.

"He's a good talker, right?" Tom says.

Caitlin looks at him quizzically, because with one segment to go it's a little bit late to be asking such questions. It's not like she can rebook it. And, hello? This guest has been on a hundred times before. He's a paid contributor to the show.

"Uh, yeah?" she says, and then, when he turns back to watch the wall of monitors in front of him, rolls her eyes at the producer standing next to her and mouths, *"What the f—?"*

Tom looks over at the screen that is showing what's airing on *Sunrise,* the competition. There's the legal analyst, pontificating on the ramifications of Annabelle Kapner missing her day in court, and there, sitting next to him, is Alexander Churn talking about how difficult it will be for the media to cover this nonevent should it happen. Tom takes a deep breath, looks over to Carl and nods. Carl goes into the back room to have a little talk with the tech in charge of queuing up the next piece of video.

Behind the studio, behind the control room, there is another room. With thousands of wires and monitors and machines piled on top of each other, this room can make even the most experienced producers shudder a little. People who aren't on the technical staff never, ever go in there.

Carl opens the heavy steel door and enters. The six men flipping switches and entering tapes into machines stare at him. It's as if a man in a Barney's seersucker suit were to walk into a tough biker bar. He isn't welcome.

"Can I help you?" says a small man sitting on a footstool at the base of a tower housing twenty video playback decks.

Carl nods, trying to look tough. "The next segment," he says. "They gave you the wrong video." He holds a tape out to the man on the stool, but the guy just stares at it like it is a dead fish.

"I don't take tape direction from anyone but Dave." Dave, the director.

"Well, I'm above Dave," says Carl, bucking up. "I am the senior supervising producer of this broadcast, and I am telling you that this is the correct tape."

"Fucking bullshit you are," says the stool man, enjoying his petty authority. He reaches to hit the button on the intercom on the adjacent wall so he can connect directly to the control room and speak to Dave himself.

Carl smacks stool man's hand out of the way, knocking the intercom box off the wall in the process. "I said put it in."

"Shit," says stool man. "I ain't taking the heat for this." He throws up his hands, motioning with his head for Carl to inject the tape into the machine himself.

"Don't worry," says Carl. "I fully intend to take it myself."

"You're going to hear from the union. Nobody's supposed to touch these machines but us."

"That's fine. I expect to hear from a lot of people."

Carl hands the stool man his card. "In case you need to reach me," he says, but he doesn't leave the room. He remains there, standing guard, making sure nothing will go worse than he knows it already will.

34

"So, what do you think?"

Galina looks up from her metal folding chair at the guard standing next to her. She shakes her head slowly from side to side. "I think," she says, "she is, how you say? Screwy?"

"Screwed," corrects the starched and uniformed officer. "Not gonna be able to make her case on TV, huh?"

Galina wrinkles her nose as if sniffing bad cheese. "What you think? They talk about Hollywood money. Three days until trial. It not looking good. Man," she says, pronouncing it main, "can you Americans ever talk about what is news?"

Galina gestures to the television, where Faith Heide is speaking to contributor Brock Bender about how Hollywood might have to scale back on the blockbusters this summer.

"Those special effects are getting costly, Faith. A thirty-second scene from the forthcoming Corpfilm release *Blazing Dawn* cost seven million dollars. And that is just a tiny fraction of the cost of the entire film."

Faith, looking like she is feigning shock, which she most likely is if she read the producer's notes from the preinterview, leans forward to pat Brock's knee in her signature style, and gazes at the camera.

"Why don't we take a look at it," she says, as if the idea to view the visual extravaganza they are talking about just occurred to her. She turns to watch the title *Blazing Dawn* flash across the enormous plasma screen placed just to the side of the interview area.

Tom Tatcher, back in the control room, briefly closes his eyes the way people do when they know something very scary is about to pop up in front of them.

Carl, still hanging with stool man, is anxiously monitoring how the recording tower shuttles from deck to deck. He watches as small blinking lights announce the fact that the tape he just injected is about to roll.

A few blocks north and east, Max Meyer steps out of the shower, toweling off his extremely short and somewhat limited white hair, and looks to see how his company's movie division's latest venture is being promoted. He sits down on the corner of the bed, causing Stacia to bounce a little.

A few thousand miles east and south, unbeknownst to him, Mark Thurber's wristwatch is running thirty seconds fast. So when he and John Mitchell watch the satellite feed of the movie graphics flash across the screen (and not having heard otherwise from Karen), they figure their window of opportunity to air their story has been missed, and they finally concede that things are not looking good. Mark turns off the set and walks back into the other room to try to console Annie—and to come up with plan Z, the rest of the alphabet having already been torn through.

John Mitchell, however, has other plans.

"For fuck sake!" he shouts as he throws his cell phone at the

wide-screen television set, shattering both appliances completely—not a great state of affairs, since it is the only working
satellite TV in all of Fardistan, or the former state of Fardistan,
whatever you want to call it.

Ratings points don't count illegal satellite feeds into Fardish
refugee camps, anyway, but if one were able to catch an instanta-
neous glimpse of the rest of the viewership of *New Day USA* over
the next thirty or so seconds, one would see that some five million
other people are tuned in. Yes, the show has quickly slipped out of
first place and is pushing third, but it still has a substantial number
of viewers. And they include a number of substantial people.

The viewers watch as the picture cuts from Faith and Brock to
the movie clip, full frame.

Three, two . . . Tom thinks as he opens his eyes and watches a car,
careening off a cliff, exploding into a ball of flames, the ball then
flying forward as if it were about to knock the camera, the
audience, the world off the map.

Boom!

An explosion rips across the screen, so detailed, so intense, that
it looks three dimensional.

One.

And the video cuts to something entirely different.

A small group of young girls, all wearing the colorful embroi-
dered skirts, shirts and scarves that the Fards are famous for, are
dancing around a pole, interlacing long ribbons as they skip and sing.
The video slows down, zooms in. We see their faces up close. We
see their Kewpie-doll cheeks, their wide-set eyes, and then we see
(supertight shot) that their lips are covered with bandages and scars.

Underneath the video of them, a man begins to speak.

"They are the victims of an old CIA project that spun out of control," he says. And then the man's face, John Mitchell's face, shows up on the screen. "And some of the most powerful people in America have profited from this pain."

Galina jumps out of her seat and starts shouting in Slavic, words of jubilation and hope. Some two hundred miles away, Max Meyer is also shouting, but his words aren't so sweet.

"Stacia! Throw me the fucking phone!" His wife does as told, and as Max reaches to catch the flying receiver, his towel drops to the floor. Naked, he hits speed dial, cursing before anyone even picks up.

At the other end should be Tom Tatcher. But at the other end Tom sees the so-called "bat phone" light up and ignores it.

His cell phone starts vibrating in his pant leg.

His BlackBerry is practically bouncing off his belt.

One minute, fifteen seconds to go. He can hold off. He can do this.

"Tom," says one of the young, nubile production assistants who, having the unfortunate luck of having to answer the control room phone, is now tapping his shoulder, "Max is trying—"

"I know," says Tom, swiping the poor young thing's hand away, his eyes never leaving the monitors. "Tell him I'll call him back."

"But—"

"Tell him."

One minute five seconds.

On the screen and around the world is a shot of a still-blond Annabelle (with a handkerchief tied around her head in an attempt to hide that fact). She has a dead snake in one hand, a microphone in the other and she is talking to a man who looks vaguely familiar, a man who in truth has no reason to talk to her except that now he is far away and pretty much untouchable. He's told her that he is getting a mildly masochistic kick out of the fact that she was able to find him, and that the story has finally gotten out. Anyway, at this point, he has nothing to lose.

"Yes," squeaks a thinned down but still smarmy looking Douglas Purnell, "the venom from the Fardish stiletto viper can safely cause lips to swell, if used in the proper dosage."

"And if used improperly?" says Annie.

"Well, I believe you've seen some of those results."

The video cuts to a grainy still shot of young Fida, looking adorable and exceedingly marketable, what with her large eyes, her rosy cheeks, her exceedingly plump lips.

"This is a cell phone photo I took of twelve-year-old Fida when I met her three months ago," Annie narrates. "She and her sister, Lida, were the face of Vanity's Cosmetic Relief project." Cut to a shot of a Vanity lip gloss, still in its packaging, the two girls smiling on the cardboard backing. "This is Fida a few months before I met her, after she first tested the products." The still photograph is wiped off the screen to reveal video of Fida, lips blistered and bloody, with some scabs peeling off.

Dave, the director, realizing that what he is seeing on monitor B isn't a clip from *Blazing Dawn,* hits the intercom that connects him to the tech room.

"Sal, what the fuck is this?" he shouts into the microphone.

Sal doesn't respond. Sal, in fact, doesn't even know that Dave is trying to talk to him because, thanks to Carl, the intercom isn't working.

Forty-five seconds.

Tom yells across the control room to tell Dave it's okay, let it run.

The whole staff sits back, agape and riveted.

Annie and Purnell are back on the screen. His beard is longer now and he's rubbing it. "Yes," he is saying, "we discovered these cosmetic properties back in the sixties when we, under the direction of Howard Hacker, now the vice president of the United States, were exploring the usage of the venom in our interrogation techniques."

"Jesus!" Max shoved one leg, then the other, into the pants he had thrown on the floor the night before, the phone still cradled into his ear. "Yes! I know where I called! Yes, I know this is Corpcom's engineering headquarters. This is Max Meyer! I'm the boss, you idiot! I need someone to break the feed! Now!" he is demanding of whichever entry-level technician it is that picked up the phone. But the technician is clearly not impressed. Max lobs the phone across the room, causing its plastic backing to shatter against the side of the television set at the foot of the bed.

On said set, the camera is scanning across stacks and stacks of files, files covered with webs of dust and layers of grime. It shows Annie opening one seemingly at random, and then zooms in to reveal a black-and-white photograph of a man, lips full as a pillow, sitting under a harsh white lamp.

Alexander Churn, his segment on *Sunrise* now over, is sitting in that show's green room, watching in awe.

Carl, observing the feed in the small square monitor on the face of the playback deck, looks at his watch.

Thirty seconds.

And it's too bad that right now, instead of seeing herself on the screen, telling and showing the whole world about how she found evidence and witnesses to prove that not only was Vanity Cosmetics' most marketable product conceived out of a dangerously toxic substance, but of how the research into the substance was directed by one of the men once at the helm of the CIA, the same man who is now the vice president of the United States, and of how Purnell (no innocent himself), had taken the old research and, now (years later) that the warring had simmered down and it is easier to navigate the corrupt Fardish terrain, decided to profit from it, Annie is balled up on a hard daybed with her face in her knees.

Purnell was no fool. He knew he had to keep a good hand in play, so just in case, he had hidden copies of all the memos. Certain people had reasons to want to keep them hidden.

Cut to a still shot, a man, who, if you aged him about forty or fifty years and thinned out his extremely full lips, would look exactly like Vice President Hacker does today.

Ten seconds.

Annie is standing in front of what appears to be a makeshift beauty parlor, complete with cheesy photographs of excessively laminated fingernails on the wall, and a row of women, faces covered but heads under drying lamps to set their curls. "In our next segment," she says, "we look into how this seemingly well-intentioned microdevelopment program had the potential to make a few Americans very rich, but for the Fardish girls and women it aimed to help, did more damage than good. And," she says as the camera pushes a little tighter into her face, "we learn how *New Day USA,* the program I worked for, became part of the problem."

Fade to black.

"Go to commercial," says Tom, and he starts to pack up his briefcase and get ready to go.

35

Lots of people want to ride with you in the limo, but what you want is someone who will take the bus with you when the limo breaks down.

—Oprah Winfrey

When I was in seventh grade, the biggest night of the year was the Wonderland Ball. The alumni committee of my private school used that event to plant the seeds for future endowments, teasing the kids with moments that would become indelible memories: tables decorated to look like overgrown mushrooms, performance artists dressed like court jesters and grinning cats, tube tunnels set up to be rabbit holes, taking you from one room to another. But for all the decorations and thought the adults poured into it, the true reason it was the night to end all nights was because school tradition had it that the eighth graders (the graduating class) would secretly spike one of the punches with cups and cups of Spanish fly. There was no scientific proof that the powder actually had an aphrodisiac effect (or proof that anyone ever actually did spike the punch), but for one hundred seventh and eighth graders, the suggestion was powerful enough. By the end of the evening, the dance floor was always empty. The kids were off necking in the rabbit holes, feeling each other up under the mushroom tops. If you didn't hook up with anyone, if you didn't partake, your status in school immediately slipped. It was, needless to say, a night not to be missed.

Unfortunately, I slept right through it. I had been up late the night before, cramming for an upcoming algebra exam, and decided to take a beauty nap. The next thing I knew, my mother—not Timothy Wilder, as I had hoped—was lifting up my party dress and putting me into pajamas.

"Dear Diary," I began writing the very next morning. "I hate myself and I want to die." But just then, my mother knocked on my door to tell me Timothy was on the phone, asking for me.

"Hi," I said, embarrassed but excited all the same.

"Hi," he said. "I hear you didn't make it to the dance, either."

Which is how thirteen-year-old Timothy became the love of my twelve-year-old life.

Love through fear of rejection, I guess.

As they say, history repeats itself. Because now, eighteen years later, I am sitting next to Mark, wondering if the thing that will bring us together once and for all, the twist that after all the fits and starts will finally seal the deal, is that we have absolutely nowhere else to turn.

"It's going to be okay," Mark says as he gently strokes my hair. We are sitting on one of the myriad carpets strewn about the guest quarters in Alfiedazied's home, packing up our things. I can feel the scratchiness of the wool through my thin cotton pants.

It's been almost a full day since my breakdown, and now that

I've sobbed and cried and carried on, I've pretty much resigned myself to the fact that I need to return to the States to face the music. No question, they will toss me straight in the crapper.

"Maybe it will be okay," I say, "in about twenty-five to life."

"Ha, ha," he says, and then takes my hand. "You know it won't be that bad."

"Ten?" I say, because that is probably what I am actually looking at.

Mark smiles, trying to be encouraging and sympathetic at the same time.

I look at him.

Those dimples.

"So, are you going to visit me?"

"Definitely," he says. "If I'm not doing time myself."

I giggle, because, really, what are laughs but tension relievers.

"Mark," I say, taking my hand away and crossing my arms as I prepare to ask what I have been afraid to ask for so long now. "I don't understand you. You should hate me. I ruined your career, I destroyed your reputation. And now you are probably facing a not too insignificant prison term. I don't get it. Why?" I don't need to expand on the why—it's clear: why did he help me? Why did he even like me? Yes, yes, he's told me a thousand times that he thinks I am innocent, that he wants to help, that the more he learned about Hacker, the more he needed to clear his own name as well. But, seriously, for what?

At first he doesn't say anything. He takes the laptop out of his bag and turns it on. Once the movie maker program opens, he hits Play.

"Watch this again, Annie. This is the best work I have ever done. Honestly."

We watch.

We watch as I interview Mitchell, Purnell, the girls, snake farmers, former political prisoners. We watch as I flip through reams of files, of documents and proof. From my reporting it is patently clear that the vice president had a lot to hide, and it is fairly obvious that the security forces that arrested me were really just protecting him.

But television is teamwork. Someone has to be holding the camera while the other person is asking the questions. Someone has to be talking the way into unfriendly places while the other one is carrying the bags. And, as it is in most of the world's creative occupations, two chefs usually are better than one. Even print journalists have editors. I couldn't have done any of this without Mark. He certainly couldn't have done any of it without me.

"I'm sorry this has to end. I'm sorry it didn't work out like we planned," he says, a small tear rolling down his cheek.

I lean over and kiss it.

"It isn't ending," I say. I can't let it.

He looks at me, slightly confused, but with tenderness.

This is the point that, were we in a film, the screen would subtly go gauzy and the light would soften out. Gentle music would seep underneath our dialogue as we slowly but hungrily started to devour each other, body and soul. But that's not what happens. What happens is that a lightbulb finally goes off in my head. Instead of getting fuzzy and soft, my world suddenly becomes quite clear.

I push Mark off of me. Not in a rejecting way, but in a revelatory one, if that makes any sense.

"You've totally changed my life," I say.

"I know. I am so sorry that this all—"

"No." I take his hand. "I mean, thank you. Whatever happens. You've changed my life."

He places his hand on top of mine and we look at each other. Mark, with his now matted beard and greasy hair, me with my dark roots and blackened fingernails, and each of us about twenty pounds too thin.

And then we start to laugh.

Really hard. In a really good way.

I wipe some of the new, happy tears that are falling down Mark's cheeks and he, almost heaving with laughter, gives me his sleeve to wipe my nose. We fall over onto the floor, in each others arms, and just giggle.

It is absolutely and totally wonderful.

"So, what now?" says Mark once we have settled down, once the laughs have turned to satisfied sighs and we pull ourselves back up to sitting. "Pen pals from prison?"

He always did like to alliterate.

"No," I say. "I don't think so."

"Why? What do you—"

"No, I mean, I don't think that's part of my plan. I mean going to trial, all that. Not part of my plan. Not anymore." I wave my finger, no, no.

"You realize what you are saying, right?"

I do. Not showing up for trial is even worse than running out on my bail. Not showing up for trial would mean that if (really when) I got caught, I would pretty much be guaranteeing myself—and Mark—a much, much worse outcome than we might otherwise have had. But not showing up for trial would also mean that we have a little more time to try to get the story told, a slightly better chance of having the case dismissed, and a much better chance of being able to feel good about my place in this world (even if it means reflecting on that place from behind bars).

Galina once told me about how in her country, journalists used to be jailed for telling the truth. They went to prison camps, hard labor, but upon release, some of them went right back at it. I am sure that, in and of itself, that wasn't what brought the Soviet Union to an end, but I am sure it didn't hurt. And for the first time in my professional (and personal) life, I actually believe in what I am doing. I know Mark does, too.

"We're posting online," I say, standing up to get to the cord for the modem. "I don't care if it isn't as credible. At least someone might see it. Who knows, maybe some bloggers might even link to it. It's better than nothing, right?"

Mark pulls me in tight and gives me a big, extremely confident kiss. "Let me do it," he says, standing up and walking across the room to connect the computer up to the modem.

Getting online from Fardistan isn't so easy. You have to hook up the satellite, pray for a connection, hope the clouds are steady and the wind isn't shifting too fast. But, if the Gods are good, you've got mail, so to speak.

And we do. We haven't checked our mail for days because, honestly, there didn't seem to be any need. Sam Fox could only contact us through Karen, and Karen knew that to contact us, she was better off calling Mitchell. No paper trace, just some calls to a phone registered in Virginia. Everyone else knew that, for their own legal protection, it was best not to contact us at all.

The computer chimes.

"Holy cow," says Mark.

I am completely speechless.

Because, there it is in our in-box:

From: Karen
To: Mark and Annie
Re: Tell John Mitchell to answer his fucking phone!!!!!!!

I look at Mark. He looks at me. We both say at once, "The phone. He broke the phone."

And then we look at the computer and hungrily scroll down. There are scores of e-mails from Karen, each sighting one newspaper headline after the next.

Click, click, click…

The *New York Herald*
PRODUCER CLAIMS BLAME FOR GLOSSGATE LIES WITH VICE PRESIDENT
In Rare Television Appearance Annabelle Kapner Shows Documentation Implicating Hacker, reveals conflict of interest with network chief.

Click, click, click…

The *Washington Eagle*
LETHAL LIP GLOSS
Little Girls Used as Testing Bunnies in Humanitarian Cosmetics Concern.

Click, click, click…

PR Daily
SAGE FACTS
Veteran TV News Producer John Mitchell Sage Emerges as
Voice of Oppressed

Mark and I take a quick look at each other, jump up, grab the
laptop and run out of the compound and over the hill to the small
tent that houses the neighborhood opium den. Mitchell is there,
stoned, but not so stoned that when we open the laptop he doesn't
realize the import of this:

Click, click, click...

The *New York Spectator*
MORNING GLORY
Morning News Program Makes News; Network Suits Show
Their Worth.
By Alexander Churn
New York Spectator Media Critic
Bravo. Bravo. Bravo.
What can I say? Someone actually listened to me for a change.
Max Meyer, you are a brave soul, a soul I can now respect. You
allowed your dirty laundry to hit your airwaves, and for doing
so, I commend you. In this media-opic day and age, there is no
escaping our conflicted interests, but at least you allowed yours
to be exposed for all to see. You are a man now. Mazel tov.

"Holy cow!" says Mitchell, leaping to his feet and causing his
fellow loungers to all sit up a bit. "We did it! It aired! I can't believe
it aired! How did we miss this?"

"Your phone, John," says Mark. "You busted it. Karen couldn't reach us."

Sometimes talking to a stoned person is like talking to a baby. But sometimes, like right now, who gives a damn?

Mitchell is so happy he is practically skipping.

"I'll be right back!" he says, and dashes out of the bar, leaving me and Mark and our laptop surrounded by about twenty men who are high as kites.

We decide to ignore them, and settle down into a corner to read through some more.

"Look at this," Mark says, pointing to the next paragraph in the Churn article. "He says that our little renegade team could sweep the Emmys."

"Don't we need to be nominated first?" I say.

"Annie," says Mark. "Enjoy this. Don't tear it apart."

"Right. Okay. But I think I need to fix my hairstyle before the ceremony." I smile, because really, it is hard to imagine myself looking good right now, regardless of how excited I might be. Which, I quickly find out, is an unfortunate thing.

John Mitchell returns to the room, holding a new satellite phone in my face.

"What?"

"It's Alfiedazied's," he says. "I've got Carl Van Dunt on the line. They want you both live on the show tomorrow. The crew is already on the plane."

"That's awesome!" I say, grabbing the receiver.

"You ready for this, kid?" says Carl. "Your big moment in the limelight?"

"Totally ready. Who's producing it?"

"I figure with you and John there, you've got it covered," he says jokingly. "Just don't forget to powder your nose."

"Carl," I say with a laugh. "I don't have any powder. I didn't even pack a lip gloss."

36

"Thirty seconds to air!" The stage manager skips over the wires strewn about the floor and jumps behind the row of semirobotic cameras.

"Shit!" The frail makeup artist rushes forward, armed with a powder puff, and dives for Ken Klark's shiny, pert nose. The white dust settles and she is gone, out of the shot.

"Ten seconds!"

Klark pulls his blue blazer down, making sure it isn't bunching at the collar.

"Five seconds!"

Tom and Carl, standing in the back of the control room, look at each other and, under the console so no one can see, give each other a little high five.

"Three! Two!" On the unspoken count of "One," the stage manager mimes a gunshot at Klark, who smiles, leans a bit forward, waiting a beat for the zooming camera lens to settle on him.

"Good morning, everyone! It's a New Day, USA!" Ken Klark says in his distinctive deep baritone, looking more energetic and radiant than he has in months. "Today is August 5th. I'm Ken Klark." He turns to his cohost as the camera widens to reveal her to one and all. "And I would in particular like to wish a good morning to our correspondent Natasha Spark, who will be sitting in as guest co-anchor while Faith Heide is on an extended vacation. Welcome, Natasha."

Natasha, Annie's correspondent friend. Carl promised that there would be a more journalistically solid interviewer, and here she is.

"Thank you, Ken. I am thrilled to be here," says Natasha. "What a show we have today."

"Indeed it is, Natasha," he says with a sparkle in his eye, a glimmer to acknowledge the millions of viewers tuning in for the special event, viewers from Park Avenue to Fardistan to, yes, the detention center in Alexandria, Virginia.

Galina, with the pride and anxiety a parent might have before his or her kid's valedictorian speech, can't even sit down. She paces across the cement floor of the recreation room as she waits for Ken and Natasha to work their way through the perfunctory news packages and segment teasers.

"Up next," Natasha finally says, "an exclusive live interview from a Fardish refugee camp with Annabelle Kapner and her boyfriend, Mark Thurber. Stay tuned."

The commercial jingle percolates across Max Meyer's kitchen and into his bedroom, but he isn't there. Why would he be? This is the biggest event to hit his news division's air since the investigative unit ran never before seen footage of Princess Diana's adolescent years, with some twenty-five million viewers tuning in. No, Meyer is standing right behind Tom and Carl, with Stacia at his side, her perfume nearly suffocating the control room crew.

* * *

"Ready, guys?" says Tony, the cameraman I worked with oh so many months ago.

I turn to Mark. "How do I look?" I ask a bit sheepishly.

"Honestly?"

I hit him playfully on the shoulder. The truth is I know I don't look all that great. Neither of us does. The crew offered me some makeup, some powder, and yes, some lip gloss, but I declined. Because honestly, it really doesn't matter how I look. So the whole world will see my bleached blond hair and the horrendous dark roots that are growing in. So they'll see Mark's scraggily beard. As far as all the weight loss, well, at least the camera will add ten pounds. What matters is that we are here. And, honestly, I always thought it looked stupid when correspondents appeared all groomed and immaculate while reporting from refugee camps and war zones.

"Testing." Tony points at me. "Annie, can you hear Natasha through your IFB?"

"Annie?" she is saying. "Can you hear me?"

I smile, look straight into the lens, touch my earpiece and wave. "Hey, Natasha. I hear you just fine."

Being on this side of the camera is probably not something I'll get used to anytime soon, especially the live stuff. It just feels weird, looking into nothing but a camera lens, but knowing there are millions and millions of people looking right back at me.

I hear Dave, the director, say, "Fifteen seconds!"

I grab Mark's hand and take a deep, long yogic breath. *Thank you, Faith.*

It all goes extremely fast.

Just as the interview begins, Natasha announces the breaking news hot off the wires: citing lack of evidence, the government has decided to drop my case. It's pretty hard to say anything coherent after that, but I think Mark and I cobble together a fairly articulate account of everything that has happened. We discuss how John Mitchell first contacted me, how I had hoped to report the story right, how I got hold of Purnell's keys, and how Karen and Mark discovered the link between the Fardish snakes, Douglas Purnell and Vice President Hacker. We explain how Purnell decided he could create a profitable cosmetics business using some properties of the snake venom; how we don't think anyone on the American side knew what was really going on or how the cosmetics were tested. We talk about the corporate conflicts and tease the tape package about it that will air tomorrow. And then suddenly Natasha is thanking us for our hard work and our time.

"I am so glad we could do this," I say, which is probably the biggest understatement of my life.

"Stay tuned tomorrow when Annie and Mark join us again," says Natasha to the audience, not to me.

And so, assuming we are done, and without missing a beat, Mark sweeps me off my feet and gives me a huge kiss on the lips.

"Um," I hear Natasha in my IFB, "Annie? Mark?"

Oh, shit. We're still on the air.

The hell with it. We might as well give them what they really want.

Quite a few seconds pass before we hear Ken Klark teasing the upcoming cooking segment, followed by an ebullient sounding Tom Tatcher.

"Go to commercial," he says.

EPILOGUE

I guess you could say Ron Ruby was right. Or maybe you could say this was my second coming. Or something. But long story short, it did happen like he said it would. Sort of. I mean, it's not like we're sitting in our home overlooking the Hollywood Hills, sipping chardonnay. I don't even like chardonnay. Neither does Mark. But, yeah, things aren't bad on the road. The deals are in place and the money is there, which makes Sam Fox happy (he still gets ten percent), but more importantly, which means that we have an outlet and the funds for the work our production team produces. Not that it would be hard to find one. Tom and Carl offered us a regular spot on *New Day* right off the bat, but breakfast television is breakfast television, and we knew that once our fifteen minutes started to fade, which they already have, the audience wouldn't have the appetite for our stories, especially if they were sandwiched between cooking segments and celebrity chats. So, even though I had sworn I would never work for ZBC News again, we worked it out with Max Meyer to give us an hourly special three times a year. John Mitchell was named our supervising producer, Mark does most of the producing, and, although I am still not totally comfortable with it (and I still think I look like a Muppet), I am the on-camera talent. And, yes, I do powder my nose before the camera starts rolling.

Anyway, the plan is to keep traveling, keep finding worthy stories that have otherwise been ignored, and dig in. There is a lot of work to be done, needless to say, but that's just fine with me. It's fine for Mark, as well. He's reluctant to return to the States just yet, anyway. Too much pressure. There are swarms of people lobbying for him to run for office, and really, going back into politics is the last thing he wants to do, even if Hacker is no longer in the game.

Life has changed for pretty much everyone, actually. I paid Ron Ruby to represent Galina, and he got her out on some obscure technicality. Now she's living in my apartment with Margarita and working for Carl as his news editor. He said he needed someone on board who could keep him honest. I just hope he keeps her from wasting her paycheck on the Virtual Shopping Network. That might not be too difficult, though; Faith Heide is the host over there now and she's pretty hard to watch. Of course, Sam Fox is thrilled. Because of the contract he negotiated, Max and friends are still stuck paying Faith's *New Day* salary, regardless of the fact that she is no longer on their air. I guess they figured it was worth the money to keep her away. Tom Tatcher has been trying hard to find a better balance of real news and the infotainment that is the lifeblood of morning television, and Faith was too much of a distraction. From what I can tell from Alexander Churn's column, Tatcher is doing a pretty good job. So I guess the only person whose life really hasn't changed all that much is Karen, but she says she is happy this way, back in the lab, away from the limelight, quietly dissecting her pigs and frogs.

Oh, and I guess Douglas Purnell (or whatever his real name is— we never found out). He's disappeared into some cave again. I am sure he'll crop up when he figures out the next carpet to bag, or whatever. I suppose if I really wanted to I could tell the feds where to look for him, but honestly, that's not my job. I mean, as a journalist, I need to protect my sources, even if they are slimy as all heck. That's the way it works, right? Otherwise, no one would talk to me and we wouldn't have any stories to tell.

But I digress. Simply put, things are pretty good for me right now, and even though I haven't solved the problems of the world or fixed the state of the media, I am happy to report that every now and then, something good does come out; every now and then there is an important story that doesn't get glossed over.